A CLASSIC OF PARALLEL-TIME AND ALTERNATE-HISTORY ADVENTURE!

Corporal Calvin Morrison of the Pennsylvania State police was scared. Unsnapping the remaining strap of his holster, he started towards the farmhouse where a murderer with a rifle was waiting. Then it happened. There was a blinding flash, and a hemisphere of flickering light glowed all around him, and an oval desk with an instrument panel appeared, and a young man was rising from a swivel-chair with a weapon in his hand . . .

Morrison, fired, flung himself to one side and rolled until he was out of the dome of light and came bumping up against a tree. The light disappeared, and he lay still for a moment in relief. Until he realized that there weren't any trees here! Not in twentieth-century Pennsylvania, anyway. Corporal Calvin Morrison had to absorb the fact that he knew *where* he was. But he hadn't the slightest inkling of *when* he was . . .

Gunpowder God

H. BEAM PIPER

SPHERE BOOKS LIMITED
30/32 Gray's Inn Road, London WC1X 8JL

First published in Great Britain by Sphere Books Ltd 1978
Copyright © 1965 by Ace Books Inc.
Published by arrangement with Ace Books (a division of
Charter Communications Inc./a Grosset & Dunlap company)
and their British agent.

Gunpowder God is published in the United States of America
under the title *Lord Kalvan of Otherwhen*. A shorter version
was originally published under the title *Gunpowder God* in the
magazine *Analog Science Fact/Science Fiction* in November
1964.

Set in Linotype Pilgrim

Printed in Great Britain by
Hunt Barnard Printing Ltd.,
Aylesbury, Bucks.

ONE

I

Tortha Karf, Chief of Paratime Police, told himself to stop
fretting. He was only three hundred years old, so by the
barest life-expectancy of his race he was good for another
two centuries. Two hundred more days wouldn't matter.
Then it would be Year-End Day, and, precisely at midnight,
he would rise from his chair, and Verkan Vall would sit
down in it, and after that he would be free to raise grapes
and lemons and wage guerrilla war against the rabbits on
the island of Sicily, which he owned outright on one un-
inhabited Fifth Level time-line. He wondered how long it
would take Vall to become as tired of the Chief's seat as he
was now.

Actually, Karf knew, Verkan Vall had never wanted to be
Chief. Prestige and authority meant little to him, and freedom much. Vall liked to work outtime. But it was a job
somebody had to do, and it was the job for which Vall had
been trained, so he'd take it, and do it, Karf suspected, better
than he'd done it himself. The job of policing a near-infinity
of worlds, each of which was this same planet Earth, would
be safe with Verkan Vall.

Twelve thousand years ago, facing extinction on an
exhausted planet, the First Level race had discovered the
existence of a second, lateral, time-dimension and a means
of physical transposition to and from a near-infinity of
worlds of alternate probability parallel to their own. So the
conveyers had gone out by stealth, bringing back wealth
to Home Time Line – a little from this one, a little from that,
never enough to be missed any when.

It all had to be policed. Some Paratimers were less than
scrupulous in dealing with outtime races – he'd have retired

ten years ago except for the discovery of a huge para-temporal slave-trade, only recently smashed. More often, somebody's bad luck or indiscretion would endanger the Paratime Secret, or some incident – nobody's fault, something that just happened – would have to be explained away. But, at all costs, the Paratime Secret must be preserved. Not merely the actual technique of transposition – that went without saying – but the very existence of a race possessing it. If for no other reason (and there *were* many others), it would be utterly immoral to make any outtime race live with the knowledge that there were among them aliens indistinguishable from themselves, watching and exploiting. It was a big police-beat.

Second Level : that had been civilised almost as long as the First. but there had been dark-age interludes. Except for paratemporal transposition, most of its sectors equalled First Level, and from many Home Time Line had learned much. The Third Level civilisations were more recent, but still of respectable antiquity and advancement. Fourth Level had started late and progressed slowly; some Fourth Level genius was first domesticating animals long after the steam engine was obsolescent all over the Third. And Fifth Level : on a few sectors, subhuman brutes, speechless and fireless, were cracking nuts and each other's heads with stones, and on most of it nothing even vaguely humanoid had appeared.

Fourth Level was the big one. The others had devolved from low-probability genetic accidents; it was the maximum probability. It was divided into many sectors and subsectors, on most of which human civilisation had first appeared in the valleys of the Nile and Tigris-Euphrates, and on the Indus and Yangtze. Europo-American Sector : they might have to pull out of that entirely, but that would be for Chief Verkan to decide. Too many thermonuclear weapons and too many competing national sovereignties. That had happened all over Third Level at one time or another within Home Time Line experience. Alexandrian-Roman : off to a fine start with the pooling of Greek theory and Roman engineering talent, and then, a thousand years ago, two half-forgotten religions had been rummaged out of the dustbin and fanatics had begun massacring one another. They were still at it, with pikes and matchlocks, having lost the ability to make anything better. Europo-American could come to that if its rival political and economic sectarians kept on. Sino-Hindic: that wasn't a civilisation; it was a bad case of cultural paralysis. And so was Indo-Turanian – about where Europo-American had been ten centuries ago.

And Aryan-Oriental: the Aryan migration of three thousand years ago, instead of moving west and south, as on most sectors, had rolled east into China. And Aryan-Transpacific, an offshoot: on one sector, some of them had built ships and sailed north and east along the Kuriles and the Aleutians and settled in North America, bringing with them horses and cattle and iron-working skills, exterminating the Amerinds, warring with one another, splitting into diverse peoples and cultures. There was a civilisation, now decadent, on the Pacific coast, and nomads on the central plains herding bison and cross-breeding them with Asian cattle, and a civilisation around the Great Lakes and one in the Mississippi Valley, and a new one, five or six centuries old, along the Atlantic and in the Appalachians. Technological level pre-mechanical, water-and-animal power; a few subsectors had gotten as far as gunpowder.

But Aryan-Transpacific was a sector to watch. They were going forward; things were ripe to start happening soon.

Let Chief Varkan watch it, for the next couple of centuries. After Year-End Day, ex-Chief Tortha would have his vineyards and lemon-groves to watch.

II

Rylla tried to close her mind to the voices around her in the tapestried room, and stared at the map spread in front of her and her father. There was Tarr-Hostigos overlooking the gap, only a tiny fleck of gold on the parchment, but she could see it in her mind's eye – the walled outer bailey with the sheds and stables and workshops inside, the inner bailey and the citadel and keep, the watchtower pointing a blunt finger skyward. Below, the little Darro flowed north to join the Listra and, with it, the broad Athan to the east. Hostigos Town, white walls and slate roofs and busy streets; the checkerboard of fields to the west and south; the forest, broken by farms, to the west.

A voice, louder and harsher than the others, brought her back to reality. Her cousin, Sthentros.

'He'll do nothing at all? Well, what in Dralm's holy name is a Great King for, but to keep the peace?'

She looked along the table, from one to another. Phosg, the speaker for the peasants, at the foot, uncomfortable in his feast-day clothes and ill at ease seated among his betters. The speakers for the artisans' guilds, and for the merchants and the townsfolk; the lesser family members and marriage-kin; the barons and landholders. Old Chartiphon, the chief-captain, his golden beard streaked with grey like the lead-splotches on his gilded breastplate, his long sword on the table in front of him. Xentos, the cowl of his priestly robe thrown back from his snowy head, his blue eyes troubled. And beside her, at the table's head, her father, Prince Ptosphes, his mouth tight between pointed grey moustache and pointed grey beard. How long it had been since she had seen her father smile!

Xentos passed a hand negatively across his face.

'King Kaiphranos said that it was every Prince's duty to guard his own realm; that it was for Prince Ptosphes, not for him, to keep bandits out of Hostigos.'

'Bandits? They're Nostori soldiers!' Sthentros shouted. 'Gormoth of Nostor means to take all Hostigos, as his grand-father took Sevenhills Valley after the traitor we don't name sold him Tarr-Dombra.'

That was a part of the map her eyes had shunned: the bowl valley to the east, where Dombra Gap split the Mountains of Hostigos. It was from thence that Gormoth's mercenary cavalry raided into Hostigos.

'And what hope have we from Styphon's House?' her father asked. He knew the answer; he wanted the others to hear it at first hand.

'The Archpriest wouldn't talk to me; the priest of Styphon hold no speech with priests of other gods,' Xentos said.

'The Archpriest wouldn't talk to me, either,' Chartiphon said. 'Only one of the upperpriests of the temple. He took our offerings and said he would pray to Styphon for us. When I asked for fireseed, he would give me none.'

'None at all?' somebody down the table cried. 'Then we are indeed under the ban.'

Her father rapped with the pommel of his poignard.

8

'You've heard the worst, now. What's in your minds that we should do? You first, Phosg.'

The peasant representative rose and cleared his throat.

'Lord Prince, this castle is no more dear to you than my cottage is to me. I'll fight for mine as you would for yours.'

There was a quick mutter of approval along the table. 'Well said, Phosg!' 'An example for all of us!' The others spoke in turn; a few tried to make speeches. Chartiphon said only: 'Fight. What else.'

'I am a priest of Dralm,' Xentos said, 'and Dralm is a god of peace, but I say, fight with Dralm's blessing. Submission to evil men is the worst of all sins.'

'Rylla,' her father said.

'Better die in armour than live in chains,' she replied. 'When the time comes, I will be in armour with the rest of you.'

Her father nodded. 'I expected no less from any of you.' He rose, and all with him. 'I thank you. At sunset we will dine together; until then servants will attend you. Now, if you please, leave me with my daughter. Chartiphon, you and Xentos stay.'

Chairs scraped and feet scuffed as they went out. The closing door cut off the murmur of voices. Chartiphon had begun to fill his stubby pipe.

'I know there's no use looking to Balthar of Beshta,' she said, 'but wouldn't Sarrask of Sask aid us? We're better neighbours to him than Gormoth would be.'

'Sarrask of Sask's a fool,' Chartiphon said shortly. 'He doesn't know that once Gormoth has Hostigos, his turn will come next.'

'He knows that,' Xentos differed. 'He'll try to strike before Gormoth does, or catch Gormoth battered from having fought us. But even if he wanted to help us, he dares not. Even King Kaiphranos dares not aid those whom Styphon's House would destroy.'

'They want that land in Wolf Valley, for a temple-farm,' she considered. 'I know that would be bad, but . . .'

'Too late,' Xentos told her. 'They have made a compact with Gormoth, to furnish him fireseed and money to hire mercenaries, and when he has conquered Hostigos he will give them the land.' He paused and added: 'And it was on my advice, Prince, that you refused them.'

9

'I'd have refused against your advice, Xentos,' her father said. 'Long ago I vowed that Styphon's House should never come into Hostigos while I lived, and by Dralm and by Galzar neither shall they! They come into a princedom, they build a temple, they make temple-farms, and slaves of everybody on them. They tax the Prince, and make him tax the people, till nobody has anything left. Look at that temple-farm in Sevenhills Valley!'

'Yes, you'd hardly believe it,' Chartiphon said. 'Why, they even make the peasants for miles around cart their manure in, till they have none left for their own fields. Dralm only knows what they do with it.' He puffed at his pipe. 'I wonder why they want Sevenhills Valley.'

'There's something in the ground there that makes the water of those springs taste and smell badly,' her father said.

'Sulphur,' said Xentos. 'But why do they want sulphur?'

III

Corporal Calvin Morrison, Pennsylvania State Police, squatted in the brush at the edge of the old field and looked across the small brook at the farmhouse two hundred yards away. It was scabrous with peeling yellow paint, and festooned with a sagging porch-roof. A few white chickens pecked disinterestedly in the littered barnyard; there was no other sign of life, but he knew that there was a man inside. A man with a rifle, who would use it; a man who had murdered once, broken jail, would murder again.

He looked at his watch; the minute-hand was squarely on the nine. Jack French and Steve Kovac would be starting down from the road above, where they had left the car. He rose, unsnapping the retaining-strap of his holster.

'Watch that middle upstairs window,' he said. 'I'm starting now.'

'I'm watching it.' Behind him, a rifle-action clattered softly as a cartridge went into the chamber. 'Luck.'

He started forward across the seedling-dotted field. He was scared, as scared as he had been the first time, back in '51, in Korea, but there was nothing he could do about that. He just told his legs to keep moving, knowing that in a few moments he wouldn't have time to be scared.

He was within a few feet of the little brook, his hand close to the butt of the Colt, when it happened.

There was a blinding flash, followed by a moment's darkness. He thought he'd been shot; by pure reflex, the .38-special was in his hand. Then, all around him, a flickering iridescence of many colours glowed, a perfect hemisphere fifteen feet high and thirty across, and in front of him was an oval desk with an instrument-panel over it, and a swivel-chair from which a man was rising. Young, well-built; a white man but, he was sure, not an American. He wore loose green trousers and black ankle-boots and a pale green shirt. There was a shoulder holster under his left arm, and a weapon in his right hand.

He was sure it was a weapon, though it looked more like an electric soldering-iron, with two slender rods instead of a barrel, joined, at what should be the muzzle, by a blue ceramic or plastic knob. It was probably something that made his own Colt Official Police look like a kid's cap-pistol, and it was coming up fast to line on him.

He fired, held the trigger back to keep the hammer down on the fired chamber, and flung himself to one side, coming down, on his left hand and left hip, on a smooth, polished floor. Something, probably the chair, fell with a crash. He rolled, and kept on rolling until he was out of the nacreous dome of light and bumped hard against something. For a moment he lay still, then rose to his feet, letting out the trigger of the Colt.

What he'd bumped into was a tree. For a moment he accepted that, then realised that there should be no trees here, nothing but low brush. And this tree, and the ones all around, were huge; great rough columns rising to support a green roof through which only a few stray gleams of sunlight leaked. Hemlocks; must have been growing here while Columbus was still conning Isabella into hocking her jewellery. He looked at the little stream he had been about to cross when this had happened. It was the one thing about this that wasn't completely crazy. Or maybe it was the craziest thing of all.

He began wondering how he was going to explain this.

'While approaching the house,' he began, aloud and in a formal tone, 'I was intercepted by a flying saucer landing in front of me, the operator of which threatened me with a ray-pistol. I defended myself with my revolver, firing one round . . . '

No. That wouldn't do at all.

He looked at the brook again, and began to suspect that there might be nobody to explain to. Swinging out the cylinder of his Colt, he replaced the fired round. Then he decided to junk the regulation about carrying the hammer on an empty chamber, and put in another one.

IV

Verkan Vall watched the landscape outside the almost invisible shimmer of the transposition-field; now he was in the forests of the Fifth Level. The mountains, of course, were always the same, but the woods around flickered and shifted. There was a great deal of randomness about which tree grew where, from time-line to time-line. Now and then he would catch fleeting glimpses of open country, and the buildings and airports installations of his own people. The red light overhead went off and on, a buzzer sounding each time. The conveyer dome became a solid iridescence, and then a mesh of cold inert metal. The red light turned green. He picked up a sigma-ray needler from the desk in front of him and holstered it. As he did, the door slid open and two men in Paratime Police green, a lieutenant and a patrolman, entered. When they saw him, they relaxed, holstering their own weapons.

'Hello, Chief's Assistant,' the lieutenant said. 'Didn't pick anything up, did you?'

In theory, the Ghaldron-Hesthor transposition-field was impenetrable; in practice, especially when two paratemporal vehicles going in opposite 'directions' interpenetrated, the field would weaken briefly, and external objects, sometimes alive and hostile, would intrude. That was why Paratimers kept weapons ready to hand, and why conveyers were checked immediately upon materialising. It was also why some Paratimers didn't make it home.

'Not on this trip. Is my rocket ready?'

'Yes, sir. Be a little delay about an aircar for the rocketport.' The patrolman had begun to take the transposition record-tapes out of the cabinet. 'They'll call you when it's ready.'

He and the lieutenant strolled out into the noise and colourful confusion of the conveyer-head rotunda. He got out his cigarette case and offered it; the lieutenant flicked his lighter. They had only taken a few puffs when another conveyer quietly materialised in a vacant circle a little to their left.

A couple of Paracops strolled over as the door opened, drawing their needlers, and peeped inside. Immediately, one backed away, snatching the handphone of his belt radio and speaking quickly into it. The other went inside. Throwing away their cigarettes, he and the lieutenant hastened to the conveyer.

Inside the chair at the desk was overturned. A Paracop lay on the floor, his needler a few inches from his outflung hand. His tunic was off and his shirt, pale green, was darkened by blood. The lieutenant, without touching him, bent over him.

'Still alive,' he said. 'Bullet, or sword-thrust.'

'Bullet. I smell nitro powder.' Then he saw the hat lying on the floor, and stepped around the fallen man. Two men were entering with an antigrav stretcher; they got the wounded man on to it and floated him out. 'Look at this, Lieutenant.'

The lieutenant looked at the hat – grey felt, wide-brimmed, the crown peaked by four indentations.

'Fourth Level,' he said. 'Europo-American, Hispano-Columbian Subsector.'

He picked up the hat and glanced inside. The lieutenant was right. The sweat-band was stamped in golden Roman-alphabet letters, JOHN B. STETSON COMPANY, PHILA-DELPHIA, PA., and, hand-inked, *Cpl. Calvin Morrison, Penn'a State Police*, and a number.

'I know that crowd,' the lieutenant said. 'Good men, every bit as good as ours.'

'One was a split second better than one of ours.' He got out his cigarette case. 'Lieutenant, this is going to be a real baddie. This pickup's going to be missed, and the people who'll miss him will be one of the ten best constabulary organisations in the world, on their time-line. We won't satisfy them with the kind of lame-brained explanations that usually get by in that sector. And we'll have to find out where he emerged, and what he's doing. A man who can beat a Paracop to the draw after being sucked into a conveyer won't just sink into obscurity on any time-line. By the time we get to him, he'll be kicking up a small fuss.'

'I hope he got dragged out of his own subsector. Suppose he comes out on a next-door time-line, and reports to his police post, where a duplicate of himself, with duplicate fingerprints, is on duty.'

'Yes. Wouldn't that be dandy, now?' He lit a cigarette. 'When the aircar comes, send it back. I'm going over the photo-records myself. Have the rocket held; I'll need it in a few hours. I'm making this case my own personal baby.'

TWO

Calvin Morrison dangled his black-booted legs over the edge of the low cliff and wished, again, that he hadn't lost his hat. He knew exactly where he was: he was right at the same place he had been, sitting on the little cliff above the road where he and Larry Stacey and Jack French and Steve Kovac had left the car, only there was no road there now, and never had been one. There was a hemlock, four feet thick at the butt, growing where the farmhouse should have been, and no trace of the stonework of the foundations of house or barn. But the really permanent features, like the Bald Eagles to the north and Nittany Mountain to the south, were exactly as they should be.

That flash and momentary darkness could have been subjective; put that in the unproven column. He was sure the strangely beautiful dome of shimmering light had been real, and so had the desk and the instrument-panel, and the man with the odd weapon. And there was nothing at all subjective about all this virgin timber where farmlands should have been. So he puffed slowly on his pipe and tried to remember and to analyse what had happened to him.

He hadn't been shot and taken to hospital where he was now lying delirious, he was sure of that. This wasn't delirium. Nor did he consider for an instant questioning either his sanity or his senses, nor did he indulge in dirty language like 'incredible' or 'impossible'. Extraordinary — now there was a good word. He was quite sure that something extraordinary had happend to him. It seemed to break into two parts: one, blundering into that dome of pearly light, what had happened inside of it, and rolling out of it;

and two, this same-but-different place in which he now found himself.

What was wrong with both was anachronism, and the anachronisms were mutually contradictory. None of the first part belonged in 1964 or, he suspected, for many centuries to come; portable energy-weapons, for instance. None of the second part belonged in 1964, either, or for at least a century in the past.

His pipe had gone out. For a while he forgot to relight it, while he tossed those two facts back and forth in his mind. He still didn't use those dirty words. He used one small boys like to scribble on privy walls.

In spite – no, because – of his clergyman father's insistence that he study for and enter the Presbyterian ministry, he was an agnostic. Agnosticism, for him, was refusal to accept or to deny without proof. A good philosophy for a cop, by the way. Well, he wasn't going to reject the possibility of time-machines; not after having been shanghaied aboard one and having to shoot his way out of it. That thing had been a time-machine, and whenever he was now, it wasn't the Twentieth Century, and he was never going to get back to it. He settled that point in his mind and accepted it once and for all.

His pipe was out; he started to knock out the heel, then stirred it with a twig and relit it. He couldn't afford to waste anything now. Sixteen rounds of ammunition; he couldn't do a hell of a lot of Indian-fighting on that. The blackjack might be some good at close quarters. The value of the handcuffs and the whistle was problematical. When he had smoked the contents of his pipe down to ash, he emptied and pocketed it and climbed down from the little cliff, going to the brook and following it down to where it joined a larger stream.

A bluejay made a fuss at his approach. Two deer ran in front of him. A small black bear regarded him suspiciously and hastened away. Now, if he could only find some Indians who wouldn't throw tomahawks first and ask questions afterwards . . .

A road dipped in front of him to cross the stream. For an instant he accepted that calmly, then caught his breath. A real, wheel-rutted road. And brown horse-droppings in it – they were the most beautiful things he had ever seen. They meant he hadn't beaten Columbus here, after all. Maybe he might have trouble giving a plausible account of himself, but at least he could do it in English. He waded through the little ford and started down the road, towards where he thought Bellefonte ought to be. Maybe he was in time to get into the Civil War. That would be more fun than Korea had been.

The sun went down in front of him. By now he was out of the big hemlocks; they'd been lumbered off on both sides of the road, and there was a respectable second growth, mostly hardwoods. Finally, in the dusk, he smelled freshly turned earth. It was full dark when he saw a light ahead.

The house was only a dim shape; the light came from one window on the end and two in front, horizontal slits under the roof overhang. Behind, he thought, were stables. And a pigpen – his nose told him that. Two dogs, outside, began whauff-whauffing in the road in front of him.

'Hello, in there!' he called.

Through the open windows, too high to see into, he heard voices: a man's, a woman's, another man's. He called again, and came closer. A bar scraped, and the door swung open. For a moment a heavy-bodied woman in a sleeveless dark dress stood in it. Then she spoke to him and stepped aside. He entered.

It was a big room, lighted by two candles, one on a table spread with a meal and the other on the mantel, and by the fire on the hearth. Double-deck bunks along one wall, fireplace with things stacked against it. There were three men and another, younger, woman, beside the one who had admitted him. Out of the corner of his eye he could see children peering around a door that seemed to open into a shed-annexe. One of the men, big and blond-bearded, stood with his back to the fireplace, holding what looked like a short gun.

No, it wasn't, either. It was a crossbow, bent, with a quarrel in the groove.

The other two men were younger – probably his sons. Both were bearded, though one's beard was only a blond fuzz. He held an axe; his older brother had a halberd. All three wore sleeveless leather jerkins, short-sleeved shirts, and cross-gartered hose. The older woman spoke in a whisper to the younger woman, who went through the door at the side, hustling the children ahead of her.

He raised his hands pacifically as he entered. 'I'm a friend,' he said. 'I'm going to Bellefonte; how far is it?'

The man with the crossbow said something. The woman replied. The youth with the axe said something, and they all laughed.

'My name is Morrison. Corporal, Pennsylvania State Police.' Hell, they wouldn't know the State Police from the Swiss Marines. 'Am I on the road to Bellefonte?' They ought to know where that was, it'd been settled in 1770, and this couldn't be any earlier than that.

More back-and-forth. They weren't talking Pennsylvania Dutch – he knew a little of it. Maybe Polish . . . no, he'd heard enough of that in the hard-coal country to recognise it, at least. He looked around while they argued, and noticed, on a shelf in the far corner, three images. He meant to get a closer look at them. Roman Catholics used images, so did Greek Catholics, and he knew the difference.

The man with the crossbow laid the weapon down, but kept it bent with the quarrel in place, and spoke slowly and distinctly. It was no language he had ever heard before. He replied, just as distinctly, in English. They looked at one another, and passed their hands back and forth across their faces. On a thousand-to-one chance, he tried Japanese. It didn't pay off. By signs, they invited him to sit and eat with them, and the children, six of them, trooped in.

The meal was ham, potatoes and succotash. The eating tools were knives and a few horn spoons; the plates were slabs of corn-bread. The men used their belt-knives. He took out his jackknife, a big switchblade he'd taken off a j.d. arrest, and caused a sensation with it. He had to demonstrate several times. There was also elderberry wine, strong but not particularly good. When they left the table for the women to clear, the men filled pipes from a tobacco-jar on the mantel, offering it to him. He filled his own, lighting it, as they had, with a twig from the hearth. Stepping back, he got a look at the images.

The central figure was an elderly man in a white robe with a blue eight-pointed star on his breast. Flanking him, on the left, was a seated female figure, nude and exaggeratedly pregnant, crowned with wheat and holding a cornstalk; and on the right a masculine figure in a mail shirt, holding a spiked mace. The only really odd thing about him was that he had the head of a wolf. Father-god, fertility-goddess, war-god. No, this crowd weren't Catholics – Greek, Roman or any other kind.

He bowed to the central figure, touching his forehead, and repeated the gesture to the other two. There was a gratified murmur behind him; anybody could see he wasn't any heathen. Then he sat down on a chest with his back to the wall.

They hadn't re-barred the door. The children had been herded back into the annexe by the younger woman. Now that he recalled, there'd been a vacant place, which he had taken, at the table. Somebody had gone off somewhere with a message. As soon as he finished his pipe, he pocketed it, managing, unobtrusively, to unsnap the strap of his holster.

Some half an hour later, he caught the galloping thud of hooves down the road – at least six horses. He pretended not to hear it; so did the others. The father moved to where he had put down the crossbow; the older son got hold of the halberd, and the fuzz-chinned youth moved to the door. The horses stopped outside; the dogs began barking frantically. There was a clatter of accoutrements as men dismounted. He slipped the .38 out and cocked it.

The youth went to the door, but before he could open it, it flew back in his face, knocking him backwards, and a man – bearded face under a high-combed helmet, steel long sword in front of him. There was another helmeted head behind, and the muzzle of a musket. Everybody in the room shouted in alarm; this wasn't what they'd been expecting, at all. Outside, a pistol banged, and a dog howled briefly.

Rising from the chest, he shot the man with the sword. Half-cocking with the double-action and thumbing the hammer back the rest of the way, he shot the man with the musket, which went off into the ceiling. A man behind him caught a crossbow quarrel in the forehead and pitched forward, dropping a long pistol unfired.

Shifting the Colt to his left hand, he caught up the sword the first man had dropped. Double-edged, with a swept guard, it was lighter than it looked, and beautifully balanced. He stepped over the body of the first man he had shot, to be confronted by a swordsman from outside, trying to get over the other two. For a few moments they cut and parried, and then he drove the point into his opponent's unarmoured face, then tugged his blade free as the man went down. The boy, who had got hold of the dropped pistol, fired past him and hit a man holding a clump of horses in the road. Then he was outside, and the man with the halberd along with him, chopping down another of the party. The father followed; he'd got the musket and a powder-flask, and was reloading it.

Driving the point of the sword into the ground, he holstered his Colt and as one of the loose horses passed, caught the reins, throwing himself into the saddle. Then, when his feet had found the stirrups, he stooped and retrieved the sword, thankful that even in a motorised age the State Police taught their men to ride.

The fight was over, at least here. Six attackers were down, presumably dead; two more were galloping away. Five loose horses milled about, and the two young men were trying to catch them. Their father had charged the short musket, and was priming the pan.

This had only been a sideshow fight, though. The main event was a half mile down the road; he could hear shots, yells and screams, and a sudden orange glare mounted into the night. While he was quieting the horse and trying to accustom him to the change of ownership, a couple more fires blazed up. He was wondering just what he had cut himself in on when the fugitives began streaming up the road. He had no trouble identifying them as such; he'd seen enough of that in Korea.

There were more than fifty of them – men, women and children. Some of the men had weapons : spears, axes, a few bows, one musket almost six feet long. His bearded host shouted at them, and they paused.

'What's going on down there?' he demanded.

Babble answered him. One or two tried to push past; he cursed them luridly and slapped at them with his flat. The words meant nothing, but the tone did. That had worked for him in Korea, too. They all stopped in a clump, while the bearded man spoke to them. A few cheered. He looked them over; call it twenty effectives. The bodies in the road were stripped of weapons; out of the corner of his eye he saw the two women passing things out the cottage door. Four of the riderless horses had been caught and mounted. More fugitives came up, saw what was going on, and joined.

'All right, you guys! You want to live forever?' He swung his sword to include all of them, then pointed down the road, to where a whole village must now be burning. 'Come on, let's go get them!'

A general cheer went up as he started his horse forward, and the whole mob poured after him, shouting. They met more fugitives, who saw that a counter-attack had been organised, if that was the word for it. The shooting ahead had stopped. Nothing left in the village to shoot at, he supposed.

Then, when they were within four or five hundred yards of the burning houses, there was a blast of forty or fifty shots in less than ten seconds, and loud yells, some in alarm. More shots, and then mounted men came pelting towards them. This wasn't an attack; it was a rout. Whoever had raided that village had been hit from behind. Everybody with guns or bows let fly at once. A horse went down, and a saddle was emptied. Remembering how many shots it had taken for one casualty in Korea, that wasn't bad. He stood up in his stirrups, which were an inch or so too short for him to begin with, waved his sword, and shouted, 'Chaaarge!' Then he and the others who were mounted kicked their horses into a gallop, and the infantry – axes, scythes, pitchforks and all – ran after them.

A horseman coming in the opposite direction aimed a sword-cut at his bare head. He parried and thrust, the point glancing from a breastplate. Before either could recover, the other man's horse had carried him on past and among the spears and pitchforks behind. Then he was trading thrusts for cuts with another rider, wondering if none of these imbeciles had ever heard that a sword had a point. By this time the road for a hundred yards in front, and the fields on either side, were full of horsemen, chopping and shooting at one another in the firelight.

He got his point in under his opponent's arm, the memory-voice of a history professor of long ago reminded him of the gap in a cuirass there, and almost had the sword wrenched from his hand before he cleared it. Then another rider was coming at him, unarmoured, wearing a cloak and a broad hat, aiming a pistol almost as long as the arm that held it. He swung back for a cut, urging his horse forward, and knew

21

he'd never make it. *All right, Cal; your luck's run out!*

The was an upflash from the pan, a belch of flame from the muzzle, and something hammered him in the chest. He hung on to consciousness long enough to kick his feet free of the stirrups. In that last moment, he realised that the rider who had shot him had been a girl.

THREE

I

Rylla sat with her father at the table in the small study. Chartiphon was at one end and Xentos at the other, and Harmakros, the cavalry captain, in a chair by the hearth, his helmet on the floor beside him. Vurth, the peasant, stood facing them, a short horseman's musketoon slung from his shoulder and a horn flask and bullet-bag on his belt.

'You did well, Vurth,' her father commended. 'By sending the message, and in the fighting, and by telling Princess Rylla that the stranger was a friend. I'll see you're rewarded.'

Vurth smiled. 'But, Prince, I have this gun, and fireseed for it,' he replied. 'And my son caught a horse, with all its gear, even pistols in the holsters, and the Princess says we may keep it all.'

'Fair battle-spoil, yours by right. But I'll see that something's sent to your farm tomorrow. Just don't waste that fireseed on deer. You'll need it to kill more Nostori before long.'

He nodded in dismissal, and Vurth grinned and bowed, and backed out, stammering thanks. Chartiphon looked after him, remarking that there went a man Gormoth of Nostor would find costly to kill.

'He didn't pay cheaply for anything tonight,' Harmakros said. 'Eight houses burned, a dozen peasants butchered, four of our troopers killed and six wounded, and we counted better than thirty of his dead in the village on the road, and six more at Vurth's farm. And the horses we caught, and the weapons.' He thought briefly. 'I'd question if a dozen of them got away alive and hale.'

Her father gave a mirthless chuckle. 'I'm glad some did. They'll have a fine tale to carry back. I'd like to see Gormoth's face at the telling.'

'We owe the stranger for most of it,' she said. 'If he hadn't rallied those people at Vurth's farm and led them back, most of the Nostori would have got away. And then I had to shoot him myself!'

'You couldn't know, kitten,' Chartiphon told her. 'I've been near killed by friends myself, in fights like that.' He turned to Xentos. 'How is he?'

'He'll live to hear our thanks,' the old priest said. 'The ornament on his breast broke the force of the bullet. He has a broken rib, and a nasty hole in him – our Rylla doesn't load her pistols lightly. He's lost more blood than I'd want to, but he's young and strong, and Brother Mytron has much skill. We'll have him on his feet again in a half-moon.'

She smiled happily. It would be terrible for him to die, and at her hand, a stranger who had fought so well for them. And such a handsome and valiant stranger, too. She wondered who he was. Some noble, or some great captain, of course.

'We owe much to Princess Rylla,' Harmakros insisted. 'When this man from the village overtook us, I was for riding back with three or four to see about this stranger of Vurth's, but the Princess said, "We've only Vurth's word there's but one; there may be a hundred Vurth hasn't seen." So back we all went, and you know the rest.'

'We owe most of all to Dralm,' Old Xentos's face lit with a calm joy. 'And Galzar Wolfhead, of course,' he added. 'It is a sign that the gods will not turn their backs upon Hostigos. This stranger, whoever he may be, was sent by the gods to be our aid.'

II

Verkan Vall put the lighter back on the desk and took the cigarette from his mouth, blowing a streamer of smoke.

'Chief, it's what I've been saying all along. We'll have to do something.' After Year-End Day, he added mentally, I'll do something. 'We know what causes this: conveyers interpenetrating in transposition. It'll have to be stopped.'

Tortha Karf laughed. 'The reason I'm laughing,' he explained, 'is that I said just that, about a hundred and fifty years ago, to old Zarvan Tharg, when I was taking over from him, and he laughed at me just as I'm laughing at you, because he'd said the same thing to the retiring Chief when he was taking over. Have you ever seen an all-time-line conveyer-head map?'

No. He couldn't recall. He blanked his mind to everything else and concentrated with all his mental power.

'No, I haven't.'

'I should guess not. With the finest dots, on the biggest map, all the inhabited areas would be indistinguishable blotches. There must be a couple of conveyers interpenetrating every second of every minute of every day. You know,' he added gently, 'we're rather extensively spread out.'

'We can cut it down.' There had to be *something* that could be done. 'Better scheduling, maybe.'

'Maybe. How about this case you're taking an interest in?'

'Well, we had one piece of luck. The pickup time-line is one we're on already. One of our people, in a newspaper office in Philadelphia, messaged us that same evening. He says the press associations have the story, and there's nothing we can do about that.'

'Well, just what did happen?'

'This man Morrison, and three other State Police officers, were closing in on a house in which a wanted criminal was hiding. He must have been a dangerous man – they don't go out in force like that for chicken-thieves. Morrison and another man were in front; the other two were coming in from behind. Morrison started forward, with his companion covering for him with a rifle. This other man is the nearest thing to a witness there is, but he was watching the front of the house and only marginally aware of Morrison. He says he heard the other two officers pounding on the back door and demanding admittance, and then the man they were after burst out the front door with a rifle in his hands. This officer – Stacey's his name – shouted to him to drop the rifle and put up his hands. Instead, the criminal tried to raise it to his shoulder; Stacey fired, killing him instantly. Then, he says, he realised that Morrison was nowhere in sight.

'He called, needless to say without response, and then he and the other two hunted about for some time. They found nothing, of course. They took this body in to the county seat and had to go through a lot of formalities; it was evening before they were back at the substation, and it happened that a reporter was there, got the story, and phoned it to his paper. The press associations then got hold of it. Now the State Police refuse to discuss the disappearance, and they're even trying to deny it.'

'They think their man's nerve snapped, he ran away in a panic, and is ashamed to come back. They wouldn't want a story like that getting around; they'll try to cover up.'

'Yes. This hat he lost in the conveyer, with his name in it – we'll plant it about a mile from the scene, and then get hold of some local, preferably a boy of twelve or so, give him narco-hyp instructions to find the hat and take it to the State Police substation, and then inform the reporter responsible for the original news-break by an anonymous phone call. After that, there will be the usual spate of rumours of Morrison being seen in widely separated localities.'

'How about his family?'

'We're in luck there, too. Unmarried, parents both dead, no near relatives.'

The Chief nodded. 'That's good. Usually there are a lot of relatives yelling their heads off. Particularly on sectors where they have inheritance laws. Have you located the exit time-line?'

'Approximated it; somewhere on Aryan-Transpacific. We can't determine the exact moment at which he broke free of the field. We have one positive indication to look at the scene.'

The Chief grinned. 'Let me guess. The empty revolver cartridge.'

'That's right. The things the State Police use don't eject automatically; he'd have to open it and take the empty out by hand. And as soon as he was outside the conveyer and no longer immediately threatened, that's precisely what he'd do: open his revolver, eject the empty, and replace it with a live round. I'm as sure of that as though I watched him do it. We may not be able to find it, but if we do it'll be positive proof.'

FOUR

Morrison woke, stiff and aching, under soft covers, and for a moment lay with his eyes closed. Near him, something clicked with soft and monotonous regularity; from somewhere an anvil rang, and there was shouting. Then he opened his eyes. It was daylight, and he was on a bed in a fairly large room with panelled walls and a white plaster ceiling. There were two windows at one side, both open, and under one of them a woman, stout and grey-haired, in a green dress, sat knitting. It had been her needles that he had heard. Nothing but blue sky was visible through the windows. There was a table, with things on it, and chairs, and, across the room, a chest on the top of which his clothes were neatly piled, his belt and revolver on top. His boots, neatly cleaned, stood by the chest, and a long unsheathed sword with a swept guard and a copper pommel leaned against the wall.

The woman looked up quickly as he stirred, then put her knitting on the floor and rose. She looked at him, and went to the table, pouring a cup of water and bringing it to him. He thanked her, drank, and gave it back. The cup and pitcher were of heavy silver, elaborately chased. This wasn't any peasant cottage. Replacing the cup on the table, she went out.

He ran a hand over his chin. About three days' stubble. The growth of his fingernails checked with that. The whole upper part of his torso was tightly bandaged. Broken rib, or ribs, and probably a nasty hole in him. He was still alive after three days. Estimating the here-and-now medical art from the general technological level as he'd seen it so far, that probably meant that he had a fair chance of continuing so. At least he was among friends and not a prisoner. The presence of the sword and the revolver proved that.

The woman returned, accompanied by a man in a blue robe with an eight-pointed white star on the breast, the colours of the central image on the peasants' god-shelf reversed. A priest, doubling as doctor. He was short and chubby, with a pleasant round face; advancing, he laid a hand on Morrison's brow, took his pulse, and spoke in a cheerfully optimistic tone. The bedside manner seemed to be a universal constant. With the woman's help, he got the bandages, yards of them, off. He did have a nasty wound, uncomfortably close to his heart, and his whole left side was black and blue. The woman brought a pot from the table; the doctor-priest smeared the wound with some dirty-looking unguent, they put on fresh bandages, and the woman took out the old ones. The doctor-priest tried to talk to him : he tried to talk to the doctor-priest. The woman came back with a bowl of turkey-broth, full of finely minced meat, and a spoon. While he was finishing it, two more visitors arrived.

One was a man, robed like the doctor, his cowl thrown back from his head, revealing snow-white hair. He had a gentle, kindly face, and was smiling. For a moment Morrison wondered if this place might be a monastery of some sort, and then saw the old priest's definitely un-monastic companion.

She was a girl, twenty, give or take a year or so, with blonde hair cut in what he knew as a page-boy bob. She had blue eyes and red lips and an impudent tilty little nose dusted with golden freckles. She wore a jerkin of something like brown suede, sewn with gold thread, and a yellow under-tunic with a high neck and long sleeves, and brown knit hose and thigh-length jackboots. There was a gold chain around her neck, and gold-hilted dagger on a belt of gold links. No, this wasn't any monastery, and it wasn't any peasant hovel, either.

As soon as he saw her, he began to laugh. He'd met that young lady before.

'You shot me!' he accused, aiming an imaginary pistol and saying 'Bang!' and then touching his chest.

She said something to the older priest, he replied, and she said something to Morrison, pantomiming sorrow and shame, covering her face with one hand, and winking at him over it. Then they both laughed. Perfectly natural mistake – how could she have known which side he'd been on?

The two priests held a colloquy, and then the younger brought him about four ounces of something dark brown in a glass tumbler. It tasted alcoholic and medicinally bitter. They told him, by signs, to go back to sleep, and left him, the girl looking back over her shoulder as she went out.

He squirmed a little, decided that he was going to like it, here-and-now, and dozed off.

Late in the afternoon he woke again. A different woman, thin, with mouse-brown hair, sat in the chair under the window, stitching on something that looked like a shirt. Outside, a dog was barking, and farther off somebody was drilling troops – a couple of hundred, from the amount of noise they were making. A voice was counting cadence: *Heep, heep, heep, heep!* Another universal constant.

He smiled contentedly. Once he got on his feet again, he didn't think he was going to be on unemployment very long. A soldier was all he'd ever been, since he'd stopped being a theological student at Princeton between sophomore and junior years. He'd owed a lot of thanks to the North Korean Communists for starting that war; without it, he might never have found the moral courage to free himself from the career into which his father had been forcing him. His enlisting in the Army had probably killed his father; the Rev. Alexander Morrison simply couldn't endure not having his own way. At least, he died while his son was in Korea.

Then there had been the year and a half, after he came home, when he'd worked as a bankguard, until his mother died. That had been soldiering of a sort; he'd worked armed and in uniform, at least. And then, when he no longer had his mother to support, he'd gone into the State Police. That had really been soldiering, the nearest anybody could come to it in peacetime.

And then he'd blundered into that dome of pearly light, that time-machine, and come out of it into – into here-and-now, that was all he could call it.

Where *here* was was fairly easy. It had to be somewhere within, say, ten or fifteen miles of where he had been time-shifted, which was just over the Clinton County line, in Nittany Valley. They didn't use helicopters to evacuate the wounded, here-and-now, that was sure.

When *now* was was something else. He lay on his back, looking up at the white ceiling, not wanting to attract the attention of the woman sewing by the window. It wasn't the past. Even if he hadn't studied history – it was about the only thing at college he had studied – he'd have known that Penn's Colony had never been anything like this. It was more like Sixteenth Century Europe, though any Sixteenth Century French or German cavalryman who was as incompetent a swordsman as that gang he'd been fighting wouldn't have lived to wear out his first pair of issue boots. And enough Comparative Religion had rubbed off on him to know that those three images on that peasant's shelf didn't belong in any mythology back to Egypt and Sumeria.

So it had to be the future. A far future, long after the world had been devastated by atomic war, and man, self-blasted back to the Stone Age, had bootstrapped himself back this far. A thousand years, ten thousand years; ten dollars if you guess how many beans in the jar. The important thing was that here-and-now was when/where he would stay, and he'd have to make a place for himself. He thought he was going to like it.

That lovely, lovely blonde! He fell asleep thinking about her.

Breakfast the next morning was cornmeal mush cooked with meat-broth and tasting rather like scrapple, and a mug of sassafras tea. Coffee, it seemed, didn't exist here-and-now, and *that* he was going to miss. He sign-talked for his tunic to be brought, and got his pipe, tobacco and lighter out of it. The woman brought a stool and set it beside the bed to put things on. The lighter opened her eyes a trifle, and she said something, and he said something in a polite voice, and she went back to her knitting. He looked at the tunic; it was torn and blood-soaked on the left side, and the badge was lead-splashed and twisted. That was why he was still alive.

The old priest and the girl were in about an hour later. This time she was wearing a red and grey knit frock that could have gone into Bergdorf-Goodman's window with a $200 price-tag any day, though the dagger on her belt wasn't exactly Fifth Avenue. They had slates and soapstone sticks with them; paper evidently hadn't been rediscovered yet. They greeted him, then pulled up chairs and got down to business.

First, they taught him the words for *you* and *me* and *he* and *she*, and, when he had that, names. The girl was Rylla. The old priest was Xentos. The younger priest, who dropped in for a look at the patient, was Mytron. The names, he thought, sounded Greek; it was the only point of resemblance in the language.

Calvin Morrison puzzled them. Evidently they didn't have surnames, here-and-now. They settled on calling him Kalvan. There was a lot of picture-drawing on the slates, and play-acting for verbs, which was fun. Both Rylla and Xentos smoked; Rylla's pipe, which she carried on her belt with her dagger, had a silver-inlaid redstone bowl and a cane stem. She was intrigued by his Zippo, and showed him her own lighter. It was a tinderbox, with a flint held down by a spring against a quarter-circular striker pushed by hand and returned by another spring for another push. With a spring to drive instead of return the striker would have done for a gun-lock. By noon, they were able to tell him that he was their friend, because he had killed their enemies, which seemed to be the definitive test of friendship, here-and-now, and he was able to assure Rylla that he didn't blame her for shooting him in the skirmish on the road.

They were back in the afternoon, accompanied by a gentleman with a grey imperial, wearing a garment like a fur-collared bathrobe and a sword-belt over it. He had a most impressive gold chain around his neck. His name was Ptosphes, and after much sign-talk and picture-making, it emerged that he was Rylla's father, and also Prince of this place. This place, it seemed, was Hostigos. The raiders with whom he had fought had come from a place called Nostor, to the north and east. Their Prince was named Gormoth, and Gormoth was not well thought of in Hostigos.

The next day, he was up in a chair, and they began giving him solid food, and wine to drink. The wine was excellent; so was the local tobacco. Maybe he'd get used to sassafras tea instead of coffee. The food was good, though sometimes odd. Bacon and eggs, for instance; the eggs were turkey eggs. Evidently they didn't have chickens, here-and-now. They had plenty of game, though. The game must have come back nicely after the atomic wars.

Rylla was in to see him twice a day, sometimes alone and sometimes with Xentos, or with a big man with a greying beard, Chartiphon, who seemed to be Ptosphes's top soldier. He always wore a sword, long and heavy, with a two-hand grip; not a real two-hander, but what he'd known as a hand-and-a-half, or bastard, sword. Often he wore a gilded back-and-breast, ornately wrought but nicked and battered. Sometimes, too, he visited alone, or with a young cavalry officer, Harmakros.

Harmakros wore a beard, too, obviously copied after Prince Ptosphes's. He decided to stop worrying about getting a shave; you could wear a beard, here-and-now, and no-body'd think you were either an Amishman or a beatnik. Harmakros had been on the patrol that had hit the Nostori raiders from behind at the village, but, it appeared, Rylla had been in command.

'The gods,' Chartiphon explained, 'did not give our Prince a son. A Prince should have a son, to rule after him, so our little Rylla must be as a son to her father.'

The gods, he thought, ought to provide Prince Ptosphes with a son-in-law, name of Calvin Morrison . . . or just Kalvan. He made up his mind to give the gods some help on that.

There was another priest in to see him occasionally: a red-nosed, grey-bearded character named Tharses, who had a slight limp and a scarred face. One look was enough to tell which god he served; he wore a light shirt of finely linked mail and a dagger and a spiked mace on his belt, and a wolf-skin hood topped with a jewel-eyed wolf head. As soon as he came in, he would toss that aside, and as soon as he sat down somebody would provide him with a drink. He almost always had a cat or a dog trailing him. Everybody called him Uncle Wolf.

Chartiphon showed him a map, elaborately illuminated on parchment. Hostigos was all Centre County, the southern corner of Clinton, and all Lycoming south of the Bald Eagles. Hostigos Town was exactly on the site of otherwhen Bellefonte; they were at Tarr-Hostigos, or Hostigos Castle, overlooking it from the end of the mountain east of the gap. To the south, the valley of the Juniata, the Besh, was the

Princedom of Beshta, ruled by a Prince Valthar. Nostor was Lycoming County north of the Bald Eagles, Tioga County to the north, and parts of Northumberland and Montour Counties, to the forks of the Susquehanna. Nostor Town would be about Hughesville. Potter and McKean Counties were Nyklos, ruled by a Prince Armanes. Blair and parts of Clearfield, Huntington and Bedford Counties made up Sask, whose prince was called Sarrask.

Prince Gormoth of Nostor was a deadly enemy. Armanes was a friendly neutral. Sarrask of Sask was no friend of Hostigos; Balthar of Beshta was no friend of anybody's.

On a bigger map, he saw that all this was part of the Great Kingdom of Hos-Harphax – all of Pennsylvania, Maryland, Delaware and southern New Jersey – ruled by a King Kaiphranos at Harphax City, at the mouth of the Susquehanna, the Harph. No, he substituted – just reigned over lightly. To judge from what he'd seen on the night of his arrival, King Kaiphranos's authority would be enforced for about a day's infantry march around his capital and ignored elsewhere.

He had a suspicion that Hostigos was in a bad squeeze between Nostor and Sask. He could hear the sounds of drilling soldiers every day, and something was worrying these people. Too often, while Rylla was laughing with him – she was teaching him to read, now, and that was fun – she would remember something she wanted to forget, and then her laughter would be strained. Chartiphon seemed always preoccupied; at times he'd forget, for a moment, what he'd been talking about. And he never saw Ptosphes smile.

Xentos showed him a map of the world. The world, it seemed, was round, but flat like a pancake. Hudson's Bay was in the exact centre, North America was shaped rather like India, Florida ran almost due east, and Cuba north and south. Asia was attached to North America, but it was all blankly unknown. An illimitable ocean surrounded everything. Europe, Africa and South America simply weren't.

Xentos wanted him to show the country from whence he had come. He'd been expecting that to come up, sooner or later, and it had worried him. He couldn't risk lying, since he didn't know on what point he might be tripped up, so he had decided to tell the truth, tailored to local beliefs and preconceptions. Fortunately, he and the old priest were alone at the time.

He put his finger down on central Pennsylvania. Xentos thought he misunderstood.

'No, Kalvan. This is your home now, and we want you to stay with us always. But from what place did you come?'

'Here,' he insisted. 'But from another time, a thousand years in the future. I had an enemy, an evil sorcerer, of great power. Another sorcerer, who was not my friend but was my enemy's enemy, put a protection about me, so that I might not be sorcerously slain. So my enemy twisted time for me, and hurled me far back into the past, before my first known ancestor had been born, and now here I am and here I must stay.'

Xentos's hand described a quick circle around the white star on his breast, and he muttered rapidly. Another universal constant.

'How terrible! Why, you have been banished as no man ever was!'

'Yes. I do not like to speak, or even think, of it, but it is right that you should know. Tell Prince Ptosphes, and Princess Ryalla, and Chartiphon, pledging them to secrecy, and beg them not to speak of it to me. I must forget my old life, and make a new one here and now. For all others, it may be said that I am from a far country. From here.' He indicated what ought to be the location of Korea on the blankness of Asia. 'I was there, once, fighting in a great war.'

'Ah! I knew you had been a warrior.' Xentos hesitated, then asked: 'Do you also know sorcery?'

'No. My father was a priest, as you are, and our priests hated sorcery.' Xentos nodded in agreement with that. 'He wished me also to become a priest, but I knew that I would not be a good one, so when this war came, I left my studies and joined the army of my Great King, Truman, and went away to fight. After the war, I was a warrior to keep the peace in my own country.'

Xentos nodded again. 'If one cannot be a good priest, one should not be a priest at all, and to be a good warrior is the next best thing. What gods did your people worship?'

'Oh, my people had many gods. There was Conformity, and Authority, and Expense Account, and Opinion. And there was Status, whose symbols were many, and who rode in the great chariot Cadillac, which was almost a god itself. And there was Atom-bomb, the dread destroyer, who would some day come to end the world. None were very good gods, and I worshipped none of them. Tell me about your gods, Xentos.'

Then he filled his pipe and lit it with the tinderbox that replaced his now fuelless Zippo. He didn't need to talk any more; Xentos was telling him about his gods. There was Dralm, to whom all men and all other gods bowed; he was a priest of Dralm himself. Yirtta Allmother, the source of all life. Galzar the Wargod, all of whose priests were called Uncle Wolf; lame Tranth, the craftman-god; fickle Lytris, the Weather-Goddess; all the others.

'And Styphon,' he added grudgingly. 'Styphon is an evil god, and evil men serve him, but to them he gives wealth and great power.'

FIVE

After that, he began noticing a subtle change in manner towards him. Occasionally he caught Rylla regarding him in awe tinged with compassion. Chartiphon merely clasped his hand and said, 'You'll like it here, Lord Kalvan.' It amused him that he had accepted the title as though born to it. Prince Ptosphes said casually, 'Xentos tells me there are things you don't want to talk about. Nobody will speak of them to you. We're all happy that you're with us; we'd like you to make this your home always.'

The others treated him with profound respect; the story for public consumption was that he was a Prince from a distant country, beyond the Western Ocean and around the Cold Lands, driven from his throne by treason. That was the ancient and forgotten land of wonder; that was the Home of the Gods. And Xentos had told Mytron, and Mytron told everybody else, that the Lord Kalvan had been sent to Hostigos by Dralm.

As soon as he was on his feet again, they moved him to a suite of larger rooms, and gave him personal servants. There were clothes for him, more than he had ever owned at one time in his life, and fine weapons. Rylla contributed a pair of her own pistols, all of two feet long but no heavier than his Colt .38-special, the barrels tapering to almost paper thinness at the muzzles. The locks worked like the tinder-boxes, flint held tightly against moving striker, like wheel-locks but with simpler and more efficient mechanism.

'I shot you with one of them,' she said.

'If you hadn't,' he said, 'I'd have ridden on, after the fight, and never come to Tarr-Hostigos.'

'Maybe it would have been better for you if you had.'

'No, Rylla. This is the most wonderful thing that ever happened to me.'

As soon as he could walk unaided, he went down and outside to watch the soldiers drilling. They had nothing like uniforms, except blue and red scarves or sashes, Prince Ptosphes's colours. The flag of Hostigos was a blue halberd-head on a red field. The infantry wore canvas jacks sewn with metal plates, or brigandines, and a few had mail shirts; their helmets weren't unlike the one he had worn in Korea. A few looked like regulars; most of them were peasant levies. Some had long pikes; more had halberds or hunting-spears or scythe-blades with the tangs straightened and fitted to eight-foot staves, or woodcutters' axes with four-foot helves.

There was about one firearm to three polearms. Some were huge muskets, five to six feet long, eight- to six-bore, aimed and fired from rests. There were arquebuses, about the size and weight of an M-1 Garrand, sixteen- to twenty-bore, and calivers about the size of the Brown Bess musket of the Revolution and the Napoleonic Wars. All were fitted with the odd back-acting flintlocks; he wondered which had been adapted from which, the gunlock or the tinderbox. There were also quite a few crossbowmen.

The cavalry wore high-combed helmets, and cuirasses; they were armed with swords and pistols, a pair in saddle-holsters and, frequently, a second pair down the boot-tops. Most of them also carried short musketoons or lances. They all seemed to be regulars. One thing puzzled him : while the crossbowmen practised constantly, he never saw a firearm discharged at a target. Maybe a powder-shortage was one of the things that was worrying the people here.

The artillery was laughable; it would have been long out of date in the Sixteenth Century of his own time. The guns were all wrought-iron, built up by welding bars together and strengthened with shrunk-on iron rings. They didn't have trunnions; evidently nobody here-and-now had ever thought of that. What passed for field-pieces were mounted on great timbers, like oversized gunstocks, and hauled on four-wheel carts. They ran from four to twelve pound bore. The fixed guns on the castle walls were bigger, some huge bombards firing fifty, one hundred, and even two hundred pound stone balls.

Fifteenth Century stuff; Henry V had taken Harfleur with

37

just as good, and John of Bedford had probably bombarded Orleans with better. He decided to speak to Chartiphon about this.

He took the broadsword he had captured on the night of his advent here-and-now to the castle bladesmith, to have it ground down into a rapier. The bladesmith thought he was crazy. He found a pair of wooden practise swords and went outside with a cavalry lieutenant to demonstrate. Immediately, the lieutenant wanted a rapier, too. The bladesmith promised to make real ones, to his specifications, for both of them. His was finished the next evening, and by that time the bladesmith was swamped with orders for rapiers.

Almost everything these people used could be made in the workshops inside the walls of Tarr-Hostigos, or in Hostigos Town, and he seemed to have an unlimited expense-account with them. He began to wonder what, besides being the guest from the Land of the Gods, he was supposed to do to earn it. Nobody mentioned that; maybe they were waiting for him to mention it.

He brought the subject up, one evening, in Prince Ptosphes's study, where he and the Prince and Rylla and Xentos and Chartiphon were smoking over a flagon of after-dinner wine.

'You have enemies on both sides – Gormoth of Nostor and Sarrask of Sask – and that's not good. You have taken me in and made me one of you. What can I do to help against them?'

'Well, Kalvan,' Ptosphes said, 'perhaps you could better tell us that. We don't want to talk of what distresses you, but you must come of a very wise people. You've already taught us new things, like the thrusting-sword' – he looked admiringly at the new rapier he had laid aside – 'and what you've told Chartiphon about mounting cannon. What else can you teach us?'

Quite a lot, he thought. There had been one professor at Princeton whose favourite pupil he had been, and who had been his favourite teacher. A history prof, and an unusual one. Most academic people at the middle of the Twentieth Century took the same attitude towards war that their Victorian opposite numbers had towards sex: one of those deplorable facts nice people don't talk about, and maybe if you don't look at the horrid thing it'll go away. This man had been different. What happened in the cloisters and the guildhalls and the parliaments and council-chambers was important, but none of them went into effect until ratified on the battlefield. So he had emphasised the military aspect of history in a freshman from Pennsylvania named Morrison, a divinity student, of all unlikely things. So, while he should have been studying homiletics and scriptural exegesis and youth-organisation methods, that freshman, and a year later, that sophomore, had been reading Sir Charles Oman's *Art of War*.

'Well, I can't tell you how to make weapons like that six-shooter of mine, or ammunition for it,' he began, and then tried, as simply as possible, to explain about mass production and machine industry. They only stared in incomprehension and wonder. 'I can show you a few things you can do with the things you have. For instance, we cut spiral grooves inside the bores of our guns, to make the bullet spin. Such guns shoot harder, straighter and farther than smoothbores. I can show you how to build cannon that can be moved rapidly and loaded and fired much more rapidly than what you have. And another thing.' He mentioned never having seen any practise firing. 'You have very little powder – fireseed, you call it. Is that it?'

'There isn't enough fireseed in all Hostigos to load all the cannon of this castle for one shot,' Chartiphon told him. 'And we can get no more. The priests of Styphon have put us under the ban and will let us have none, and they send cartload after cartload to Nostor.'

'You mean you get your fireseed from the priests of Styphon? Can't you make your own?'

They all looked at him as though he were a cretin.

'Nobody can make fireseed but the priests of Styphon,' Xentos told him. 'That was what I meant when I told you that Styphon's House has great power. With Styphon's aid, they alone can make it, and so they have great power, even over the Great Kings.'

'Well I'll be Dralm-damned!'

He gave Styphon's House that grudging respect any good cop gives a really smart crook. Brother, what a racket! No wonder this country, here-and-now, was divided into five Great Kingdoms, and each split into a snakepit of warring Princes and petty barons. Styphon's House wanted it that way; it was good for business. A lot of things became clear. For instance, if Styphon's House did the weaponeering as well as the powder-making, it would explain why small-arms were so good; they'd see to it that nobody without fireseed stood an outside chance against anybody with it. But they'd keep the brakes on artillery development. Styphon's House wouldn't want bloody or destructive wars – they'd be bad for business. Just wars that burned lots of fireseed; that would be why there were all these great powder-hogs of bombards around.

And no wonder everybody in Hostigos had monkeys on their backs. They knew they were facing the short end of a war of extermination. He set down his goblet and laughed.

'You think nobody but those priests of Styphon can make fireseed?' There was nobody here that wasn't security-cleared for the inside version of his cover-story. 'Why, in my time, everybody, even the children, could do that.' (Well, children who'd got as far as high school chemistry; he'd almost been expelled, once . . .) 'I can make fireseed right here on this table.' He refilled his goblet.

'But it is a miracle; only by the power of Styphon . . . ' Xentos began.

'Styphon's a big fake!' he declared. 'A false god; his priests are lying swindlers.' That shocked Xentos; good or bad, a god was a god and shouldn't be talked about like that. 'You want to see me do it? Mytron has everything in his dispensary I'll need. I'll want sulphur, and saltpetre.' Mytron prescribed sulphur and honey (they had no molasses here-and-now), and saltpetre was supposed to cool the blood. 'And charcoal, and a brass mortar and pestle, and a flour-sieve and something to sift into, and a pair of balance-scales.' He picked up an unused goblet. 'This'll do to mix it in.'

Now they were all staring at him as though he had three heads, and a golden crown on each one.

'Go on, man! Hurry!' Ptosphes told Xentos. 'Have everything brought here at once.'

Then the Prince threw back his head and laughed – maybe a trifle hysterically, but it was the first time Morrison had heard Ptosphes laugh at all. Chartiphon banged his fist on the table.

'Ha, Gormoth!' he cried. 'Now see whose head goes up over whose gate!'

Xentos went out. Morrison asked for a pistol, and Ptosphes brought him one from a cabinet behind him. It was loaded; opening the pan, he spilled out the priming on a sheet of parchment and touched a lighted splinter to it. It scorched the parchment, which it shouldn't have done, and left too much black residue. Styphon wasn't a very honest powder maker; he cheapened his product with too much charcoal and not enough saltpetre. Morrison sipped from his goblet. Saltpetre was seventy-five per cent, charcoal fifteen, sulphur ten.

After a while Xentos returned, accompanied by Mytron, bringing a bucket of charcoal, a couple of earthern jars, and the other things. Xentos seemed slightly dazed; Mytron was frightened and making a good game try at not showing it. He put Mytron to work grinding saltpetre into the mortar. The sulphur was already pulverised. Finally, he had about a half pint of it mixed.

'But it's just dust,' Chartiphon objected.

'Yes. It has to be moistened, worked into dough, pressed into cakes, dried, and ground. We can't do all that here. But this will flash.'

Up to about 1500, all gunpowder had been like that – meal powder, they had called it. It had been used in cannon for a long time after grain powder was being used in small-arms. Why, in 1588, the Duke of Medina-Sidonia had been very happy that all the powder for the Armada was corned arquebus powder, and not meal-powder. He primed the pistol with a pinch from the mixing goblet, aimed at a half-burned log in the fireplace, and squeezed. Outside somebody shouted, feet pounded up the hall, and a guard with a halberd burst into the room.

'The Lord Kalvan is showing us something about a pistol,' Ptosphes told him. 'There may be more shots; nobody is to be alarmed.'

'All right,' he said, when the guard had gone out and closed the door. 'Now let's see how it'll fire.' He loaded with a blank charge, wadding it with a bit of rag, and handed it to Rylla. 'You fire the first shot. This is a great moment in the history of Hostigos. I hope.'

She pushed down the striker, set the flint down, aimed at the fireplace, and squeezed. The report wasn't quite as loud, but it did fire. Then they tried it with a ball, which went

41

a half inch into the log. Everybody thought that was very good. The room was full of smoke, and they were all coughing, but nobody cared. Chartiphon went to the door and shouted into the hall for more wine.

Rylla had her arms around him. 'Kalvan! You really did it!' she was saying.

'But you said no prayers,' Mytron faltered. 'You just made fireseed.'

'That's right. And before long, everybody'll be just making fireseed. Easy as cooking soup.' And when that day comes, he thought, the priests of Styphon will be out on the sidewalk, beating a drum for pennies.

Chartiphon wanted to know how soon they could march against Nostor. 'It will take more fireseed than Kalvan can make on this table,' Ptosphes told him. 'We will need saltpetre, and sulphur, and charcoal. We will have to teach people how to get the sulphur and the saltpetre for us, and how to grind and mix them. We will need many things we don't have now, and tools to make them. And nobody knows all about this but Kalvan, and there is only one of him.'

Well, glory be! Somebody had got something from his lecture on production, anyhow.

'Mytron knows a few things, I think.' He pointed to the jars of sulphur and saltpetre. 'Where did you get these?' he asked.

Mytron had gulped his first goblet of wine without taking it from his lips. He had taken three gulps to the second. Now he was working on his third, and coming out of shock nicely. It was about as he thought. The saltpetre was found in crude lumps under manure-piles, then refined; the sulphur was evaporated out of water from the sulphur springs in Wolf Valley. When that was mentioned, Ptosphes began cursing Styphon's House bitterly. Mytron knew both processes, on a quart-jar scale. He explained how much of both they would need.

'But that'll take time,' Chartiphon objected. 'And as soon as Gormoth hears that we're making our own fireseed, he'll attack at once.'

'Don't let him hear about it. Clamp down the security.' He had to explain about that. Counter-intelligence seemed to be unheard of, here-and-now. 'Have cavalry patrols on all the roads out of Hostigos. Let anybody in, but let nobody out. Not just to Nostor; to Sask and Beshta, too.' He thought for a moment. 'And another thing. I'll have to give orders people aren't going to like. Will I be obeyed?'

'By anybody who wants to keep his head on his shoulders,' Ptosphes said. 'You speak with my voice.'

'And mine, too!' Chartiphon cried, reaching his sword across the table for him to touch the hilt. 'Command me and I will obey, Lord Kalvan.'

He established himself, the next morning, in a room inside the main gateway to the citadel, across from the guardroom, a big flagstone-floored place with the indefinable but unmistakable flavour of a police-court. The walls were white plaster; he could write and draw diagrams on them with charcoal. Nobody, here-and-now, knew anything about paper. He made a mental note to do something about that, but no time for it now. Rylla appointed herself his adjutant and general Girl Friday. He collected Mytron, the priest of Tranth, all the master-craftsmen in Tarr-Hostigos, some of the craftsmen's guild people from Hostigos Town, a couple of Chartiphon's officers, and half a dozen cavalrymen to carry messages.

Charcoal would be no problem – there was plenty of that, burned exclusively in the iron-works in the Listra Valley and extensively elsewhere. There was coal, from surface outcroppings to the north and west, and it was used for a number of purposes, but the sulphur content made it unsuitable for iron-furnaces. He'd have to do something about coke some time. Charcoal for gunpowder, he knew, ought to be willow or alder or something like that. He'd do something about that, too, but at present he'd have to use what he had available.

For quantity evaporation of sulphur he'd need big iron pans, and sheet-metal larger than skillets and breastplates didn't seem to exist. The iron-works were forges, not rolling mills. So they'd have to beat the sheet-iron out in two-foot squares and weld them together like patch quilts. He and Mytron got to work on planning the evaporation works. Unfortunately, Mytron was not pictorial-minded, and made little or no sense of the diagrams he drew.

Saltpetre could be accumulated all over. Manure-piles would be the best source, and cellars and stables and underground drains. He set up a saltpetre commission, headed by one of Chartiphon's officers, with authority to go anywhere and enter any place, and orders to behead any subordinate who misused his powers and to deal just as summarily with anybody who tried to obstruct or resist. Mobile units, wagons and oxcarts loaded with cauldrons, tubs, tools and the like, to go from farm to farm. Peasant women to be collected and taught to leech nitrated soil and purify nitrates. Equipment, manufacture of.

Grinding mills : there was plenty of water-power, and by good fortune he didn't have to invent the waterwheel. That was already in use, and the master-millwright understood what was needed in the way of converting a gristmill to a fireseed mill almost at once. Special grinding equipment, invention of. Sifting screens, cloth. Mixing machines; these would be big wine-casks, with counter-revolving paddle-wheels inside. Presses to squeeze dough into cakes. Mills to grind caked powder; he spent considerable thought on regulations to prevent anything from striking a spark around them, with bloodthirsty enforcement threats.

During the morning he managed to grind up the cake he'd made the evening before from what was left of the first experimental batch, running it through a sieve to about FFFg fineness. A hundred grains of that drove a ball from an eight-bore musket an inch deeper into a hemlock log than an equal charge of Styphon's Best.

By noon he was almost sure that almost all of his War Production Board understood most of what he'd told them. In the afternoon there was a meeting, in the outer bailey, of as many people who would be working on fireseed production as could be gathered. There was an invocation of Dralm by Xentos, and an invocation of Galzar by Uncle Wolf, and an invocation of Tranth by his priest. Ptosphes spoke, emphasising that the Lord Kalvan had full authority to do anything, and would be backed to the limit, by the headsman if necessary. Chartiphon made a speech, picturing the howling wilderness they would shortly make of Nostor. (Prolonged cheering.) He made a speech, himself, emphasising that there was nothing of a supernatural nature whatever about fireseed, detailing the steps of manufacture, and trying to give some explanation of what made it explode. The meeting then broke up into small groups, everybody having

44

his own job explained to him. He kept running back and forth, explaining to the explainers.

In the evening they had a feast. By that time he and Rylla had got a rough table of organisation charcoaled on to the wall of his headquarters.

Of the next four days, he spent eighteen hours each in that room, talking to six or eight hundred people. Some of them he suffered patiently if not gladly; they were trying to do their best at something they'd never been expected to do before. Some he had trouble with. The artisans' guilds bickered with one another about jurisdiction, and they all complained about peasants invading their crafts. The masters complained that the journeymen and apprentices were becoming intractable, meaning that they'd started thinking for themselves. The peasants objected to having their byres invaded and their dunghills forked down, and to being put to unfamiliar work. The landlords objected to having their peasants taken out of the fields, predicting that the year's crop would be lost.

'Don't worry about that,' he told them. 'If we win, we'll eat Gormoth's crops. If we lose, we'll all be too dead to eat.'

And the Iron Curtain went down. Within a few days, indignant pack-traders and wagoners were being collected in Hostigos Town, trapped for the duration, protesting vehemently but unavailingly. Sooner or later, Gormoth and Sarrask would begin to wonder why nobody was coming out of Hostigos, and would send spies slipping through the woods to find out. *Counter-espionage; organise soonest.* And a few of his own spies in Sask and Nostor. And an anti-Styphon fifth column in both princedoms. *Discuss with Xentos.*

By the fifth day, the Wolf Valley sulphur-evaporation plant was ready to go into operation, and saltpetre production was up to some ten pounds a day. He put Mytron in charge at Tarr-Hostigos, hoping for something better than the worst, and got into his new armour. He and Rylla and a half dozen of Harmakros's cavalrymen trotted out the gate and down the road from the castle into Hostigos Gap. It was the first time he'd been outside the castle since he had been brought there unconscious, tied on to a horse-litter.

It was not until they were out of the gap and riding towards the town, spread around the low hill above the big spring, that he turned in his saddle to look back at the castle. For a moment he couldn't be certain what was wrong, but he knew something was. Then it struck him.

There was no trace whatever of the great stone-quarries.

There should have been. No matter how many thousands of years had passed since he had been in and out of that dome of shifting light that had carried him out of his normal time, there would have been some evidence of quarrying there. Normal erosion would have taken, not thousands, but hundreds of thousands, of years to obliterate those stark man-made cliffs, and enough erosion to have done that would have reduced the whole mountain by half. He remembered how unchanged the little cliff, under which he and Larry and Jack and Steve had parked the car, had been when he had . . . emerged. No. That mountain had never been quarried, at any time in the past.

So he wasn't in the future; that was sure. And he wasn't in the past, unless every scrap of history everybody had ever written or taught was an organised lie, and that he couldn't swallow.

Then when the hell was he?

Rylla had reined in her horse and stopped beside him. The six troopers came to an unquestioning halt.

'What is it, Kalvan?'

'I was just . . . just thinking of the last time I saw this place.'

'You mustn't think about that, any more.' Then, after a moment : 'Was there somebody . . . somebody you didn't want to leave?'

He laughed. 'No, Rylla. The only somebody like that is right beside me, now.'

They shook their reins and started off again, the six troopers clattering behind them.

SIX

I

Verkan Vall watched Tortha Karf spin the empty revolver cartridge on his desk. It was a very valuable empty cartridge; it had taken over forty days and cost ten thousand man-hours of crawling on hands and knees and pawing among dead hemlock needles to find it.

'That was a small miracle, Vall,' the Chief said. 'Aryan-Transpacific?'

'Oh, yes; we were sure of that from the beginning. Styphon's House Subsector.' He gave the exact numerical designation of the time-line. 'They're all basically alike; the language, culture, taboo and situation-response tapes we have will do.'

The Chief was fiddling with the selector for the map screen; when he had got geographical area and run through Level and Sector, he lit it with a map of Eastern North America, divided into five Great Kingdoms. First, Hos-Zygros – he chose to identify it in the terms the man he was hunting would use – its use – its capital equivalent with Quebec, taking in New England and southeastern Canada to Lake Ontario. Second, Hos-Agrys : New York, western Quebec Province and northern New Jersey. Third, Hos-Harphax, where the pickup incident had occurred. Fourth, Hos-Ktemnos : Virginia and North Carolina. Finally, Hos-Bletha, south from there to the tip of Florida and west along the Gulf to Mobile Bay. And also Trygath, which was not Hos-, or *great*, in the Ohio Valley. Glancing at a note in front of him, Tortha Karf made a dot of light in the middle of Hos-Harphax.

'That's it. Of course, that was over forty days ago. A man can go a long way, even on foot, in that time.'

47

The Chief knew that. 'Styphon's House,' he said. 'That's that gunpowder theocracy, isn't it?'

It was. He'd seen theocracies all over Paratime, and liked none of them; priests in political power usually made themselves insufferable, worse than any secular despotism. Styphon's House was a particularly nasty case in point. About five centuries ago, Styphon had been a minor healer-god; still was on most of Aryan-Transpacific. Some deified ancient physician, he supposed. Then, on one time-line, some priest experimenting with remedies had mixed a batch of saltpetre, sulphur and charcoal – a small batch, or he wouldn't have survived it.

For a century or so, it had merely been a temple miracle, and then the propellant properties had been discovered, and Styphon had gone out of medical practice and into the munitions business. Priestly researchers had improved the powder and designed and perfected weapons to use it. Nobody had discovered fulminating powder and invented the percussion-cap, but they had everything short of that. Now, through their monopoly on this essential tool for maintaining or altering the political status quo, Styphon's House ruled the whole Atlantic seaboard, while the secular sovereigns merely reigned.

He wondered if Calvin Morrison knew how to make gunpowder, and while he was wondering silently, the Chief did so aloud, adding:

'If he does, we won't have any trouble locating him. We may, afterwards, though.'

That was how pickup jobs usually were, on the exit end; the pickup either made things easy or impossibly difficult. Many of these paratemporal DP's, suddenly hurled into an unfamiliar world, went hopelessly insane, their minds refusing to cope with what common sense told them was impossible. Others were quickly killed through ignorance. Others would be caught by the locals, and committed to mental hospitals, imprisoned, sold as slaves, executed as spies, burned as sorcerers, or merely lynched, depending on local mores. Many accepted and blended into their new environment and sank into traceless obscurity. A few created commotions and had to be dealt with.

'Well, we'll find out. I'm going outtime myself to look into it.'

'You don't need to, Vall. You have plenty of detectives who can do that.'

He shook his head obstinately. 'On Year-End Day, that'll be a hundred and seventy-four days, I'm going to be handcuffed to that chair you're sitting in. Until then, I'm going to do as much outtime work as I possibly can.' He leaned over and turned a dial on the map-selector, got a large-scale map of Hos-Harphax and increased the magnification and limited the field. He pointed. 'I'm going in about there. In the mountains in Sask, next door. I'll be a pack-trader – they go everywhere and don't have to account for themselves to anybody. I'll have a saddle-horse and three pack-horses loaded with wares. It'll take about five or six days to collect and verify what I'll take with me. I'll travel slowly, to let word seep ahead of me. It may be that I'll hear something about this Morrison before I enter Hostigos.'

'What'll you do about him when you find him?'

That would depend. Sometimes a pickup would be taken alive, moved to Police Terminal on the Fifth Level, given a complete memory obliteration, and then returned to his own time-line. An amnesia case; that was always a credible explanation. Or he would be killed, with a sigma-ray needler which left no traceable effects. Heart failure, or, 'He just died'. Amnesia and heart failure were wonderful things, from the Paratime Police viewpoint. Anybody with any common sense would accept either. Common sense was a wonderful thing, too.

'Well, I don't want to kill the fellow; after all, he's a police officer, too. But with the explanation we're cobbling up for his disappearance, returning him to his own time-line wouldn't be any favour to him.' He paused, thinking. 'We'll have to kill him, I'm afraid. He knows too much.'

'What does he know, Vall?'

'One, he's seen the inside of a conveyer, something completely alien to his own culture's science. Two, he knows he's been shifted in time, and time-travel is a common science-fiction concept in his own world. If he can disregard verbalisms about fantasies and impossibilities, he will deduce a race of time-travellers.

'Only a moron, which no Pennsylvania State Police officer is, would be so ignorant of his own world's history as to think for a moment that he'd been shifted into the past. And he'll know he hasn't been shifted into the future, because that area, on all of Europo-American, is covered with truly permanent engineering works of which he'll find no trace. So what does that leave?'

'A lateral shift in time, and a race of lateral time travellers,' the Chief said. 'Why, that's the Paratime Secret itself!'

II

They were feasting at Tarr-Hostigos that evening. All morning, pigs and cattle had been driven in, lowing and squealing, to be slaughtered in the outer bailey. Axes thudded for firewood; the roasting-pits were being cleaned out from the last feast; casks of wine were coming up from the cellars. Morrison wished the fireseed mills were as busy as the castle bakery and kitchen.

A whole day's production shot to hell. He said as much to Rylla.

'But, Kalvan, they're all so happy.' She was pretty happy, herself. 'And they've worked so hard.'

He had to grant that, and maybe the morale gain would offset the production loss. And they did have something to celebrate: a full hundredweight of fireseed, fifty per cent better than Styphon's Best, and half of it made in the last two days.

'It's been so long since any of us had anything to be really happy about,' she was saying. 'When we'd have a feast, everybody'd try to get drunk as soon as they could, to keep from thinking about what was coming. And now maybe it won't come at all.'

And now, they were all drunk on a hundred pounds of black powder. Five thousand caliver or arquebus rounds at most. They'd have to do better than twenty-five pounds a day – get it up above a hundred at least. Saltpetre production was satisfactory, and Mytron had figured a couple of angles at the evaporation plant that practically gave them sulphur running out of their ears. The bottleneck was mixing and caking, and grinding the cakes. That meant more machinery, and there weren't enough men competent to build it. It would mean stopping work on the other things.

The carriages for the new light four-pounders. The iron-works had turned out four of them, so far – welded wrought-iron, of course, since nobody knew how to cast iron, here-and-now, and neither did he – but made with trunnions. They only weighed four hundred pounds, the same as Gustavus Adolphus's, and with four horses the one prototype already completed could keep up with cavalry on any kind of decent ground. He was happier about that little gun than anything else – except Rylla, of course.

And they were putting trunnions on some old stuff, big things, close to a ton metal-weight but only six- and eight-pounders, and he hoped to get field-carriages under them, too. They'd take eight horses apiece, and they would never keep up with cavalry.

And rifling-benches – long wooden frames in which the barrel would be clamped, with grooved wooden cylinders to slide in guides to rotate the cutting-heads. One turn in four feet – that, he remembered, had been the usual pitch for the Kentucky rifles. So far, he had one, in the Tarr-Hostigos gunshop.

And drilling troops – he had to do most of that himself, too, till he could train some officers. Nobody knew anything about foot-drill by squads; here-and-now troops manoeuvred in columns of droves.

It would take a year to build the sort of an army he wanted. And Gormoth of Nostor would give him a month, at most.

He brought that up at the General Staff meeting that afternoon. Like rifled firearms and trunnions on cannon, General Staffs hadn't been invented here-and-now, either. You just hauled a lot of peasants together and armed them; that was Mobilisation. You picked a reasonably passable march-route; that was Strategy. You lined up your men and shot or hit anything in front of you; that was Tactics. And Intelligence was what mounted scouts, if any, brought in at the last minute from a mile ahead. It cheered him to recall that that would probably be Prince Gormoth's notion of the Art of War. Why, with twenty thousand men, Gustavus Adolphus, or the Duke of Parma, or Gonzalo de Córdoba, could have gone through all five of these Great Kingdoms like a dose of croton oil. And what Turenne could have done!

Ptosphes and Rylla were present as Prince and Heiress-Apparent. The Lord Kalvan was Commander-in-Chief of the Armed Forces of Hostigos. Chartiphon, gratifyingly un-resentful at seeing an outlander promoted over his head, was Field Marshal and Chief of Operations. An elderly 'captain' — actual functioning rank about brigadier-general — was quartermaster, paymaster, drillmaster, inspector-general and head of the draft board. A civilian merchant, who wasn't losing any money at it, had charge of procurement and supply. Mytron was surgeon-general, and the priest of Tranth had charge of production. Uncle Wolf Tharses was Chief of Chaplains. Harmakros was G2, mainly because his cavalry were patrolling the borders and keeping the Iron Curtain tight, but he'd have to be moved out of that. He was too good a combat man to be stuck with a Pentagon job, and Xentos was now doing most of the Intelligence work. Besides his ecclesiastical role as high priest of Dralm, and his political function as Ptosphes's Chancellor, he was in contact with his co-religionists in Nostor, all of whom hated Styphon's House inexpressibly and were organising an active Fifth Column. Like Iron Curtain, Fifth Column was now part of the local lexicon.

The first blaze of optimism, he was pleased to observe, had died down on the upper echelon.

'Dralm-damn fools!' Chartiphon was growling. 'One keg of fireseed — they'll want to shoot that all away tonight celebrating — and they think we're saved. Making our own fireseed's given us a chance, and that's all.' He swore again, this time an oath that made Xentos frown. 'We have three thousand under arms; if we take all the boys with bows and arrows and all the old peasants with pitchforks, we might get that up to five thousand, but not another child or dotard more. And Gormoth'll have ten thousand: four thousand of his own people and those six thousand mercenaries he has.'

'I'd call it eight thousand,' Harmakros said. 'He won't take the peasants out of the fields; he needs them there.'

'Then he won't wait till the harvest's in; he'll invade sooner,' Ptosphes said.

He looked at the relief-map on the long table. The idea that maps were important weapons of war was something else he'd have to introduce. This one was only partly finished; he and Rylla had done most of the work on it, in time snatched from everything else that ought to have been done last week at the latest. It was based on what he remembered from the U.S. Geological Survey quadrangle sheets he'd used on the State Police, on interviews with hundreds of soldiers, woodsmen, peasants and landlords, and on a good bit of personal horseback reconnaissance.

Gormoth could invade up the Listra Valley, crossing the river at the equivalent of Lock Haven, but that wouldn't give him a third of Hostigos. The whole line of the Bald Eagles was strongly defended everywhere but at Dombra Gap. Tarr-Dombra, guarding it, had been betrayed, seventy-five years ago, to Prince Gormoth's grandfather, and Sevenhills Valley with it.

'Then we'll have to do something to delay him. This Tarr-Dombra . . . say we take that, and occupy Sevenhills Valley. That'll cut off his best invasion route.'

They all stared at him, just as he'd been stared at when he'd first spoken of making fireseed. It was Chartiphon who first found his voice:

'Man! You never saw Tarr-Dombra, or you wouldn't talk like that! Nobody can take Tarr-Dombra, unless they buy it, like Prince Galtrath did, and we haven't enough money for that.'

'That's right,' said the retread 'captain' who was G1 and part of G4. 'It's smaller than Tarr-Hostigos, of course, but it's twice as strong.'

'Do the Nostori think it can't be taken, too? Then it can be. Prince, are there any plans of that castle here?'

'Well, yes. On a big scroll, in one of my coffers. It was my grandfather's, and we've always hoped that some time . . .'

'I'll want to see that. Later will do. Do you know if any changes have been made since the Nostori got it?'

None on the outside, at least. He asked about the garrison; five hundred, Harmakros thought. A hundred of Gormoth's regulars, and four hundred mercenary cavalry, to patrol Sevenhills Valley and raid into Hostigos.

'Then we stop killing raiders who can be taken alive. Prisoners can be made to talk.' He turned to Xentos. 'Is there a priest of Dralm in Sevenhills Valley? Can you get in touch with him, and will he help us? Explain to him that this is not a war against Prince Gormoth, but against Styphon's House.'

'He knows that, and he will help as much as he can, but he can't get into Tarr-Dombra. There is a priest of Galzar there, for the mercenaries, and a priest of Styphon for the lord of the castle and his gentlemen, but among the Nostori, Dralm is but a god for the peasants.'

Yes, and that rankled, too. The priests of Dralm would help, all right.

'Good enough. He can talk to people who can get inside, can't he? And he can send messages, and organise an espionage apparatus. I want to know everything that can be found out about Tarr-Dombra, no matter how trivial. Particularly, I want to know the guard-routine, and I want to know how the castle is supplied. And I want it observed at all times. Harmakros, you find men to do that. I take it we can't storm the place. Then we'll have to get in by trickery.'

III

Verkan the pack-trader went up the road, his horse plodding unhurriedly and the three pack-horses on the lead-line trailing behind. He was hot and sticky under his steel back-and-breast, and sweat ran down his cheeks from under his helmet into his new beard, but nobody ever saw an unarmed pack-trader, so he had to endure it. A Paratimer had to be adaptable, if nothing else. The armour was from an adjoining nearly identical time-line, and so were his clothes, the short carbine in the saddle-sheath, his sword and dagger, the horse-gear, and the loads of merchandise – all except the bronze coffer on one pack-load.

Reaching the brow of the hill, he started slowly down the other side, and saw a stir in front of a whitewashed and thatched-roofed roadside cottage. Men mounting horses, sun-glints on armour, and the red and blue colours of Hostigos. Another cavalry post, the third since he'd crossed the border from Sask. The other two had ignored him, but this crowd meant to stop him. Two had lances, and a third a musketoon, and a fourth, who seemed to be in command, had his holsters open and his right hand on his horse's neck. Two more, at the cottage, were getting into the road on foot with musketoons.

He pulled up; the pack-horses, behind, came to a well trained stop.

'Good cheer, soldiers,' he greeted.

'Good cheer, trader,' the man with his hand close to his pistol-butt replied. 'From Sask?'

'Sask latest. From Ulthor, this trip; Grefftscharr by birth.' Ulthor was the lake port in the north; Grefftscharr was the kingdom around the Great Lakes. 'I'm for Agrys City.'

One of the troopers chuckled. The sergeant asked: 'Have you fireseed?'

He touched the flask on his belt. 'About twenty charges. I was going to buy some in Sask Town, but when the priests heard I was passing through Hostigos they'd sell me none. Doesn't Styphon's House like you Hostigi?'

'We're under the ban.' The sergeant didn't seem greatly distressed about it. 'But I'm afraid you'll not get out of here soon. We're on the edge of war with Nostor, and Lord Kalvan wants no tales carried to him, so he's ordered that none may leave Hostigos.'

He cursed; that was expected of him. The Lord Kalvan, now?

'I'd feel ill-used, too, in your place, but you know how it is,' the sergeant sympathised. 'When lords command, commonfolk obey, if they want to keep their heads on. You'll make out all right, though. You'll find ready sale for all your wares at good price, and then if you're skilled at any craft, work for good pay. Or you might take the colours. You're well horsed and armed, and Lord Kalvan welcomes all such.'

'Lord Kalvan? I thought Ptosphes was Prince of Hostigos. Or have there been changes?'

'No; Dralm bless him, Ptosphes is still our Prince. But the Lord Kalvan, Dralm bless him too, is our new warleader. It's said he's a Prince himself, from a far land, which he well could be. It's also said he's a sorcerer, but that I doubt.'

'Yes. Sorcerers are more heard of than seen,' Vall commented. 'Are there many more traders caught here as I am?'

'Oh, the Styphon's own lot of them; the town's full of them. You'd best go to the Sign of the Red Halberd; the better sort of them all stay there. Give the landlord my name' – he repeated it several times to make sure it would be remembered – 'and you'll fare well.'

He chatted pleasantly with the sergeant and his troopers, about the quality of local wine and the availability of girls and the prices things fetched at sale, and then bade them good luck and rode on.

The Lord Kalvan, indeed! Deliberately, he willed himself no longer to think of the man in any other way. And a Prince from a far country, no less. He passed other farmhouses; around them some work was going on. Men were forking down dunghills and digging under them, and cauldrons steamed over fires. He added that to the cheerfulness with which the cavalrymen had accepted the ban of Styphon's House.

Styphon, it appeared, had acquired a competitor.

Hostigos Town, he saw, was busier and more crowded than Sask Town had been. There were no mercenaries around, but many local troops. The streets were full of carts and wagons, and the artisans' quarter was noisy with the work of smiths and joiners. He found the inn to which the sergeant had directed him, mentioning his name to make sure he got his rake-off, put up his horses, safe-stowed his packs and had his saddlebags, valise and carbine carried to his room. He followed the inn-servant with the bronze coffer on his shoulder. He didn't want anybody else handling that and finding out how light it was.

When he was alone, he went to the coffer, an almost featureless rectangular block without visible lock or hinges, and pressed his thumbs on two bright steel ovals on the top. The photoelectric lock inside responded to his thumbprint patterns with a click, and the lid rose slowly. Inside were four globes of gleaming coppery mesh, a few instruments with dials and knobs, and a little sigma-ray needler, a ladies' model, small enough to be covered by his hand but as deadly as the big one he usually carried.

There was also an antigrav unit attached to the bottom of the coffer; it was on, with a tiny red light glowing. When he switched it off, the floorboards under the coffer creaked. Lined with collapsed metal, it now weighed over half a ton. He pushed down the lid which only his thumbprints could open, and heard the lock click.

The common-room downstairs was crowded and noisy. He found a vacant place at one of the long tables, across from a man with a bald head and a straggling red beard, who grinned at him.

'New fish in the net?' he asked. 'Welcome, brother. Where from?'

'Ulthor, with three horse-loads of Grefftscharr wares. My name's Verkan.'

'Mine's Skranga.' The bald man was from Agrys City, on the island at the mouth of the Hudson. He had been trading for horses in the Trygath country.

'These people here took the lot, fifty of them. Paid me less than I asked, but more than I expected, so I guess I got a fair price. I had four Trygathi herders – they all took the colours in the cavalry. I'm working in the fireseed mill, till they let me leave here.'

'The what?' He made his voice sound incredulous. 'You mean they're making their own fireseed? But only the priests of Styphon can do that.'

Skranga laughed. 'That's what I used to think, too, but anybody can do it. It's easy as boiling maple-sugar. See, they get saltpetre from under dunghills ...'

He detailed the process step by step. The man next to him joined the conversation; he even understood, roughly, the theory: the charcoal was what burned, the sulphur was the kindling, and the saltpetre made the air to blow up the fire and blow the bullet out of the gun. And there was no secrecy about it, Vall mused as he listened. If a man who had been a constabulary corporal, and a combat soldier before that, wasn't keeping any better security it was because he didn't care. Lord Kalvan just didn't want word getting into Nostor till he had enough fireseed to fight a war with.

'I bless Dralm for bringing me here,' Skranga was saying. 'When I can leave here, I'm going somewhere and set up making fireseed myself. Hos-Ktemnos – no, I don't want too close to Styphon's House Upon Earth. Maybe Hos-Bletha, or Hos-Zygros. But I'll make myself rich at it. So can you, if you keep your eyes and ears open.'

The Agrysi finished his meal, said he had to go back to work, and left. A cavalry officer, a few places down, promptly picked up his goblet and flagon and moved into the vacated seat.

'You just got in?' he asked. 'From Nostor?'

'No, from Sask.' The answer seemed to disappoint the

57

cavalryman; he went into the Ulthor-Grefftscharr routine again. 'How long will I have to stay here?'

The officer shrugged. 'Dralm and Galzar only know. Till we fight the Nostori and beat them. What do the Saski think we're doing, here?'

'Waiting for Gormoth to cut your throats. They don't know you're making your own fireseed.'

The officer laughed. 'Ha! Some of those buggers'll get theirs cut, if Prince Sarrask doesn't mind his step. You say you have three pack-loads of Grefftscharr wares. Any sword-blades?'

'About a dozen; I sold a few in Sask Town. Some daggers, a dozen gunlocks, four good shirts of rivet-link mail, a lot of bullet-moulds. And jewellery, and tools, and brassware.'

'Well, take your stuff up to Tarr-Hostigos. They have a little fair in the outer bailey each evening; you can get better prices from the castle-folk than here in town. Go early. Use my name.' He gave it, and his cavalry unit. 'See Captain Harmakros; he'll be glad of any news you can give him.'

Late in the afternoon, he re-packed his horses and went up the road to the castle on the mountain above the gap. The workshops along the wall of the outer bailey were all busy. Among other things, he saw a new carriage for a field-piece being put together – not a four-wheel cart, but two big wheels and a trail, to be hauled with a limber, which was also being built. The gun was a welded iron four-pounder, which was normal for Styphon's House Subsector, but it had trunnions, which was not. Lord Kalvan, again.

Like all the local gentry, Harmakros had a small neat beard. His armour was rich but commendably well battered; his sword, instead of the customary cut-and-thrust (mostly cut) broadsword, was a long rapier, quite new. Kalvan had evidently introduced the revolutionary concept that swords had points, which should be used. He asked a few exploratory questions, then listened to a detailed account of what the Grefftscharr trader had seen in Sask, including mercenary companies Prince Sarrask had lately hired, with the names of the captains.

'You've kept your eyes and ears open,' he commended, 'and you know what's worth telling about. I wish you'd come through Nostor instead. Were you ever a soldier?'

'All free-traders are soldiers, in their own service.'

'Yes; that's so. Well, when you've sold your loads, you'll be welcome in ours. Not as a common trooper – I know you traders too well for that. As a scout. You want to sell your pack-horses, too? We'll give you a good price for them.'

'If I can sell my loads, yes.'

'You'll have no trouble doing that. We'll buy the mail, the gunlocks, the sword-blades and that sort of thing ourselves. Stay about; have your meals with the officers here. We'll find something for you.'

He had some tools, both for wood and metal work. He peddled them among the artisans in the shops along the outer wall, for a good price in silver and a better one in information. Besides rapiers and cannon with trunnions, Lord Kalvan had introduced rifling in firearms. Nobody knew whence he had come, except that it was far beyond the Western Ocean. The more pious were positive that he had been guided to Hostigos by the very hand of Dralm.

The officers with whom he ate listened avidly to what he had picked up in Sask Town. Nostor first and then Sask seemed to be the schedule. When they talked about Lord Kalvan, the coldest expressions were of deep respect, shading from there up to hero-worship. But they knew nothing about him before the night he had appeared to rally some fleeing peasants for a counter-attack on Nostori raiders and had been shot, by mistake, by Princess Rylla herself.

Vall sold the mail and sword-blades and gunlocks as a lot, and spread his other wares for sale in the bailey. There was a crowd, and the stuff sold well. He saw Lord Kalvan, strolling about from display to display, in full armour – probably wearing it all the time to accustom himself to the weight, Vall decided. Kalvan was carrying a .38 Colt on his belt along with his rapier and dagger, and clinging to his arm was a beautiful blonde girl in male riding-dress. That would be Prince Ptosphes's daughter, Rylla. The happy possessiveness with which she clung to him, and the tenderness with which he looked at her, made him smile. Then the thought of his mission froze the smile on his lips. He didn't want to kill that man, and break that girl's heart, but . . .

They came over to his display, and Lord Kalvan picked up a brass mortar and pestle.

'Where did you get this?' he asked. 'Where did it come from?'

'It was made in Grefftscharr, Lord; shipped down the lakes by boat to Ulthor.'

'It's cast. Are there no brass foundries nearer than Grefftscharr?'

'Oh, yes, Lord. In Zygros City there are many.' Lord Kalvan put down the mortar. 'I see. Thank you. Captain Harmakros tells me he's been talking to you. I'd like to talk to you, myself. I think I'll be around the castle all morning, tomorrow; ask for me, if you're here.'

Returning to the Red Halberd, Vall spent some time and a little money in the common-room. Everybody, as far as he could learn, seemed satisfied that the mysterious Lord Kalvan had come to Hostigos in a perfectly normal manner, with or without divine guidance. Finally, he went up to his room.

Opening the coffer, he got out one of the copper-mesh globes, and from it drew a mouthpiece on a small wire, into which he spoke for a long time.

'So far,' he concluded, 'there seems to be no suspicion of anything paranormal about the man in anybody's mind. I have been offered an opportunity to take service with his army as a scout. I intend doing this; assistance can be given me in performing this work. I will find a location for an antigrav conveyer to land, somewhere in the woods near Hostigos Town; when I do, I will send a message-ball through from there.'

Then he replaced the mouthpiece, set the timer for the transportation-field generator, and switched on the antigrav. Carrying the ball to an open window, he tossed it outside, and then looked up as it vanished in the night. After a few seconds, high above, there was an instant's flash among the many visible stars. It looked like a meteor; a Hostigi, seeing it, would have made a wish.

SEVEN

Kalvan sat on a rock under a tree, wishing he could smoke, and knowing that he was getting scared again. He cursed mentally. It didn't mean anything — as soon as things started happening he'd forget about it but it always happened, and he hated it. That sort of thing was all right for a buck private, or a platoon-sergeant, or a cop going to arrest some hillbilly killer, but, for Dralm's sake, a five-star general, now!

And that made him think of what Churchill had called Hitler: the lance-corporal who had promoted himself to commander-in-chief at one jump. Corporal Morrison had done that, cut Hitler's time by quite a few years, and got into the peerage, which Hitler hadn't.

It was quiet on the mountain top, even though there were two hundred men squatting or lying around him, and another five hundred, under Chartiphon and Prince Ptosphes, five hundred yards behind. And, in front, at the edge of the woods, a skirmish line of thirty riflemen, commanded by Verkan, the Grefftscharr trader.

There had been some objections to giving so important a command to an outlander; he had informed the objector rather stiffly that until recently he had been an outlander and a stranger himself. Verkan was the best man for it. Since joining Harmakros's scouts, he had managed to get closer to Tarr-Dombra than anybody else, and knew the ground ahead better than any. He wished he could talk the Grefftscharrer into staying in Hostigos. He'd fought bandits all over, as any trader must, and Trygathi, and nomads on the western plains, and he was a natural rifle-shot and a born guerrilla. Officer type, too. But free-traders didn't stay

61

anywhere, they all had advanced cases of foot-itch and horizon-fever.

And out in front of Verkan and his twenty rifled calivers at the edge of the woods, the first on any battlefield in here-and-now history, were a dozen men with rifled eight-bore muskets, fitted with peep-sights and carefully zeroed in, in what was supposed to be the cleared ground in front of the castle gate. The condition of that approach ground was the most promising thing about the whole operation.

It had been cleared, all right – at least, the trees had been felled and the stumps rooted out. But the Nostori thought Tarr-Dombra couldn't be taken and they'd gone slack: the ground hadn't been brushed for a couple of years. There were bushes all over it as high as a man's waist, and not a few that a man could hide behind standing up. And his men would have been hard enough to see even if it had been kept like a golf-course.

The helmets and body-armour had all been carefully rusted; there'd been anguished howls about that. So had every gun-barrel and spearhead. Nobody wore anything but green or brown, and most of them had bits of greenery fastened to helmets and clothing. The whole operation had been rehearsed four times back of Tarr-Hostigos, starting with twelve hundred men and eliminating down to the eight hundred best.

There was a noise, about what a wild-turkey would make feeding, and a soft voice called, 'Lord Kalvan!' It was Verkan; he carried a rifle and wore a dirty grey-green smock with a hood; his sword and belt were covered with green and brown rags.

'I never saw you till you spoke,' Morrison commended him.

'The wagons are coming up. They're at the top switch-back now.'

He nodded. 'We start, then.' His mouth was dry. What was that thing in *For Whom the Bell Tolls* about spitting to show you weren't afraid? He couldn't have done that now. He nodded to the boy squatting beside him; the boy picked up his arquebus and started back to where Ptosphes and Chartiphon were waiting.

And Rylla. He cursed vilely – in English, since he still couldn't get much satisfaction out of taking the names of these local gods in vain. She'd announced that she was coming along. He'd told her she'd do nothing of the sort; so had her father and Chartiphon. She'd thrown a tantrum, and thrown other things as well. She had come along. He was going to have his hands full with that girl, after they were married.

'All right,' he said softly to the men around him. 'Let's start earning our pay.'

The men around and behind him rose quietly, two spears or halberds or long-handled scythe-blades to every caliver or arquebus, though some of the spearmen had pistols in their belts. He and Verkan advanced to the edge of the woods, where riflemen crouched in pairs behind trees. Across four hundred yards of clearing rose the limestone walls of Tarr-Dombra, the castle that couldn't be taken, above the chasm that had been quarried straight across the mountain top. The drawbridge was down and the portcullis up, and a few soldiers with black and orange scarves and sashes — his old college colours; he ought to be ashamed to shoot them — loitered in the gateway or kept perfunctory watch from the battlements.

Ptosphes and Chartiphon — and Rylla, damn it! — came up with the rest of the force, with a frightful clatter and brush-crashing which nobody at the castle seemed to hear. There was one pike or spear or halberd or something — too often something — to every two arquebuses or calivers. Chartiphon wore a long brown sack with arm and neck holes over his armour. Ptosphes wore brown, and browned armour; so did Rylla. They nodded greetings, and peered through the bushes to where the road from Sevenhills Valley came up to the summit of the mountain.

Finally, four cavalrymen, with black and orange pennons and scarves, came into view. They were only fake Princeton men; he hoped they'd get rid of that stuff before some other Hostigi shot them by mistake. A long ox-wagon, piled high with hay which covered eight Hostigi infantrymen, followed. Then a few false-colour cavalry, another big hay-wagon, more cavalry, and two more wagons, and a dozen cavalry behind.

The first four clattered over the drawbridge, spoke to the guards, and rode through the gate. Two wagons followed vanishing through the gate. Great Galzar, if anybody noticed anything, now! The third rumbled on to the drawbridge and stopped directly below the portcullis; that was the one with the log framework under the hay, and the log slung underneath; the driver must have cut the strap to let it drop, jamming the wagon. The fourth, the one loaded with rocks to the top of the bed, stopped on the end of the drawbridge, weighting it down.

Then a pistol banged inside, and another; there were shouts of 'Hostigos!' and 'Ptosphes!' He blew his State Police whistle, and six of the big elephant-size muskets went off in front, from places where he'd have sworn there'd been nobody at all. The rest of Verkan's rifle-platoon began firing, sharp whipcrack reports entirely different from the smoothbores. He hoped they'd remember to patch their bullets when they reloaded; that was something new for them. He blew his whistle twice and started running forward.

The men who had been showing themselves on the walls were gone, now, but a musket-shot or so showed that the snipers in front hadn't got all of them. He ran past a man with fishnet over his helmet stuck full of twigs, ramming a ball into his musket; another, near him, who had been waiting till he was half through, fired. Grey powdersmoke hung in the gateway; all the Hostigi were inside now, and there was an uproar of shouting – 'Hostigos!' 'Nostor!' – and shots and blade-clashing. He broke step to look behind him; his two hundred were pouring after him, and Ptosphes's spearmen; the arquebusiers and calivermen had advanced to two hundred yards and were plastering the battlements as fast as they could load and fire, without bothering to aim. Aimed smoothbore fire at that range was useless; they were just trying to throw as much lead as they could.

A cannon went off above him when he was almost to the end of the drawbridge, and then, belatedly, the portcullis slammed down and stopped eight feet from the ground on the log framework hidden under the hay of the third wagon. They'd tested that a couple of times with the portcullis at Tarr-Hostigos, first. All six of the oxen on the last wagon were dead; the drivers and the infantrymen inside had been furnished short broadaxes to make sure of that. The oxen of the portcullis wagon had been cut loose and driven inside. There were a lot of ripped-off black and orange scarves on the ground, and more on corpses. The gate, and the two gate-towers, had been secured.

But shots were coming from the citadel, across the bailey, and a mob of Nostori was pouring out the gate from it. This, he thought, was the time to expend some .38-specials. Standing with his feet apart and his left hand on his hip, he drew the Colt and began shooting, timed-fire rate. He killed six men with six shots (he'd done that well on silhouette targets often enough), and they were the front six men. The rest stopped, just long enough for the men behind him to come up and sweep forward, arquebuses banging. Then he holstered the empty Colt – he had only eight rounds left for it – and drew his rapier and poignard. Another cannon thundered from the outside wall; he hoped Rylla and Chartiphon hadn't been in front of it. Then he was fighting his way through the citadel gate, shoulder to shoulder with Prince Ptosphes.

Behind, in the bailey, something else besides 'Ptosphes!' and 'Gormoth!' and 'Hostigos!' was being shouted. It was:

'Mercy, comrade! Mercy; I yield! Oath to Galzar!'

There was much more of that as the morning passed; before noon, all the garrison had either cried for mercy or hadn't needed it. There had only been those two cannon-shots, though between them they had killed or wounded fifty men. Nobody would be crazy enough to attack Tarr-Dombra, so the cannon had been left empty, and they'd only had time to load and fire two.

The hardest fighting was inside the citadel. He ran into Rylla there, with Chartiphon hurrying to keep up with her. There was a bright sword-nick on her brown helmet, and blood on her light rapier; she was laughing happily. Then the melee swept them apart. He had expected that taking the keep would be even grimmer work, but as soon as they had the citadel, it surrendered. By that time, he had used the last of his irreplaceable cartridges. Muzzle-loaders for him, from now on.

They hauled down Gormoth's black flag with the orange lily and ran up the halberd-head of Hostigos. They found four large bombards, throwing hundred-pound stone balls, loaded them, hand-spiked them around, and sent the huge gunstones crashing into the roofs of the town of Dyssa, at the mouth of the Gorge River, to announce that Tarr-Dombra was under new management. They set the castle cooks to

5

work skinning and cutting up the dead wagon-oxen for a barbecue. Then they turned their attention to the prisoners, herded into the inner bailey.

First, there were the mercenaries. They all agreed to enter Prince Ptosphes's service. They couldn't be used against Gormoth until the term of their contract with him expired; they would be sent to patrol the Sask border. Then there were Gormoth's own subject troops. They couldn't be made to bear arms at all, but they could be put to work, as long as they were given soldiers' pay and soldierly treatment. Then there was the governor of the castle, a Count Pheblon, cousin to Gormoth, and his officers. They would be released, on oath to send their ransoms to Hostigos. The castle priest of Galzar, after administering the oaths, elected to go to Hostigos with his parishioners.

As for the priest of Styphon, Chartiphon wanted to question him under torture, and Ptosphes thought he should be beheaded out of hand.

'Send him to Nostor with Pheblon,' Morrison said. 'No, send him to Balph, in Hos-Ktemnos, with a letter to the Supreme Priest, Styphon's Voice, telling him that we make our own fireseed, that we will teach everybody else to make it, and that we are the enemies of Styphon's House until Styphon's House is destroyed.'

Everybody, including those who had been suggesting novel and interesting ways of putting the priest to death, shouted approval.

'And a letter to Gormoth,' he continued, 'offering him peace and friendship. Tell him we'll put his soldiers to work in the fireseed mill and teach them the whole art, and when we release them, they can teach it in Nostor.'

Ptosphes was horrified. 'Kalvan! What god has addled your wits, man? Gormoth's our enemy by birth, and he'll be our enemy as long as he lives.'

'Well, if he tries to make his own fireseed without joining us, that won't be long. Styphon's House will see to that.'

EIGHT

I

Verkan the Grefftscharr led the party that galloped back to Hostigos Town in the late afternoon with the good news — Tarr-Dombra taken, with over two hundred prisoners, a hundred and fifty horses, four tons of fireseed, twenty cannon, and rich booty of smallarms, armour and treasure. And Sevenhills Valley was part of Hostigos again. Harmakros had defeated a large company of mercenary cavalry, killing over twenty of them and capturing the rest. And he had taken the Styphon temple-farm, a nitriary, freeing the slaves and putting the priests to death. And the long-despised priest of Dralm had gathered his peasant flock and was preaching to them that the Hostigi had come not as conquerors but as liberators.

That sounded familiar to Verkan Vall; he'd heard the like on quite a few time-lines, including Morrison/Kalvan's own. Come to think of it, in the war in which Morrison had fought, both sides had made that claim.

He also brought copies of the letters Prince Ptosphes had written — more likely, that Kalvan had written and Ptosphes had signed — to Gormoth and to Sesklos, Styphon's Voice. The man was clever; those letters would do a lot of harm, where harm would do the most good.

Dropping a couple of troopers to spread the news in the town, he rode up to the castle; as he approached the gate, the great bell of the town hall began pealing. It took some time to tell the whole story to Xentos, counting interruptions while the old priest-chancellor told Dralm about it. When he got away from Xentos, he was dragged bodily into the officers' mess, where a barrel of wine had already been broached. Fortunately, he had some First Level alcodotevitimine pills with him. By the time he got down to Hostigos Town it was dark, everybody was roaring drunk, the bell was still ringing, and somebody was wasting fireseed in the square with a little two-pounder.

He was mobbed there, too; the troopers who had come in with him betrayed him as one of the heroes of Tarr-Dombra. Finally he managed to get into the inn and up to his room. Getting another message-ball and a small radio-active beacon from his coffer, he hid them under his cloak, got his horse, and managed to get out of town, riding to a little clearing two miles away.

Pulling out the mouthpiece, he recorded a message, concluding:

'I wish especially to thank Skordran Kirv and the people with him for the reconnaissance work at Tarr-Dombra, on this and adjoining time-lines. The information so secured, and the success this morning resulting from it, places me in an excellent position to carry out my mission.

'I will need the assistants, and the equipment, at once. The people should come immediately; there is a big victory celebration in the town, everybody's drunk, and they could easily slip in unnoticed. There will be a formal thanksgiving ceremony in the temple of Dralm, followed by a great feast, three days from now. At this time the betrothal of Lord Kalvan to the Princess Rylla will be announced.'

Then he set the transposition timer, put the ball on antigrav, and tossed it up with a gesture like a falconer releasing his hawk. There was a slight overcast, and it flashed just below the ceiling, but that didn't matter. On this night, nobody would be surprised at portents in the sky over Hostigos. Then, after stripping the shielding from the beacon and planting it to guide the conveyer in, he sat down with his back to a tree and lit his pipe. Half an hour transposition time to Police Terminal, maybe an hour to get the men and equipment together, and another half hour to transpose them.

He wouldn't be bored waiting. First Level people never were. He had too many interesting things in his memory, all of which were available to total recall.

Invited to sit, the Agrysi horse-trader took the chair facing the desk in the room that had been fitted up as Lord Kalvan's private office. He was partly bald, with a sparse red beard; about fifty, five-eight, a hundred and forty-five. The sort of character Corporal Calvin Morrison would have taken a professional interest in: he'd have a record, was probably wanted somewhere, for horse-theft at a guess. Shave off that beard and he'd double for a stolen-car fence he had arrested a year ago. A year before he'd gone elsewhen, anyhow. The horse-trader, Skranga, sat silently, wondering why he'd been brought in, and trying to think of something they might have on him. Another universal constant, he thought.

'Those were excellent horses we got from you,' he began. 'The officers snapped most of them up before they could get to the remount corrals.'

'I'm glad to hear you say so, Lord Kalvan,' Skranga said cautiously. 'I try to deal only in the best.'

'You've been working in the fireseed mill, since. I'm told you've learned all about making fireseed.'

'Well, Lord, I try to learn what I'm doing, when I'm supposed to do something.'

'Most commendable. Now, we're going to open the frontiers. There's no point in keeping them closed since we took Tarr-Dombra. Where had you thought of going?'

Skranga shrugged. 'Back to the Trygath country for more horses, I suppose.'

'If I were you, I'd go to Nostor, before Gormoth closes his frontiers. Speak to Prince Gormoth privately, and be sure the priests of Styphon don't find out about it. Tell him you can make fireseed, and offer to make it for him. You'll be making your fortune if you do.'

That was the last thing Skranga had expected. He was almost successful in concealing his surprise.

'But, Lord Kalvan! Prince Gormoth is your enemy.' Then he stopped, scenting some kind of top-level double-crossing. 'At least, he's Prince Ptosphes's enemy.'

'And Prince Ptosphes's enemies are mine. But I like my enemies to have all the other enemies possible, and if Styphon's House find out that Gormoth is making his own fireseed, they'll be his. You worship Dralm? Then, before you speak to Prince Gormoth, go to the Nostor temple of Dralm, speak secretly to the highpriest there, tell him I sent you, and ask his advice. You mustn't let Gormoth know about that. Dralm, or somebody, will reward you well.'

Skranga's eyes widened for a moment, then narrowed craftily.

'Ah. I understand, Lord Kalvan. And if I get into Gormoth's palace, I'll find means of sending word to the priests of Dralm, now and then. Is that it, Lord Kalvan?'

'You understand perfectly, Skranga. I suppose you'd like to stay for the great feast, but if I were you, I'd not. Go the first thing in the morning, tomorrow. And before you go, speak to Highpriest Xentos; ask the blessing of Dralm before you depart.'

He'd have to get somebody into Sask and start Prince Sarrask up in fireseed production, too, he thought. That might be a little harder. And after the feast, all these traders and wagoners who'd been caught in the Iron Curtain would be leaving, fanning out all over the five Great Kingdoms. He watched Skranga go out, and then filled and lit a pipe – not the otherwhen Dunhill, but a local corncob, regular Douglas MacArthur model – and lit it at the candle on his desk.

Styphon's House was the real enemy. Beat Gormoth properly, on his own territory, and he'd stay beaten. Sarrask of Sask was only a Mussolini to Gormoth's Hitler; a decisive defeat of Nostor would overawe him. But Styphon's House wouldn't stop till Hostigos was destroyed; their prestige, which was their biggest asset, demanded it. And Styphon's House was big; it spread over all the Great Kingdoms, from the St Lawrence to the Gulf.

Big but vulnerable, and he knew, by now, the vulnerable point. Styphon wasn't a popular god, like Dralm or Galzar or Yirtta Allmother. The priests of Styphon never tried for a following among the people, or even the minor nobility and landed gentry who were the backbone of here-and-now society. They ruled by pressure on the Great Kings and the Princes, and as soon as the pressure was relieved, as soon as the fireseed monopoly was broken, those rulers and their people with them would turn on Styphon's House. The war against Styphon's House was going to be won in little independent powder mills all over the Five Kingdoms.

But beating Gormoth was the immediate job. He didn't know how much good Skranga would be able to do, or Xentos's Dralm-temple Fifth Column. You couldn't trust that kind of thing. Gormoth would have to be beaten on the battlefield. Taking Tarr-Dombra had been a good start. The next morning two thousand Nostori troops, mostly mercenaries, had tried to force a crossing at Dyssa Ford, at the mouth of Pine Creek; they'd been stopped by artillery fire. That night, Harmakros had taken five hundred cavalry across the West Branch of Vryllos Gap, and raided western Nostor, firing thatches, running off cattle, and committing all the usual atrocities.

He frowned slightly. Harmakros was a fine cavalry leader, and a nice guy to sit down and drink with, but Harmakros was just a trifle atrocity-prone. That massacre at the Sevenhills temple-farm, for instance. Well, if that was the way they made war, here-and-now, that would be the way to make it.

Then he sat for a while longer, thinking about the Art of War, here-and-now. He hoped taking Tarr-Dombra would hold Gormoth off for the rest of this year and give him a chance to organise a real army, trained in the tactics he could remember from the history of the Sixteenth and Seventeenth Centuries of his own time.

Light cannon, the sort Gustavus Adolphus had smashed Tilly's unwieldy tercios at Breitenfeld with. And plenty of rifles, and men trained to use them. There was a lot of forest country, here-and-now, and oddly, no game laws to speak of; everybody was a hunter. And bore-standardisation, so that bullets could be issued, instead of every soldier having to carry his own bullet-mould and make his own bullets. He wondered how soon he could get socket bayonets, unknown here-and-now, produced. Not by the end of this year, not along with everything else. But if he could get rid of all these bear spears, and these scythe-blade things, whatever they were called, and get the spearmen armed with eighteen-foot Swiss pikes, then they'd keep the cavalry off his arquebusiers and calivermen.

He dug the heel out of his pipe and put it down, rising and looking at his watch (the only one in the world, and what would he do if he broke it?). It was 1700; dinner in an hour and a half. He went out, returning the salute of the halberdier at the door, and up the stairway.

His servant had the things piled on a table in his parlour, on a white sheet. The tunic with the battered badge that had saved his life; the grey shirt, torn and blood-stained. The breeches; he left the billfold in the hip pocket. He couldn't spend the paper currency of a nonexistent United States, and the identification cards belonged to a man similarly non-existent here-and-now. He didn't want the boots, either; the castle cordwainer did better work, now that he had learned to make right and left feet. The Sam Browne belt, with the empty cartridge-loops and the holster and the handcuff-pouch. Anybody you needed handcuffs for, here-and-now, you knocked on the head or shot. He tossed the blackjack down contemptuously; blackjacks didn't belong, here-and-now. Rapiers and poignards did.

He picked up the .38 Colt Official Police, swung out the cylinder and checked it by habit-reflex, and dry-practised a few rounds at a knot-hole in the panelling. He didn't want to part with that, even if there were no more cartridges for it, but the rest of this stuff would be rather meaningless without it. He slipped it into the holster and buttoned down the retaining-strap.

'That's the lot,' he told the servant. 'Take them to High-priest Xentos.'

The servant put them compactly together, one boot on either side, and wrapped them in the sheet. Tomorrow, at the thanksgiving ceremony, they would be deposited as votive offerings in the temple of Dralm. He didn't believe in Dralm, or any other god, but now, besides being a general and an ordnance engineer and an industrialist, he had to be a politician and no politician can afford to slight his con-stituents' religion. If nothing else, a parsonage childhood had given him a talent for hypocritical lip-service.

He watched the servant carry the bundle out. There goes Corporal Calvin Morrison, he thought. Long live Lord Kalvan of Hostigos.

Verkan Vall, his story finished, relaxed in his chair and sipped his tall drink. There was no direct light on the terrace, only a sky-reflection of the city lights below, dim enough that the tip of Tortha Karf's cigarette glowed visibly. There were four of them around the low table : the Chief of Paratime Police; the Director of the Paratime Commission, who acted only on the Chief's suggestion; the Chairman of the Paratemporal Trade Board, who did as the Commission Director told him; and himself, who, in a hundred and twenty-odd days, would have all Tortha Karf's power and authority – and all his headaches.

'You took no action?' the Paratime Commission Director was asking.

'None whatever. None was needed. The man knows he was in some kind of a time-machine, which shifted him, not into the past or future of his own world, but laterally, in another time-dimension, and from that he can deduce the existence, somewhen, of a race of lateral time-travellers. That, in essence, is the Paratime Secret, but this Calvin Morrison – Lord Kalvan, now is no threat to it. He's doing a better job of protecting it in his own case than we could. He has good reason to.

'Look what he has, on his new time-line, that his old one could never have given him. He's a great nobleman; they've gone out of fashion on Europo-American, where the Common Man is the ideal. He's going to marry a beautiful princess, and they've even gone out of fashion for children's fairy-tales. He's a sword-swinging soldier of fortune, and they've vanished from a nuclear-weapons world. He's commanding a good little army, and making a better one of it, the work he loves. And he has a cause worth fighting for and an enemy worth beating. He's not going to jeopardise his position with those people.

'You know what he did? He told Xentos, under pledge of secrecy, that he had been banished by sorcery from his own time, a thousand years in the future. Sorcery, on that time-line, is a perfectly valid explanation for anything. With his permission, Xentos gave that story to Rylla, Ptosphes and Chartiphon; they handed it out that he is an exiled Prince from a country completely outside local geographical knowledge. See what he has? Regular defence in depth; we couldn't have done nearly as well ourselves.'

'Well, how'd it leak to you?' the Board Chairman wanted to know.

'From Xentos, at the big victory feast. I got him off to one side, got him into a theological discussion, and spiked his drink with some hypno truth-drug. He doesn't even remember, now, that he told me.'

'Nobody on that time-line'll get it that way,' the Board Chairman agreed. 'But didn't you take a chance on getting that stuff of his out of the temple?'

He shook his head. 'We ran a conveyor in, the night of the feast, when it was empty. The next morning, when the priests discovered that the uniform and the revolver and the other things had vanished, they cried, "Lo! Dralm has accepted the offering! A miracle!" I was there, and saw it. Kalvan doesn't believe in any miracles; he thinks some of these transients that left Hostigos that day when the borders were opened stole the stuff. I know Harmakros's cavalry were stopping people at all the exit roads and searching wagons and packs. Publicly, of course, Kalvan had to give thanks to Dralm for accepting the offering.'

'Well, was it necessary?'

'Not on that time-line. On the pickup line, yes. The stuff will be found . . . first the clothing and the badge with his number on it. Not too far from where he vanished; I think at Altoona. We have a man planted on the city police force there. Later, maybe in a year, the revolver will turn up, in connection with a homicide we will arrange. The Sector Regional Subchief can take care of that. There are always plenty of prominent people on any time-line who wouldn't be any great loss.'

'But that won't explain anything,' the Commission Director objected.

'No; it'll be an unsolved mystery. Unsolved mysteries are just as good as explanations, as long as they're mysterious within a normal framework.'

'Well, gentlemen, all this is very interesting, but how does it concern me officially?' the Paratime Trade Board Chairman asked.

The Commission Director laughed. 'You disappoint me!

74

This Styphon's House racket is perfect for penetration of that subsector, and in a couple of centuries, long before either of us retire, it'll be a good area to have penetrated. We'll just move in on Styphon's House and take over the same way we did the Yat-Zar temples on the Hulgun Sector, and build that up to general political and economic control.'

'You'll have to stay off Morrison's — Kalvan's — time-line,' Tortha Karf said.

'I should say they will! You know what's going to be done with that? We're going to turn that over to the University of Dhergabar, as a study-area, and five adjoining time-lines for controls. You know what we have here?' He was becoming excited about it. 'We have the start of an entirely new subsector, identified from the exact point of divarication, something we've never been able to do before, except from history. I'm already established on that time-line as Verkan the Grefftscharr trader; Kalvan thinks that I'm travelling on horseback to Zygros City to recruit brass-founders for him, to teach his people how to cast brass cannon. In about forty or so days, I can return with them. They will, of course, be the University study-team. And I will be back, every so often, as often as horse travel rates would plausibly permit. I'll put in a trade depot, which can mask the conveyer-head . . .'

Thortha Karf began laughing. 'I knew you'd figure yourself some way! And, of course, it's such a scientifically important project that the Chief of Paratime Police would have to give it his personal attention, so you'll be getting outtime even after I retire and you take over.'

'Well, all right. We all have our hobbies; you've been going to that farm of yours on Fifth Level Sicily for as long as I've been on the Paracops. Well, my hobby farm's going to be Kalvan Subsector, Fourth Level Aryan Transpacific. I'm only a hundred and thirty; by the time I'm ready to retire . . .'

NINE

I

In the quiet of the Innermost Circle, in Styphon's House Upon Earth, at Balph, the great image looked down, and Sesklos, Supreme Priest and Styphon's Voice, returned the carven stare almost as stonily. Sesklos did not believe in Styphon or in any other god; if he had, he wouldn ot be sitting here. The policies of Styphon's House were too important to entrust to believers, and such could never hope to rise above the white robed outer circle, or at most don the black robes of underpriests. None might wear the yellow robe, let alone the flame-coloured robe of primacy. The image, he knew, was of a man – the old highpriest who had, by discovering the application of a minor temple secret, taken the cult of a minor healer-god out of its mean back-street shrines and made it the power that ruled the rulers of all the Five Kingdoms. If it had been in Sesklos to worship anything, he would have worshipped the memory of that man.

And now, the first Supreme Priest looked down upon the last one. Sesklos lowered his eyes to the sheets of parchment in front of him, flattening one with his hands to read again :

> PTOSPHES, Prince of Hostigos, to SESKLOS, calling himself Styphon's Voice, these:
> False priest of a false god, impudent swindler, liar and cheat!
> Know that we in Hostigos, by simple mechanic arts, now make for ourselves that fireseed which you pretend to be the miracle of your fraudulent god, and that we purpose teaching these arts to all, that hereafter Kings and Princes minded to make war may do so for their own defence and

advancement, and not to the enrichment of Styphon's House of Iniquities.

In proof thereof, we send fireseed of our own make, enough for twenty musket charges, and set forth how it is made, thus:

To three parts of refined saltpetre and three fifths of one part of charcoal add two fifths of one part of sulphur, all ground to the fineness of bolted wheat flour. Mix thoroughly, moisten the mixture, and work it to a heavy dough, then press into cakes and dry them, and when they are fully dry, grind and sieve them.

And know that we hold you and all in Styphon's House of Iniquities our deadly enemies, and the enemies general of all men, to be dealt with as wolves are, and that we will not rest content until Styphon's House of Iniquities is utterly cast down and destroyed.

PTOSPHES,
Prince of and for the nobles and people of Hostigos.

That had been the secret of the power of Styphon's House. No ruler, Great King or petty lord, could withstand his enemies if they had fireseed and he had none; no ruler sat secure upon his throne except by the favour of Styphon's House. Given here, armies marched to victory; withheld there, terms of peace were accepted. In every council of state, Styphon's House spoke the deciding word. Wealth poured in to be loaned out again at usury and return more wealth.

And now, the contemptible Prince of a realm a man could ride across without tiring his horse was bringing it down, and Styphon's House had provoked him to it. There had been sulphur springs in Hostigos, and of Styphon's Trinity, sulphur was hardest to get. Well, they'd demanded the land of him, and he'd refused, and none could be allowed to defy Styphon's House, so his enemy, Prince Gormoth, had been given gifts of money and fireseed. Things like that were done all the time.

Three moons ago, Ptosphes and his people had been desperate; now he was writing thus, to Styphon's Voice Himself. The impiety of it shocked Sesklos. Then he pushed aside Ptosphes's letter and looked again at the one from

77.

Vyblos, the highpriest at Nostor Town. Three moons ago, a stranger, calling himself Kalvan and claiming to be an exiled Prince from a far country, had appeared in Hostigos. A moon later, Ptosphes had made this Kalvan commander of all his soldiers, and had set guards on his borders, that none might leave. He had been informed of that, but had thought nothing of it.

Then, six days ago, the Hostigi had taken Tarr-Dombra, the castle securing Gormoth's best route of invasion into Hostigos, and a black-robe priest who had been there had been released to bear this letter to him. Vyblos had sent the letter on by swift couriers; the priest was following more slowly to tell his tale in person.

It had, of course, been this Kalvan who had given Ptosphes the fireseed secret. He wondered briefly if this Kalvan might be some renegade from Styphon's House, then shook his head. No; the full secret, as Ptosphes had set it down, was known only to yellow-robe priests of the Inner Circle, upper-priests, highpriests and Archpriests. If one of these had absconded, the news would have reached him as fast as relays of galloping horses could bring it. Some Inner Circle priests might have written it down, a thing utterly forbidden, and the writing might have fallen into unconsecrated hands, but he doubted that. The proportions were different: more saltpetre and less charcoal. He would have Ptosphes's sample tried; he suspected that it might be better than their own.

A man, then, who had rediscovered the secret for himself? That could be, though it had taken many years and the work of many priests to perfect the process, especially the caking and grinding. He shrugged. That was not important. The important thing was that the secret was out. Soon everybody would be making fireseed, and then Styphon's House would be only a name, and a name of mockery at that.

He might, however, postpone that day for as long as mattered to him. He was near his ninetieth year; he would not live to see many more, and for each man the world ends when he dies.

Letters of urgency to the Archpriests of the five Great Temples, plainly telling them all, each to tell those under him as much as he saw fit. A story to be circulated among the secular rulers, that fireseed stolen by bandits was being smuggled and sold. Prompt investigation of reports of anyone gathering sulphur or saltpetre, or building or altering grinding-mills. Death by assassination of anyone suspected of knowing the secret.

That would only do for the moment; he knew that. Something better must be devised, and quickly. And care must be taken not to spread, while trying to suppress, the news that someone outside Styphon's House was making fireseed. A Great Council of all the Archpriests, but that later.

And, of course, immediate destruction of Hostigos, and all in it, not one to be spared even for slavery. Gormoth had been waiting until his own people could harvest their crops; he must be made to move at once. An Archpriest of Styphon's House Upon Earth to be sent to Nostor, since this was entirely beyond poor Vyblos's capacities. Krastokles, he thought. Lavish gifts of fireseed and silver and arms for Gormoth.

He glanced again at Vyblos's letter. A copy of Ptosphes's letter to himself had gone to Gormoth, by the hand of the castellan of Tarr-Dombra, released on ransom-oath. Why, Ptosphes had given his enemy the fireseed secret! He rebuked himself for not having noticed that before. That had been a daring, and a fiendishly clever, thing to do.

So, with Krastokles would go fifty mounted Guardsmen of the Temple, their captain to be an upperpriest without robe. And more silver, to corrupt Gormoth's courtiers and mercenary captains.

And a special letter to the highpriest of the Sask Town temple. It had been planned to use Prince Sarrask as a counterpoise to Gormoth, when the latter had grown too great by the conquest of Hostigos. Well, the time for that was now. Gormoth was needed to destroy Hostigos; as soon as that was accomplished, he, too, must be destroyed.

Sesklos struck the gong thrice, and as he did, he thought again of this mysterious Kalvan. That was nothing to shrug off. It was important to learn who he was, and whence he had come, and with whom he had been in contact before he had appeared – he was intrigued by Vyblos's choice of the word – in Hostigos. He could have come from some far country where the making of fireseed was commonly known. He knew of none such, but the world might well be larger than he thought.

Or could there be other worlds? The idea had occurred to him, now and then, as an idle speculation.

II

The man called Lord Kalvan – except in retrospect, he never thought of himself as anything else now – sipped from the goblet and set it on the stand beside his chair. It was what they called winter-wine: set out in tubs to freeze, and the ice thrown off until it was sixty to seventy proof, the nearest they had to spirits, here-and-now. *Distillation*, he added to the long list of mental memos; *invent and introduce*. Bourbon, he thought; they grew plenty of corn.

It was past midnight; a cool breeze fluttered the curtains at the open windows, and flickered the candles. He was tired, and he knew that he would have to rise at dawn tomorrow, but he knew that he would lie awake a long while if he went to bed now. There was too much to think about.

Troop strengths: better than two to one against Hostigos. If Gormoth waited till his harvests were in and used all his peasant levies, more than that. Of course, if he waited, they'd be a little better prepared in training and matériel, but not much. Three thousand regular infantry, meaning they had been organised into companies and given a modicum of drill. Two thousand were pikemen and halberdiers, and too many of the pikes were short hunting-spears, and too many of the halberds were those scythe-blade things (he still didn't know what else to call them), and a thousand calivermen, arquebusiers and musketeers. And fifty riflemen, though in another thirty days there would be a hundred more. And eight hundred cavalry, all of whom could be called regulars – nobles and gentlemen-farmers, and their attendants.

Artillery – there was the real bright spot. Four of the light four-pounders were finished and in service, gun-crews training with them, and two more would be finished in another eight or ten days. And the old guns had been remounted; they were at least three hundred per cent better than anything Gormoth would have.

All right, they couldn't do anything about numbers; then

cut the odds by concentrating on mobility and firepower. It didn't really matter who had the mostest; just git th'ar fustest and fire the most shots and score the most hits with them. But he didn't want to think about that right now.

He emptied the goblet and debated pouring himself more, lighting his pipe. Instead, he turned to something he hadn't had time to think about lately: the question of just when now was.

He wasn't at any time in the past or the future, of May 19, 1964, when he'd walked into that dome of light. He'd settled that in his mind definitely. So what did that leave? Another time-dimension.

Say time was a plane, like a sheet of paper. *Paper; experiment with manufacture of*; that mental memo popped up automatically, and was promptly shoved down again. He wished he'd read more science fiction; time-dimensions were a regular science fiction theme, and a lot of it carefully thought out. Well, say he was an insect, capable of moving only in one direction, crawling along a line on the paper, and say somebody picked him up and set him down on another line.

That figured. And say, long ago, one of these lines of time had forked, maybe before the beginning of recorded history. Or say these lines had always existed, an infinite number of them, and on each one, things happened differently. That could be it. He was beginning to be excited; Dralm-dammit, now he'd be awake half the night, thinking about this. He got up and filled the goblet with almost-brandy.

He'd found out a little about these people's history. Their ancestors had been living on the Atlantic Coast for over five hundred years; they all spoke the same language, and were of the same stock; Zarthani. They hadn't come from across the Atlantic, but from the west, across the continent. Some of that was recorded history he had read, and some was legend; all of it was supported by the maps, which showed all the important seacoast cities at the mouths of rivers. There were no cities on the sites of such excellent harbours as Boston, Baltimore or Charleston. There was the Grefftscharr Kingdom, at the west end of the Great Lakes, and Dorg at the confluence of the Mississippi and Missouri, and Xiphlon at the site of New Orleans. But there was nothing but a trading town at the mouth of the Ohio, and the

Ohio valley was full of semi-savages. Rivers flowing east and south had been the pathway.

So these people had come from across the Pacific. But they weren't Asiatics, as he used the word; they were blond Caucasians. Aryans! Of course; the Aryans had come out of Central Asia, thousands of years ago, sweeping west and south into India and the Mediterranean basin, and west and north to Scandinavia. On this line of events, they'd gone the other way.

The names sounded Greek — all those -os and -es and -on endings — but the language wasn't even the most corrupt Greek. It wasn't even grammatically the same. He'd had a little Greek in college, dodging it as fast as it was thrown at him, but he knew that.

Wait a minute. The words for 'father' and 'mother'. German, *vater*; Spanish, *padre*; Latin, *pater*; Greek, as near that as didn't matter; Sanskrit, *pitr*. German, *mutter*; Spanish, *madre*; Latin, *mater*; Greek, *meter*; Sanskrit, *matr*. In Zarthani, they were *phadros* and *mavra*.

It was one of those small late-afternoon gatherings, nobody seeming to have a care in the world, lounging indolently, sipping tall drinks, nibbling canapés, talking and laughing. Verkan Vall held his lighter for his wife, Hadron Dalla, then applied it to his own cigarette. Across the low table, Tortha Karf was mixing himself a drink, with the concentrated care of an alchemist compounding the Elixir of Life. The Dhergabar University people — the elderly professor of Paratemporal Theory, the lady professor of Outtime History(IV), and the young man who was director of outtime study operations — were all smiling like three pussy-cats at a puddle of spilled cream.

'You'll have it all to yourselves,' Vall told them. 'The Paratime Commission has declared that time-line a study-line, and it's absolutely quarantined to everybody but University personnel and accredited students. I'm making it my personal business to see that the quarantine is enforced.'

Tortha Karf looked up. 'After I retire, I'm taking a seat on the Paratime Commission,' he said. 'I'll see to it that the quarantine isn't revoked or modified.'

'I wish we could account for those four hours from the time he got out of that transposition field until he stopped at the peasant's cottage,' the paratemporal theorist said. 'We have no idea what he was doing.'

'Wandering in the woods, trying to orient himself,' Dalla said. 'Sitting and thinking, most of the time, I'd say. Getting caught in a conveyer field must be a pretty shattering experience, if you don't know what it is, and he seems to have adjusted very nicely by the time he had those Nostori to fight. I don't believe he was changing history all by himself.'

'You can't say that,' the old professor chided. 'He could have shot a rattlesnake which would otherwise have bitten and killed a child who would otherwise have grown up to be an important personage. That sounds far-fetched and trivial, but paratemporal alternate probability is built on different trivialities. Who knows what started the Aryan migration eastward on that sector, instead of westward as on all the others? Some tribal chief's hangover; some wizard's nightmare.'

'Well, that's why you're getting those five adjoining time-lines for controls,' the outtime study operations director said. 'And I'd keep out of Hostigos on all of them. We don't want our people massacred along with the resident population by Gormoth's gang, or forced to defend themselves with Home Time Line weapons.'

'What bothers me,' the lady professor of history said, 'is Vall's beard.'

'It bothers me, too,' Dalla said, 'but I'm getting used to it.'

'He hasn't shaved it off since he came back from Kalvan's time-line, and it begins to look like a permanent fixture. And I notice Dalla's a blonde, now. Blondes are less conspicuous on Aryan-Transpacific. They're both going to be on and off that time-line all the time.'

'Well, nobody's exclusive rights to anything outtime excludes the Paratime Police. I told you I was going to give that time-line my personal attention. And Dalla is officially Special Chief's Assistant's Special Assistant, now; she'll be promoted automatically along with me.'

'Well, you won't introduce a lot of probability contamination, will you?' the elderly theorist asked anxiously. 'We want to observe the effect of this man's appearance on that time-line . . . '

'You know any kind of observation that doesn't contaminate the thing observed, professor?' Tortha Karf, who had got the drink mixed, asked.

'If anything, I'll be able to minimise the amount of contamination his study-teams introduce. I'm already well established with these people, as Verkan the Grefftscharr trader. Why, Lord Kalvan offered me a commission in his army, commanding a rifle regiment he's raising, and right now I'm supposed to be recruiting brass-founders for him in Zygross.' Vall turned to the operations director. 'I can't plausibly get back to Hostigos for another thirty days. Can you have your team ready by then? They'll have to know their trade; if they cast cannon that blow up on the first shot, I know where their heads will go, and I won't try to intervene for them.'

'Oh, yes. They have everything now but local foundry techniques and correct Zygrosi accent. Thirty days will be plenty.'

'But that's contamination!' the professor of Paratemporal Theory objected. 'You're teaching his people to make cannon, and . . . '

'Just to make better cannon, and if I didn't bring in fake Zygrosi founders, Kalvan would send somebody else to bring in real ones. I will help him in any other way a wandering pack-trader could; information and things like that. I may even go into battle with him, again – with one of those back-acting flintlocks. But I want *him* to win. I admire the man too much to want to hand him an unearned victory on a platter.'

'He sounds like a lot of man to me,' the lady historian said. 'I'd like to meet him, myself.'

'Better not, Eldra,' Dalla warned. 'That princess of his is handy with a pistol, and I don't think she cares much who she shoots.'

TEN

I

The General Staff had a big room of their own to meet in, just inside the door of the keep, and the relief map was finished and set up. The General Staff were all new at it. So was he, but he had some vague idea of what a General Staff was supposed to do, which put him several up on any of the rest of them. Xentos was reporting what he had got from the Nostori Fifth Column.

'The bakeries work night and day,' he said. 'And milk cannot be bought at any price – it is all being made into cheese. And most of the meat is being made into smoked sausages.'

Stuff a soldier could carry in a haversack and eat uncooked: field-rations. That stuff, even the bread, could be stored, Kalvan thought, but Xentos was also reporting that wagons and oxen were being commandeered, and peasants impressed as drivers. They wouldn't do that too long in advance.

'Then Gormoth isn't waiting to get his harvests in,' Ptosphes said. 'He'll strike soon, and taking Tarr-Dombra didn't stop him at all.'

'It delayed him, Prince,' Chartiphon said. 'He'd be pouring mercenaries into Nostor now through Sevenhills Valley if we hadn't.'

'I grant that.' There was a smile on Ptosphes's lips. He'd been learning to smile again, since the powder mills had gone into operation, and especially since Tarr-Dombra had fallen. 'We'll have to be ready for him a little sooner than I'd expected, that's all.'

'We'll have to be ready for him yesterday at the latest,' Rylla said. She'd picked that expression up from him. 'What do you think he'll hit us with?'

85

'Well, he's been shifting troops around,' Harmakros said. 'He seems to be moving all his mercenaries east, and all his soldiers west.

'Marax Ford,' Ptosphes guessed. 'He'll throw the mercenaries at us first.'

'Oh, no, Prince!' Chartiphon dissented. 'Go all the way around the mountains and all the way up through East Hostigos? He wouldn't do that. Here's how he'll come in.'

He drew his big hand-and-a-half sword – none of these newfangled pokers for him – and gave it a little toss in his hand to get the right grip on it, then pointed on the map to where the Listra flowed into the Athan.

'There – Listra-Mouth. He can move his whole army up the river in his own country, force a crossing here – if we let him – and take all Listra Valley to the Saski border. That's where all our iron-works are.'

Now that was something. Not so long ago, to Chartiphon, weapons had been just something you fought with; he'd taken them for granted. Now he was realising that they had to be produced.

That started an argument. Somebody thought Gormoth would try to force one of the gaps. Not Dombra; that was too strong. Maybe Vryllos Gap.

'He'll attack where we don't expect him, that's where,' Rylla declared.

'Well, that means we have to expect him everywhere.'

'Great Galzar!' Ptosphes exploded, drawing his rapier. 'That means we have to expect him everywhere from here' – he touched the point to the map to the mouth of the Listra – 'to here,' which was about where Lewisburg had been in Calvin Morrison's world. 'That means that with half Gormoth's strength, we'll have to be stronger than he is at every point.'

'Then we'll have to move what men we have around faster,' his daughter told him.

Well, good girl! She'd seen what none of the others had, what he'd been thinking about last night, that mobility could make up for lack of numbers.

'Yes,' he said. 'Harmakros, how many infantrymen could you put horses under? They don't have to be good horses, just good enough to take them where they'll fight on foot.'

Harmakros was scandalised. Mounted soldiers were

cavalry; everybody knew it took years to train a cavalry-man; he had to be practically born at it. Chartiphon was scandalised, too. Infantrymen were *foot* soldiers; they had no business on horses.

'It'll mean,' he continued, 'that in action about one out of four will have to hold horses for the others, but they'll get into action before the battle's over, and they can wear heavier armour. Now, how many infantry can you find mounts for?'

Harmakros looked at him, decided that he was serious, thought for a moment, then grinned. It always took Harmakros a moment or so to recover from the shock of a new idea, but he always came up punching before the count was over.

'Just a minute; I'll see.'

He pulled the remount officer aside; Rylla joined them with a slate and soapstone. Among other things, Rylla was the mathematician. She'd learned Arabic numerals, even the reason for having a symbol for nothing at all. Very high on the *I love Rylla*, *reasons why* list was the fact that the girl had a brain and wasn't afraid to use it.

He turned to Chartiphon and began talking about the defence of Listra-Mouth. They were still discussing it when Rylla and Harmakros came over and joined them.

'Two thousand,' Rylla said. 'They all have four legs, and we think they were all alive last evening.'

'Eighteen hundred,' Harmakros cut in. 'We'll need some for pack-train and replacements.'

'Sixteen hundred,' Kalvan decided. 'Eight hundred pikemen, with pikes and not hunting-spears or those scythe-blade things, and eight hundred arquebusiers, with arque-buses and not rabbit-guns. Can you do that, Chartiphon?'

Chartiphon could. All men who wouldn't fall off their horses, too.

'It'll make a Styphon's own hole in the army, though,' he added.

Aside from the Mobile Force, that would leave twelve hundred pikemen and two hundred with firearms. Of course, there was the militia : two thousand peasant levies, anybody who could do an hour's foot-drill without dropping dead, armed with anything at all. They would fight bravely if un-skilfully. A lot of them were going to get killed.

And, according to best intelligence estimates, Gormoth had six thousand mercenaries, of whom four thousand were cavalry, and four thousand of his own subjects, including neither the senile nor the adolescent and none of them armed with agricultural implements or crossbows. He looked at the map again. Gormoth would attack where he could use his cavalry superiority to best advantage. Either Listra-Mouth or Marax Ford.

'Good. And all the riflemen.' All fifty of them. 'Put them on the best horses, they'll have to be everywhere at once. And five hundred regular cavalry.'

Everybody howled at that. There weren't that many, not uncommitted. Swords flashed over the map, indicating places where they only had half enough now. Contradictions were shouted. One of these days somebody was going to use a sword for something besides map-pointing in one of these arguments. Finally, by robbing Peter and Paul both, they scraped up five hundred for the Mobile Force.

'And I want all those musketoons and lances turned in,' he said. 'The lances are better pikes than half our pikemen have, and the musketoons are almost as good as arquebuses. We won't have cavalrymen burdened with infantry weapons when the infantry need them as desperately as they do.'

Harmakros wanted to know what the cavalry would fight with.

'Swords and pistols. The purpose of cavalry is to scout and collect information, neutralise enemy cavalry, harass enemy movement and communications, and pursue fugitives. It is not to fight on foot – that's why we're organising mounted infantry – and it is not to commit suicide by making attacks on massed pikemen – that's why we're building these light four-pounders. The lances and musketoons will go to the infantry, and the fowling-pieces and scythe-blade things they replace can go to the militia.

'Now, you'll command this Mobile Force, Harmakros. Turn all your intelligence work over to Xentos; Prince Ptosphes and I will help him. You'll have all four of the four-pounders, and the two being built as soon as they're finished, and pick out the lightest four of the old eight-pounders. You'll be based in Sevenhills Valley; be prepared to move either east or west as soon as you have orders.

'And another thing: battle-cries.' They had to be shouted

constantly, to keep friend from killing friend. 'Besides "Ptosphes!" and "Hostigos!" we will shout "*Down Styphon!*"'

That met with general approval. They all knew who the real enemy was.

II

Gormoth, Prince of Nostor, set down the goblet, wiping his bearded lips on the back of his hand. The candles in front of him and down the long tables at the sides flickered. Tableware clattered, and voices were loud.

'Lost everything!' The speaker was a baron driven from Sevenhills Valley when Tarr-Dombra had fallen almost a moon ago. 'My house, a score of farms, a village . . .'

'You think we've lost nothing?' another noble demanded. 'They crossed the river the night after they chased you out, and burned everything on my land. It was Styphon's own miracle I got out with my own blood unspilled.'

'For shame!' cried Vyblos, the highpriest of the temple of Styphon, sitting with him at the high table. 'You speak of cow-byres and peasant-huts; what of the temple-farm of Sevenhills, a holy place pillaged and desecrated? What of fifteen consecrated priests and novices, and a score of lay guards, all cruelly murdered? "Dealt with as wolves are," ' he quoted.

'That's Styphon's business; let him look to his own,' the lord from western Nostor said. 'I want to know why our Prince isn't looking to the protection of Nostor.'

'It can be stopped, Prince.' That was the mayor, and wealthiest merchant, of Nostor Town. 'Prince Ptosphes has offered peace, now that Hostigos has Tarr-Dombra again. He's a man of his word.'

'Peace tossed like a bone to a cur?' yelled Netzigon, the chief captain of Nostor. 'Friendship shot at us out of a cannon?'

'Peace with a desecrator of holy places, and a butcher of Styphon's priests?' Vyblos fairly screamed. 'Peace with a blasphemer who pretends, with his mortal hands, to work Styphon's own miracle, and make fireseed without Styphon's aid?'

'More than pretends!' That was Gormoth's cousin, Count Pheblon. He still hadn't taken Pheblon back into his favour after losing Tarr-Dombra, but for those words he was close to it. 'By Dralm, the Hostigi burned more fireseed taking Tarr-Dombra than we thought they had in all Hostigos. I was there, which you weren't. And when they opened the magazines, they only sneered and said, "That filthy trash; don't get it mixed with ours."'

'That's all aside,' the baron from Listra-Mouth said. 'I want to know what's being done to keep their raiders out of Nostor. Why, they've harried all the strip between the mountains and the river; there isn't a house standing there now.'

Weapons clattered at the door. Somebody else sneered: 'That's Ptosphes, now! Under the tables, everybody!' A man in mail and black leather strode in, advancing and saluting; the captain of the dungeons.

'Lord Prince, the special prisoner has been made to talk. He will tell all.'

'Ha!' Gormoth knew what that meant. Then he laughed at the looks of concern on faces down the side tables. Not a few at his court had cause to dread somebody telling all about something. He drew his poignard and cut a line across the candle in front of him, a thumb's breadth from the top.

'You bring good news. I'll go to hear him in that time.'

As he nodded dismissal, the captain bowed and backed away. He rapped loudly on the table with the pommel of the dagger.

'Be silent, all of you; I've little time, so give heed. Klestreus,' he addressed the elected captain-general of the mercenary free-companies, 'you have four thousand horse, two thousand foot, and ten cannon. Add to them a thousand of my infantry and such guns of mine as you think fit. You'll cross the Athan at Marax Ford. Be on the road before the dew's off the grass tomorrow; before dawn of the next day, take and hold the ford, put the best of your cavalry across at once, and let the others follow as speedily as they can.

'Netzigon,' he told his own chief-captain, 'you'll gather every man you can, down to the very peasant rabble, and such cannon as Klestreus leaves you. Post companies to confront every pass in the mountains from across the river; use the peasants for that. With the rest of your force, march to Listra-Mouth, and Vryllos Gap. As Kestreus moves west through East Hostigos, he will attack each gap from behind; when he does, your people will cross over and give aid. Tarr-Dombra we'll have to starve out; the rest must be taken by storm. When Klestreus is as far as Vryllos Gap, you will cross the Athan and move up Listra Valley. After that, we'll have Tarr-Hostigos to take. Galzar only knows how long we'll be at that, but by the end of the moon-half all else in Hostigos should be ours.'

There were gratified murmurs all along the table; this made good hearing, and they had waited long to hear it. Only the highpriest, Vyblos, was ill-pleased.

'But why so soon, Prince?'

'Soon? By the Mace of Galzar, you've been bawling for it like a branded calf since greenleaf-time. Well, now you have your invasion – yet you object. Why?'

'A few more days would cost nothing, Prince,' Vyblos said. 'Today I had word from Styphon's House Upon Earth, from the pen of His Divinity, Styphon's Voice Himself. An Archpriest, His Sanctity Krastokles, is travelling hither with rich gifts and the blessing of Styphon. It were poor reverence not to await His Sanctity's coming.'

Another cursed temple-rat, bigger and fatter and more insolent than this one. Well, let him come after the victory, and content himself with what bones were tossed to him.

'You heard me,' he told the two captains. 'I rule here, not this priest. Be about it; send out your orders now, and move in the morning.'

Then he rose, pushing back the chair before the servant behind him could touch it. The line was still visible at the top of the candle.

Guards with torches attended him down the winding stairs into the dungeons. The air stank. His breath congealed; the heat of summer never penetrated here. From the torture chamber shrieks told of some wretch being questioned; idly he wondered who. Stopping at an iron-bound door, he unlocked it with a key from his belt and entered alone, closing it behind him.

The room within was large, warmed by a fire on a hearth in the corner and lighted by a great lantern from above.

Under it, a man bent over a littered table, working with a mortar and pestle. As the door closed, he straightened and turned. He had a bald head and a red beard, and wore a most unprisonerlike dagger on his belt. A key for the door lay on the table, and by them a pair of heavy horseman's pistols. He smiled.

'Greetings, Prince; it's done. I tried some, and it's as good as they make in Hostigos, and better than the dirt the priests sell.'

'And no prayers to Styphon, Skranga?'

Skranga was chewing tobacco. He spat brownly on the floor.

'That in the face of Styphon! You want to try it, Prince? The pistols are empty.'

There was a bowl half full of fireseed on the table. He measured a charge and poured it into one, loaded and wadded a ball on top of it, primed the pan, readied the flint and striker. Aiming at a billet of wood by the hearth, he fired, then laid the pistol down and went to probe the hole with a straw. The bullet had gone in almost a little finger's length; Styphon's powder wouldn't do that much.

'Well, Skranga!' he laughed. 'We'll have to keep you hidden for a while yet, but from this hour you're first nobleman of Nostor after myself. Style yourself Duke. There'll be rich lands for you in Hostigos, when Hostigos is mine.'

'And in Nostor the Styphon temple-farms?' Skranga asked. 'If I'm to make fireseed for you, there's all there that I'll need.'

'Yes, by Galzar, that too! After I've dealt with Ptosphes, I'll have a reckoning with Vyblos, and before I let him die, he'll be envying Ptosphes.'

Snatching up a pewter cup without looking to see if it were clean, he went to the wine-barrel and drew it full. He tasted the wine, then spat it out.

'Is this the swill they've given you to drink?' he demanded. 'Whoever's at fault won't see tomorrow's sun set!' He flung open the door and bellowed into the hall: 'Wine! Wine for Prince Gormoth and Duke Skranga! And silver cups!' He hurled the pewter, still half full of wine, at a guard. 'Move your feet, you bastard! And see it's fit for nobles to drink!'

ELEVEN

I

Mobile Force HQ had been the mansion of a Nostori noble driven from Sevenhills Valley on D-for-Dombra Day. Kalvan's name had been shouted ahead as he rode to it through the torchlit, troop-crowded village, and Harmakros and some of his officers met him at the door.

'Great Dralm, Kalvan!' Harmakros laughed. 'Don't tell me you're growing wings on horses, now. Our messengers only got off an hour ago.'

'Yes, I met them at Vryllos Gap.' They crossed the outer hall and entered the big room beyond. 'We got the news at Tarr-Hostigos, just after dark. What have you heard since?'

At least fifty candles burned in the central chandelier. Evidently the cavalry had got here before the peasants, on D-Day, and hadn't looted too destructively themselves. Harmakros led him to an inlaid table on which a map, scorched with hot needles on white deerskin, was spread.

'We have reports from all the watchtowers along the mountains. They're too far back from the river for anything but dust to be seen, but the column's over three miles long. First cavalry, then infantry, then guns and wagons, and then more infantry and some cavalry. They halted at Nirfë at dusk and built hundreds of campfires. Whether they left them burning and moved on after dark, and how far ahead the cavalry are now, we don't know. We expect them at Marax Ford by dawn.'

'We got a little more than that. The Nostor priest of Dralm got a messenger off a little after noon, but he didn't get across the river till twilight. Your column's commanded by Klestreus, the mercenary captain-general. All Gormoth's mercenaries, four thousand cavalry and two thousand infantry, a thousand of his own infantry, and fifteen guns, he didn't say what kind, and a train of wagons that must be simply creaking with loot. At the same time, Netzigon's moving west on Listra-Mouth with an all-Nostori army; dodging them was what delayed this messenger. Chartiphon's at Listra-Mouth with what he can scrape up; Ptosphes is at Vryllos Gap with a small force.'

'That's it,' Harmakros said. 'Double attack, but the one from the east will be the heavy one. We can't do anything to help Chartiphon, can we?'

'Beat Klestreus as badly as we can; that's all I can think of.' He had got out his pipe; as soon as he had filled it, one of the staff officers was offering a light. That was another universal constant. 'Thank you. What's been done here, so far?'

'I started my wagons and the eight-pounders east on the main road; they'll halt just west of Fitra, here.' He pointed on the map to a little farming village. 'As soon as I'm all collected here, I'll start down the back road, which joins the main road at Fitra. After I'm past, the heavy stuff will follow on. I have two hundred militia – the usual odds-and-sods, about half with crossbows – marching with the wagons.'

'That was all smart.'

He looked again at the map. The back road, adequate for cavalry and four-pounders but not for wagons or the heavy guns, followed the mountain and then bent south to join the main valley road. Harmakros had got the slow stuff off first, and wouldn't be impeded by it on his own march, and he was waiting to have all his force together, instead of feeding it in to be chopped up by detail.

'Where had you thought of fighting?'

'Why, on the Athan, of course.' Harmakros was surprised that he should ask. 'Klestreus will have some of his cavalry across before we get there, but that can't be helped. We'll kill them or run them back, and then defend the line of the river.'

'No.' Kalvan touched the stem of his corncob on the Fitra road-junction. 'We fight here.'

'But, Lord Kalvan! That's miles inside Hostigos!' one of the officers expostulated. Maybe he owned an estate down there. 'We can't let them get that far!'

'Lord Kalvan,' Harmakros began stiffly. He was going to

be insubordinate; he never bothered with titles otherwise. 'We cannot give up a foot of Hostigi ground. The honour of Hostigos forbids it.'

Here we are, back in the Middle Ages! He seemed to hear the voice of the history professor, inside his head, calling a roll of battles lost on points of honour. Mostly by the French, though they weren't the only ones. He decided to fly into a rage.

'To Styphon with that!' he yelled, banging his fists on the table. 'We're not fighting this war for honour, and we're not fighting this war for real-estate. We're fighting this Dralmdamned war for survival, and the only way we can win it is to kill all the damned Nostori we can, and get as few of our men killed doing it as we can.

'Now, here,' he continued quietly, the rage having served its purpose. 'Here's the best place to do it. You know what the ground's like there. Klestreus will cross here at Marax. He'll rush his best cavalry ahead, and after he's secured the ford, he'll push on up the valley. His cavalry'll want to get in on the best looting before the infantry come up. By the time the infantry are over, they'll be strung out all up East Hostigos.

'And they'll be tired, and, more important, their horses will be tired. We'll all have got to Fitra by daylight, and by the time they begin coming up, we'll have our position prepared, our horses will be fresh again, all the men will have at least an hour or so sleep, and a hot meal. You think that won't make a difference? Now, what troops have we east of here?'

A hundred-odd cavalry along the river; a hundred and fifty regular infantry, and about twice as many militia. Some five hundred, militia and some regulars, at posts in the gaps.

'All right . . . get riders off at once, somebody who won't be argued with. Have that force along the river move back, the infantry as rapidly as possible, and the cavalry a little ahead of the Nostori, skirmishing. They will not attempt to delay them; if the ones in front are slowed down, the ones behind will catch up with them, and we don't want that.'

Harmakros had been looking at the map, and also looking over the idea. He nodded.

'East Hostigos,' he declared, 'will be the graveyard of the Nostori.'

That took care of the honour of Hostigos.

'Well, mercenaries from Hos-Agrys and Hos-Ktemnos. Who hired those mercenaries, anyhow – Gormoth, or Styphon's House?'

'Why, Gormoth. Styphon's House furnished the money, but the mercenary captains contracted with Gormoth.'

'Stupid of Styphon. The reason I asked, the Rev. What's-his-name, in Nostor, included an interesting bit of gossip in his report. It seems that this morning Gormoth had one of his understewards put to death. Forced a funnel into his mouth, and had close to half a keg of wine poured into him. The wine was of inferior quality, and had been furnished to a prisoner, or supposed prisoner, for whom Gormoth had commanded good treatment.'

One of the officers made a face. 'Sounds like Gormoth.' Another laughed and named a couple of innkeepers in Hostigos town who deserved the same. Harmakros wanted to know who this pampered prisoner was.

'You know him. That Agrysi horse-trader, Skranga.'

'Yes, we got some good horses from him. I'm riding one, myself,' Harmakros said. 'Hey! He was working in the fireseed mill. Do you think he's making fireseed for Gormoth, now?'

'If he's doing what I told him to he is.' There was an outcry; even Harmakros stared at him in surprise. 'If Gormoth starts making his own fireseed, Styphon's House will find it out, and you know what'll happen. That's why I was wondering who'd be able to use those mercenaries against whom. That's another thing. We can't be bothered with Nostori prisoners, but take all the mercenaries who'll surrender. We'll need them when Sarrask's turn comes up.'

II

Dawn was only a pallor in the east, and the whitewashed walls were dim blurs under dark thatches, but the village of Fitra was awake, and the shouting began as he approached: 'Lord Kalvan! Dralm bless Lord Kalvan!' He was used to it, now; it didn't give him the thrill it had at first. Light streamed from open doors and windows, and a fire blazed on the little common, and there was a crowd of villagers and cavalrymen who had ridden on ahead. Behind him, hooves thudded on the road, and far back he could hear the four-pounders clattering over the pole bridge at the mill. He had to make a speech from the saddle, while orders were shouted and reshouted to the rear and men and horses crowded off the road to make way for the guns.

Then he and Harmakros and four or five other officers rode forward, reining in where the main road began to dip into the little hollow. The eastern pallor had become a bar of yellow light. The Mountains of Hostigos were blackly plain on the left, and the jumble of low ridges on the right were beginning to take shape. He pointed to a ravine between two of them.

'Send two hundred cavalry around that ridge and into that little valley, where those three farms are clumped together,' he said. 'They're not to make fires or let themselves be seen. They're to wait till we're engaged, here, and the second batch of Nostori come up. Then they'll come out and hit them from behind.'

An officer galloped away to attend to it. The yellow light spread; only a few of the larger and brighter stars were still visible. In front, the ground fell away to the small brook that ran through the hollow, to join a larger stream that flowed east along the foot of the mountain. The mountain rose steeply to a bench, then sloped up to the summit. On the right was broken ground, mostly wooded. In front, across the hollow, was mostly open farmland. There were a few trees around them, in the hollow, and on the other side. This couldn't have been better if he'd had Dralm create it to special order.

The yellow light had reached the zenith, and the eastern horizon was a dazzle. Harmakros squinted at it and said something about fighting with the sun in their eyes.

'No such thing; it'll be overhead before they get here. Now, you go take a nap. I'll wake you in time to give me some sack-time. As soon as the wagons get here, we'll give everybody a hot meal.'

An ox-cart appeared on the brow of the hill across the hollow, piled high, a woman and a boy trudging beside the team and another woman and some children riding. Before they were down to the brook, a wagon had come into sight. This was only the start; there'd be a perfect stream of them

Z

soon. They couldn't be allowed on the main road west of Fitra until the wagons and the eight-pounders were through.

'Have them turned aside,' he ordered. 'And use the wagons and carts for barricades, and the oxen to drag trees.'

The village peasants were coming out now, with four- and six-ox teams dragging chains. Axes began thudding. More refugees were coming in; there were loud protests at being diverted and at having wagons and oxen commandeered. The axemen were across the hollow now, and men shouted at straining oxen as felled trees were dragged in to build an abatis.

He strained his eyes against the sunrise; he couldn't see any smoke. Too far away, but he was sure it was there. The enemy cavalry had certainly crossed the Athan by now, and pyromania was as fixed in the mercenary character as kleptomania. The abatis began to take shape, trees dragged into line with the tops of the front and the butts to the rear, with spaces for three of the six four-pounders on either side of the road and a barricade of wagons and farmcarts a little in advance at either end. He rode forward now and then to get an enemy's-eye view of it. He didn't want it to look too formidable from in front, or too professional – for one thing, he wanted to make sure that the guns were completely camouflaged. Finally he began to notice smears of smoke against the horizon, maybe six or eight miles away. Klestreus's mercenaries weren't going to disappoint him after all.

A company of infantry came up. They were regulars, a hundred and fifty of them, with two pikes (and one of them a real pike) to every caliver, marching in good order. They'd come all the way from the Athan, reported fighting behind them, and were disgusted at marching away from it. He told them they'd get all they wanted before noon, and to fall out and rest. A couple of hundred militia, some with crossbows, dribbled in. There were more smokes on the eastern horizon, but he still couldn't hear firing. At seven-thirty, the supply wagons, the four eight-pounders, and the two hundred militia arrived. That was good. The refugees, now a steady stream, could be sent on up the road. He saw to it that fires were lit and a hot meal started, and then went into the village.

He found Harmakros asleep in one of the cottages,

wakened him, and gave him the situation to date.

'Send somebody to wake me,' he finished, 'as soon as you see smoke within three miles, as soon as our cavalry skirmishers start coming in, and in any case in two and a half hours.'

Then he pulled off his helmet and boots, unbuckled his sword-belt, and lay down in the rest of his armour on the cornshuck tick Harmakros had vacated, hoping that it had no small inhabitants or, if so, that none of them would find lodgement under his arming-doublet. It was cool in here behind the stone walls and under the thick thatch. The wet heat of his body became a clammy chill. He shifted positions a few times, decided that fewer things gouged into him when lying on his back, and closed his eyes.

So far, everything had gone nicely; all he was worried about was who was going to let him down, and how badly. He hoped some valiant fool wouldn't get a rush of honour to the head and charge when he ought to stand fast, like the Saxons at Hastings.

If he could bring this off just half as well as he'd planned it, which would be about par for any battle, he could go to Valhalla when he died and drink at the same table with Richard Coeur-de-Lion, the Black Prince and Henry of Navarre. A complete success would entitle him to take a salute from Stonewall Jackson. He fell asleep receiving the commendation of George S. Patton.

III

An infantry captain wakened him at a little before ten.

'They're burning Systros, now,' he said. That was a town of some two thousand, two and a half miles away. 'A couple of the cavalry who've been keeping contact with them just came in. The first batch, about fifteen hundred, are coming up fast, and there's another lot, about a thousand, a mile and a half behind them. And we've been hearing those big bombards at Narza Gap.'

Between Montoursville and Muncy; that would be Klestreus's infantry on this side, and probably some of Netzigon's ragtag and bobtail on the other. He pulled on his boots and buckled on his belt, and somebody brought him a bowl of beef stew with plenty of onion in it, and a mug of sour red wine. When his horse was brought, he rode forward to the line, noticing in passing that the Mobile Force Uncle Wolf and the village priest of Dralm and priestess of Yirtta had set up a field hospital in the common, and that pole-and-blanket stretchers were being made. He hoped he wouldn't be wounded. No anaesthetics, here-and-now, though the priests of Galzar used sandbags.

A big cloud of smoke dirtied the sky over Systros. Silly buggers – first crowd in had fired it. Here-and-now mercenaries were just the same as Tilly's or Wallenstein's. Now the ones behind would have to bypass it, which would bring them to Fitra in even worse order.

The abatis was finished, and he cantered forward for a final look at it. He couldn't see a trace of any of the guns, and it looked, as he had wanted it to, like the sort of thing a lot of peasant home-guards would throw up. At each end, between the abatis itself and the short barricades of carts, was an opening big enough for cavalry to sortie out. The mounted infantry horse-lines were back of the side road, with the more poorly armed militia holding horses.

Away off, one of the Narza Gap bombards boomed; they were still holding out. Then he began to hear the distant, and then not-so-distant, pop of smallarms. Cavalry drifted up the road, some reloading pistols as they came. The shots grew louder; more cavalry, in more of a hurry, arrived. Finally, four of them topped the rise and came down the slope; the last one over the top turned in his saddle and fired a pistol behind him. A dozen Nostori cavalry appeared as they were splashing through the brook.

Immediately, a big eight-bore rifled musket bellowed from behind the abatis, and then another and another. His horse dance-stepped daintily. Across the hollow, a horse was down, kicking, another reared, riderless, and a third, also empty saddled, trotted down to the brook and stopped to drink. The mercenaries turned and galloped away out of sight into the dead ground beyond the rise. He was wondering where Harmakros had put the rest of the riflemen when a row of smoke-puffs blossomed along the edge of the bench above the stream on the left, and shots cracked like a string of fire-crackers. There were yells from out of sight across the hollow, and musketoons thumped in reply. Wasting

Styphon's good fireseed — at four hundred yards, they couldn't have hit Grant's Tomb with smoothbores.

He wished he had five hundred rifles up there. Hell, why not wish for twenty medium tanks and half a dozen Sabre-Jets, while he was at it!

Then Klestreus's mercenary cavalry came up in a solid front on the brow of the hill — black and orange pennons and helmet-plumes and scarves, polished breastplates. Lancers all in front, musketoon-men behind. A shiver ran along the front as the lances came down.

As though that had been the signal, and it probably had been, six four-pounders and four eight-pounders went off together. It wasn't a noise, but a palpable blow on the ears. His horse started to buck; by the time he had him under control the smoke was billowing out over the hollow, and several perfect rings were floating up against the blue, and everybody behind the abatis was yelling, *'Down Styphon!'*

Roundshot; he could see where it had torn furrows back into the group of black and orange cavalry. Men were yelling, horses rearing, or down and screaming horribly, as only wounded horses can. The charge had stopped before it had started. On either side of him, gun-captains were shouting, 'Grapeshot! Grapeshot!' and cannoneers were jumping to their pieces before they had stopped recoiling with double-headed swabs, one end wet to quench lingering powder-bag sparks and one end dry.

The cavalry charge slid forward in broken chunks, down the slope and into the hollow. When they were twenty yards short of the brook, four hundred arquebuses crashed. The whole front went down, horses behind falling over dropped horses in front. The arquebusiers who had fired stepped back, drawing the stoppers of their powder-flasks with their teeth. *Spring powder-flasks, self-measuring; get made and issued soonest.* He also added cartridge-paper to the paper memo.

When they were half reloaded, the other four hundred arquebuses crashed. The way those cavalry were jammed down there, it would take an individual miracle for any bullet to miss something. The smoke was clogging the hollow like spilled cotton now, but through it he could see another wave of cavalry coming up on the brow of the opposite hill.

A four-pounder spewed grapeshot into them, then another and another, till the whole six had fired.

Gustavus Adolphus's four-pounder crews could load and fire faster than musketeers, the dry lecture-room voice was telling him. Of course, the muskets they'd been timed against had been matchlocks; that had made a big difference. Lord Kalvan's were doing almost as well: the first four-pounder had fired on the heels of the third arquebus volley. Then one of the eight-pounders fired, and that was a small miracle.

A surprising number of Klestreus's cavalry had survived the fall of their horses. Well, not so surprising; horses were bigger targets, and they didn't wear breastplates. Having nowhere else to go, the men were charging on foot, using their lances as pikes. A few among them had musketoons; they'd been in the rear. Quite a few were shot coming up, and more were piked trying to get through the abatis. A few did get through. As he galloped to help deal with one of these parties, he heard a trumpet sound on the left, and another on the right, and there was a clamour of *Down Styphon!* at both ends. That would be the cavalry going out; he hoped the artillery wouldn't get excited.

Then he was in front of a dozen unhorsed Nostori cavalrymen, pulling up his horse and aiming a pistol at them.

'Yield, comrades! We spare mercenaries!'

An undecided second and a half, then one of them lifted a reversed musketoon.

'We yield; oath to Galzar.'

That, he thought, they would keep. Galzar didn't like oath-breaking soldiers; he let them get killed at the next opportunity. *Cult of Galzar; encourage.*

Some peasants ran up, brandishing axes and pitchforks. He waved them back with his pistol, letting them have a look at the muzzle.

'Keep your weapons,' he told the mercenaries. 'I'll find somebody to guard you.'

He detailed a couple of Mobile Force arquebusiers; they impressed some militia. Then he had to save a wounded mercenary from having his throat cut. Dralm-damned civilians! He'd have to detail prisoner-guards. Disarm these mercenaries and the peasants'd cut their throats; leave them armed, and the temptation might overcome the fear of Galzar.

Along the abatis, the firing had stopped, but the hollow below was a perfect hell's bedlam – pistol shots, clashing steel, *Down Styphon!* and, occasionally, *Gormoth!* Over his shoulder he could see villagers, even women and children, replacing militiamen on the horse-lines. Captains were shouting, 'Pikes forward!' and pikemen were dodging among the branches to get through the abatis. Dimly, through the smoke, he could see red and blue on horsemen at the brow of the opposite hill. *Uniforms; do something about. Brown, or dark green.*

The road had been left unobstructed, and he trotted through and down towards the brook. What he saw in the hollow made his stomach heave, and it didn't heave easily. It was the horses that bothered him more than anything else, and he wasn't the only one. The infantry, going forward, were stopping to cut wounded horses' throats, or brain them, or shoot them with pistols from saddle-holsters. They shouldn't do that, they ought to keep on, but he couldn't stand seeing horses suffer.

Stretcher-bearers were coming forward, too, and villagers to loot. Corpse-robbing was the only way the here-and-now civil population had of getting a little of their own back after a battle. Most of them had clubs or hatchets, to make sure that what they were robbing really were corpses.

There were a lot of good weapons lying around. They ought to be collected, before they rusted into uselessness, but there was no time for that now. Stopping to do that, once, had been one of Stonewall Jackson's few mistakes. Something was being done towards that, though: he saw crossbows lying around, and each one meant a militiaman who had armed himself with an enemy cavalry musketoon.

The battle had passed on eastward; unopposed infantry were forming up, blocks of pikemen with blocks of arquebusiers between, and men were running back to bring up horses. Away ahead, there was an uproar of battle; that would be the two hundred cavalry he had posted on the far right hitting another batch of Gormoth's mercenaries, who, by now, would be disordered by fugitives streaming back from the light at the hollow. The riflemen on the bench were drifting eastward, too, firing as they went.

And enemy cavalry were coming in in groups, holding their helmets up on their sword-points, calling out, 'We yield, oath to Galzar.' One of the officers of the flanking party, with four troopers, was coming in with close to a hundred of them, regretting that so many had got away. And all the infantry who had marched in from the Athan, and many of the local militia, had mounted themselves on captured horses.

There was a clatter behind him, and he got his horse off the road to let the four-pounders pass in column. Their captain waved to him and told him, laughing, that the eights would be along in a day or so.

'Where do we get some more shooting?' he asked.

'Down the road a piece; just follow along and we'll show you plenty to shoot at.'

He slipped back the knit cuff under his mail sleeve and looked at his watch. It was still ten minutes to noon, Hostigos Standard Sundial Time.

TWELVE

I

By 1730, they were down the road a really far piece, and there had been considerable shooting on the way. Now they were two miles west of the Athan, on the road to Marax Ford, and the Nostori wagons and cannon were strung out for half a mile each way. He was sitting, with his helmet off, on an upended wine keg at a table made by laying a shed-door across some boxes, with Harmakros's pyrographed deerskin map spread in front of him, and a mug where he could reach it. Beside the road, some burned out farm buildings were still smoking, and the big oaks which shaded him were yellowed on one side from heat. Several hundred prisoners squatted in the field beyond, eating rations from their own wagons.

Harmakros, and the commander of mounted infantry, Phrames – he'd be about two-star rank – and the brigadier-general commanding cavalry, and the Mobile Force Uncle Wolf – somewhat younger than the Tarr-Hostigos priest of Galzar and about chaplain major equivalent – sat or squatted around him. The messenger from Sevenhills Valley, who had just caught up with him, paced back and forth, trying to walk the stiffness out of his legs. He drank from a mug as he talked. He was about U.S. first lieutenant equivalent.

Titles of rank; regularise. This business of calling everybody from company commander up to Commander-in-chief a captain just wouldn't do. He'd made a start with that, on the upper echelons; he'd have to carry it down to field and company level. *Rank, insignia of; establish.* He thought he'd adopt the Confederate Army system – it was simpler, with no oak and maple leaves and no gold and silver distinctions. Then he pulled his attention back to what the messenger was saying.

'That's all we know. All morning, starting before mess call, there was firing up the river. Cannon-fire, and then smallarms, and, when the wind was right, we could hear shouting. About first morning drill-break, some of our cavalry, who'd been working up the river along the mountains, came back and reported that Netzigon had crossed the river in front of Vryllos Gap, and they couldn't get through to Ptosphes and Princess Rylla.'

He cursed, first in Zarthani and then in English. 'Is she at Vryllos Gap too?'

Harmakros laughed. 'You ought to know that girl by now, Kalvan; you're going to marry her. Just try and keep her out of battles.'

That he would, by Dralm! With how much success, though, was something else.

The messenger, having taken time out for a deep drink, continued:

'Finally, a rider came in from this side of the mountain. He said that the Nostori were across and pushing Prince Ptosphes back into the gap. He wanted to know if the captain of Tarr-Dombra could send him help.'

'Well?'

The messenger shrugged. 'We only had two hundred regulars and two hundred and fifty militia, and it's ten miles to Vryllos along the river, and an even longer way around the mountains on the south side. So the captain left a few cripples and kitchen-women to hold the castle, and crossed the river at Dyssa. They were just starting when I left; I could hear cannon-fire as I was leaving Sevenhills Valley.'

'That was about the best thing he could do.'

Gormoth would have a couple of hundred men at Dyssa. Just a holding-force; they'd given up the idea of any offensive operations against Dombra Gap. If they could be run out and the town burned, it would start a scare that might take a lot of pressure off Ptosphes and Chartiphon both.

'Well, I hope nobody expects any help from us,' Harmakros said. 'Our horses are ridden into the ground; half our men are mounted on captured horses, and they're in worse shape than what we have left of our own.'

'Some of my infantrymen are riding two to a horse,' Phrames said. 'You can figure what kind of a march they'd make. They'd do almost as well on foot.'

'And it would be midnight before any of us could get to Vryllos Gap, and that would be less than a thousand.'

'Five hundred, I'd make it,' the cavalry brigadier said. 'We've been losing by attrition all the way east.'

'But I'd heard that your losses had been very light.'

'You heard? From whom?'

'Why, the men guarding prisoners. Great Galzar, Lord Kalvan, I never saw so many prisoners . . .'

'That's been our losses: prisoner-guard details. Every one of them is as much out of it as though he'd been shot through the head.'

But the army Klestreus had brought across the Athan had ceased to exist. Not improbably as many as five hundred had re-crossed at Marax Ford. Six hundred had broken out of Hostigos at Narza Gap. There would be several hundred more, singly and in small bands, dodging through the woods to the south; they'd have to be mopped up. The rest had all either been killed or captured.

First, there had been the helter-skelter chase east from Fitra. For instance, twenty riflemen, firing from behind rocks and trees, had turned back two hundred trying to get through at the next gap down. Mostly, anybody who was overtaken had simply pulled off his helmet or held up a reversed weapon and cried for quarter.

He'd only had to fight once, himself; he and two Mobile Force cavalrymen had caught up to ten fleeing mercenaries and shouted to them to yield. Maybe this crowd was tired of running, maybe they were insulted at the demand from so few, or maybe they'd just been bullheaded. Instead, they had turned and charged. He had half-dodged and half parried a lance and spitted the lancer in the throat, and then had been fighting two swordsmen, and good ones, when a dozen mounted had come up.

Then, they'd had a small battle a half-mile west of Systros. Fifteen hundred infantry and five hundred cavalry, all mercenaries, had just gotten on to the main road again after passing on both sides of the burning town when the Fitra fugitives came dashing into them. Their own cavalry were swept away, and the infantry were trying to pike off the fugitives, when mounted Hostigi infantry arrived, dismounted, gave them an arquebus volley, and then made a pike charge, and then a couple of four-pounders came up and began throwing case-shot, leather tubes full of pistol balls. The Fitra fugitives had never been exposed to case-shot before, and after about two hundred were casualties they began hoisting their helmets and invoking Galzar.

Galzar was being a big help today. Have to do something nice for him.

That had been where the mercenary general, Klestreus, had been captured. Phrames had taken his surrender; Kalvan and Harmakros had been too busy chasing fugitives. A lot of these had turned towards Narza Gap.

Hestophes, the Hostigi CO there, had been a real cool cat. He'd had two hundred and fifty men, two old bombards, and a few lighter pieces. Klestreus's infantry had attacked Nirfë Gap, the last one down, and, with the help of Netzigon's people from the other side, swamped it. A few survivors had managed to get away along the mountain top and brought him warning. An hour later, he was under attack from both sides, too.

He had beaten off three attacks, by a probable total of two thousand, and was bracing for a fourth when his lookouts on the mountain reported seeing the fugitives from Fitra and Systros streaming east. Immediately he had spiked his guns and pulled his men up the mountain. The besieging infantry on the south were swept through by fleeing cavalry, and they threw the Nostori on the other side into confusion. Hestophes spattered them generously with smallarms fire to discourage loitering and let them go to spread panic on the other side. By now, they would be spreading it in Nostor Town.

Then, just west of the river, they had run into the wagon train and artillery, inching along under ox-power, accompanied by a thousand of Gormoth's subject troops and another five hundred mercenary cavalry. This had been Systros over again, except it had been a massacre. The fugitive cavalry had tried to force a way past, the infantry had resisted them, the four-pounders – only five of them, now; one was off the road just below Systros with a broken axle – arrived and began firing case-shot, and then two eight-pounders showed up. Some of the mercenaries attempted to fight – when they later found the pay-chests in one of the wagons, they understood why – but the Nostori simply emptied their arquebuses and calivers and ran. Along with

Down Styphon! the pursuers were shouting *Dralm and no Quarter!* He wondered what Xentos would think of that; Dralm wasn't supposed to be that kind of a god, at all.

'You know,' he said, getting out his pipe and tobacco, 'we didn't have a very big army to start with. What do we have now?'

'Five hundred, and four hundred along the river,' Phrames said. 'We lost about five hundred, killed and wounded. The rest are guarding prisoners all the way back to Fitra.' He looked up at the sun. 'Back almost to Hostigos Town, by now'.

'Well, we can help Ptosphes and Chartiphon from here,' he said. 'That gang Hestophes let through Narza Gap will be in Nostor Town by now, panting their story out, and the way they'll tell it, it will be five times worse than it really was.' He looked at his watch. 'By this time, Gormoth should be getting ready to fight the Battle of Nostor.' He turned to Phrames. 'You're in charge of this stuff here. How many men do you really need to guard it? Two hundred?'

Phrames looked up and down the road, and then at the prisoners, and then, out of the corner of his eye, at the boxes under the improvised table. They hadn't got around to weighing that silver yet, but there was too much of it to be careless with.

'I ought to have twice that many.'

'The prisoners are mercenaries, and have agreed to take Prince Ptosphes' colours.' the priest of Galzar said. 'Of course, they may not bear arms against Prince Gormoth or any in his service until released from their oaths to him. In the sight of the Wargod, helping guard these wagons would be the same, for it would release men of yours to fight. But I will speak to them, and I will answer that they will not break their surrender. You will need some to keep the peasants from stealing, though.'

'Two hundred,' Phrames agreed. 'We have some walking wounded who can help.'

'All right. Take two hundred; men with the worst beat up horses and those men who are riding double, and mind the store. Harmakros, you take three hundred and two of the four-pounders, and cross at the next ford down. I'll take the other four hundred and three guns and work north and east. You might split into two columns, a hundred men and one gun, but no smaller. There'll be companies and parts of companies over there, trying to re-form. Break them up. And burn the whole country out – everything that'll catch fire and make a smoke by daylight or a blaze at night. Any refugees, head them up the river, give them a good scare and let them go. We want Gormoth to think we're across the river with three or four thousand men. By Dralm, that'll take some pressure off Ptosphes and Chartiphon!'

He rose, and Phrames took his seat. Horses were brought, and he and Harmakros mounted. The messenger from Seven-hills Valley sat down, stretching his legs in front of him. He rode slowly along the line of wagons, full of food the Nostori wouldn't eat this winter, and would curse Gormoth for it, and fireseed the Styphon temple-farm slaves would have to toil to replace. Then he came to the guns, and saw one that caught his eye. It was a long brass eighteen-pounder, on a two-wheel cart, with the long tail of the heavy timber stock supported by a four-wheel cart. There were two more behind it, and an officer with a ginger-brown beard sat morosely smoking a pipe on the limber-cart of the middle one. He pulled up.

'Your guns, Captain?'

'They were. They're Prince Ptosphes' guns now, I suppose.'

'They're still yours, if you take our colours, and good pay for the use of them. We have other enemies besides Gormoth, you know.'

The captain grinned. 'So I've heard. Well, I'll take Ptosphes' colours. You're the Lord Kalvan? Is it true that you people make your own fireseed?'

'What do you think we were shooting at you, sawdust? You know what the Styphon stuff's like. Try ours and see the difference.'

'Well, Down Styphon, then!'

They chatted for a little. The mercenary artillery-man's name was Alkides; his home, to the extent that any free-captain had one, was in Agrys City, on Manhattan Island. His guns, of which he was inordinately proud, and almost tearfully happy at being able to keep, had been cast in Zygros City. They were very good; if Verkan could collect a few men capable of casting guns like that, with trunnions . . .

'Well, go back there by that burned house, by those big

trees. You'll find one of my officers, Count Phrames, and Uncle Wolf, there. You'll find a keg of something, too. Where are your men?'

'Well, some were killed, before we cried quits. The rest are back with the other prisoners.'

'Gather them up. Tell Count Phrames you're to have oxen – we have no horses to spare – and get your company and guns on the road for Hostigos Town as soon as you can. I'll talk to you later. Good luck, Captain Alkides.'

Or *Colonel* Alkides; if he was as good as he seemed to be, maybe Brigadier-General Alkides.

There were dead infantry all along the road, mostly killed from behind. Another case of cowardice carrying its own penalty; infantry who stood against cavalry had a chance, often a good one, but infantry who turned tail and ran had none. He didn't pity them a bit.

It grew progressively worse as he neared the river, where the crews of the four-pounders and the two eight-pounders were swabbing and polishing their pieces, and dark birds rose cawing and croaking and squawking when disturbed. Must be every crow and raven and buzzard in Hos-Harphax; he even saw eagles.

The river, horse-knee deep at the ford, was tricky; his mount continually stumbled on armour-weighted corpses. That had been case-shot, mostly, he thought.

THIRTEEN

I

'So your boy did it, all by himself,' the lady historian professor was saying.

Verkan Vall grinned. They were in a seminar room at the University, their chairs facing a big map of Fourth Level Aryan-Transpacific Hostigos, Nostor, northeastern Sask and northern Beshta. The pinpoints of light he had been shifting back and forth on it were out, now.

'Didn't I tell you he was a genius?'

'Just how much genius did it take to lick a bunch of klunks like that?' said Talgan Dreth, the outtime studies director. 'The way I heard it, they licked themselves.'

'Well, considerable, to predict their errors accurately and plan to exploit them,' argued old Professor Shalgro, the paratemporal probability theorist. To him, it was a brilliant theoretical achievement, and the battle was merely the experiment which had vindicated it. 'I agree with Chief's Assistant Verkan; the man is a genius, and the fact that he was only able to become a minor police officer on his own time-line shows how these low-order cultures allow genius to go to waste.'

'He knew the military history of his own time-line, and he knew how to apply it on Aryan-Transpacific.' The historian wasn't letting her own subject be slighted. 'Actually, I think Gormoth planned an excellent campaign – against people like Ptosphes and Chartiphon. If it hadn't been for Kalvan, he'd have won.'

'Well, Chartiphon and Ptosphes fought a battle of their own and won it, didn't they?'

'More or less.' He began punching buttons on the arm of his chair and throwing on red and blue lights. 'Netzigon was supposed to wait here, at Listra-Mouth, till Klestreus got up to here. Chartiphon began cannonading him – ordnance engineering by Lord Kalvan – and Netzigon couldn't take it. He attacked prematurely.'

'Why didn't he just pull back? He had that river in front of him. Chartiphon couldn't have got his guns across that, could he?' Talgan Dreth asked.

'Oh, that wouldn't have been honourable. Besides, he didn't want the mercenaries to win the war; he wanted the glory of winning it himself.'

The historian laughed. 'How often I've heard *that*!' she said. 'But don't these Hostigi go in for all this honour and glory jazz too?'

'Sure – till Kalvan talked them out of it. As soon as he started making fireseed, he established a moral ascendancy. And then, the new tactics, the new swordplay, the artillery improvements; now it's "Trust Lord Kalvan. Lord Kalvan is always right." '

'He'll have to work at that, now,' Dreth said. 'He won't dare make any mistakes. What happened to Netzigon?'

'He made three attempts to cross the river, which is a hundred yards wide, in the face of artillery superiority. That was how he lost most of his cavalry. Then he threw his infantry across here at Vryllos, pushed Ptosphes back into the gap, and started a flank attack up the south bank on Chartiphon. Ptosphes wouldn't stay pushed; he waited till Netzigon was between the river and the mountain, and then counter-attacked. Then Rylla took what cavalry they had across the river, burned Netzigon's camp, butchered some camp-followers, and started a panic in his rear. That was when everything came apart and the pieces began breaking up, and then the commander at Tarr-Dombra, there, took some of his men across, burned Dyssa, and started another panic.'

'It was too bad about Rylla,' the lady historian said.

'Yes.' He shrugged. 'Things like that happen, in battles.' That was why Dalla was always worried when she heard he'd been in one. 'We had a couple of antigrav conyeyers in, after dark. They had to stay up to twenty thousand feet, since we didn't want any heavenly portents on top of everything else, but they got some good infrared telephoto views. Big fires all over western Nostor, and around Dyssa, and more of them, the whole countryside, in the southwest – that was Kalvan and Harmakros. And a lot of hasty fortifying and entrenching around Nostor Town; Gormoth seems to think he's going to have to fight the next battle there.'

'Oh, that's ridiculous,' Talgan Dreth said. 'It'll be a couple of weeks before Kalvan has his army in shape for an offensive, after those battles. And how much powder do you think he has left?'

'Six or seven tons. That came in just before I came here, from our people in Hostigos Town. After he crossed the river last evening, Harmakros captured a big wagon train. A Styphon's House Archpriest, on his way to Nostor Town, with four tons of fireseed and seven thousand ounces of gold. Subsidies for Gormoth.'

'Now that's what's called making war support war,' the history professor commented.

'And another ton or so in Klestreus's supply train, and the pay-chests for his army,' he added. 'Hostigos came out of this all right.'

'Wait till I get this all worked up,' old Professor Shalgro was gloating. 'Absolute proof of the decisive effect of one superior individual on the course of history. Kalthar Morth and his Historical Inevitability, and his vast, impersonal social forces, indeed!'

'Well, what are we going to do, now?' Talgan Dreth asked. 'We have the study-team organised, the five men who'll be the brass-founders, and the three girls who'll be the pattern-makers.'

'Well, we have horseback travel-time between Zygros City and Hostigos Town to allow for. They've been familiarising on adjoining near-identical time-lines? Send them all to Zygros City on the Kalvan time-line. I have a couple of Paracops planted there already. Let them make local contacts and call attention to themselves. Dalla and I will do the same. Then we won't have to worry about some traveller from Zygros showing up in Hostigos Town and punching holes in our stories.'

'How about conveyer-heads?'

He shook his head. 'You'll have to have your team established in Hostigos Town before they can put one in there. You have a time-line for operations on Fifth Level, of course;

work from there. You'll have to get on to Kalvan Time-Line by an antigrav conveyer drop.'

'Horses and all?'

'Horses and all. That will be mounts for myself and Dalla, for two Paracops who will pose as hired guards, and for your team. Seventeen saddle-horses. And twelve pack horses, with loads of Zygrosi and Grefftscharr wares. Lord Kalvan's friend Verkan is a trader; traders have to have merchandise.'

Talgan Dreth whistled softly. 'That'll mean at least two hundred-foot conveyers. Where had you thought of landing them?'

'Up here.' He twisted the dial; the map slid down, until he had the southern corner of the Princedom of Nyklos, north and west of Hostigos. 'About here,' he said, making a spot of light.

II

Gormoth of Nostor stood inside the doorway of his presence-chamber, his arm over the shoulder of the newly ennobled Duke Skranga, and together they surveyed the crowd within. Netzigon, who had come stumbling in after midnight with all his guns and half his army lost and the rest a frightened rabble. His cousin, Count Pheblon, his ransom still unpaid; he'd hoped Ptosphes wouldn't be alive to be paid by the moon's end. The nobles of the Elite Guard, who had attended him here at Tarr-Hostigos, waiting for news of victory until news of defeat had come in. Three of Klestreus's officers, who had broken through at Narza Gap to bring it, and a few more who had got over Marax Ford and back to Nostor alive. And Vyblos, the Highpriest, and with him the Archpriest Krastokles from Styphon's House Upon Earth, and his black-armoured guard-captain, who had arrived at dawn with half a dozen troopers on broken-down horses.

He hated the sight of all of them, and the two priests most of all. He cut short their greetings.

'This is Duke Skranga,' he told them. 'Next to me, he is the first nobleman of Nostor. He takes precedence over all here.' The faces in front of his went slack with amazement, then stiffened angrily. A mutter of protest was hushed almost as soon as it began. 'Do any object? Then it had better be one who's served me at least half as well as this man, and I see none such here.' He turned to Vyblos. 'What do you want, and who's this with you?'

'His Sanctity, the Archpriest Krastokles, sent by His Divinity, Styphon's Voice,' Krastokles began furiously. 'And how has he fared since entering your realm? Set upon by Hostigi heathens, hounded like a deer through the hills, his people murdered, his wagons pillaged . . .'

'His wagons, you say? Well, great Galzar, what of my gold and my fireseed, sent me by Styphon's Voice in his care, and look how he's cared for them, he and Styphon between them.'

'You blaspheme!' Archpriest Krastokles cried. 'And it was not your gold and fireseed, but the god's, to be given you in the god's service at my discretion.'

'And lost at your discretion. You witless fool in a yellow bedgown, didn't you know a battle when you were riding into one?'

'Sacrilege!'

A dozen voices said it at once: Vyblos's and Krastokles's, and, among others, Netzigon's. By the Mace of Galzar, now didn't he have a fine right to open his mouth here? Anger almost sickened him; in a moment he was afraid that he would vomit pure bile. He strode to Netzigon, snatching the golden chief-captain's chain from over his shoulder.

'All the gods curse you, and all the devils take you! I told you to wait at Listra-Mouth for Klestreus, not to throw your army away along with his. By Galzar, I ought to have you flayed alive!' He struck Netzigon across the face with the chain. 'Out of my sight, while you're still alive!' Then he turned to Vyblos. 'You, too – out of here, and take the Arch-pimp Krastokles with you. Go to your temple and stay there; return here either at my bidding or at your peril.'

He watched them leave: Netzigon shaken, the black-armoured captain stolidly, Vyblos and Krastokles stiff with rage. A few of Netzigon's officers and gentlemen attended him; the rest drew back from them as though from contamination. He went to Pheblon and threw the golden chain over his head.

'I still don't thank you for losing me Tarr-Dombra, but that's a handful of dried peas to what that son of a horse-leech's daughter cost me. Now, Galzar help you, you'll have to make an army out of what he left you.'

'My ransom still needs paying,' Pheblon reminded him. 'Till that's done, I'm oath-bound to Prince Ptosphes and Lord Kalvan.'

'So you are; twenty thousand ounces of silver for you and those taken with you. You know where to find it? I don't.'

'I do, Prince,' Duke Skranga said. 'There's ten times that in the treasure-vault of the temple of Styphon.'

III

Count Netzigon waited until he was outside to touch a handkerchief to his cheek. It was bleeding freely, and had dripped on to his doublet. Now by Styphon, the cleaning of that would cost Gormoth dear!

It wasn't his fault, anyhow. Great Styphon, was he to sit still while Chartiphon cannonaded him from across the river? And how had he known what sort of cannon Chartiphon had? The Hostigi really must be making fireseed; he hadn't believed that until yesterday. Three times he had sent his cavalry splashing into the river, and three times the guns had murdered them. He'd never seen guns throw small-shot so far. So then he'd sent his infantry over at Vryllos, and driven those with Prince Ptosphes back into the gap, and then, while he was driving against Chartiphon's right and the day had seemed won, Ptosphes had brought his beaten soldiers back, fighting like panthers, and that she-devil daughter of his – He'd heard, later, that she'd been killed. Styphon bless whoever did it!

Then everything had gone down in bloody ruin. Driven back across the river again, the Hostigi pouring after them, and then riders from Nostor Town with word that Klestreus's army was beaten in East Hostigos and orders to fall back, and they had retreated, with the whole country burning around them, fire and smoke at Dyssa and fugitives screaming that a thousand Hostigi were pouring out of Dombra Gap, and his worthless peasant levies throwing away their weapons and taking to their heels . . .

Sorcery, that's what it was! That cursed foreign wizard, Kalvan!

Someone touched his arm. His hand flew to his poignard,

and then he saw that it was the Archpriest's guard-captain. He relaxed.

'You were ill-used, Count Netzigon,' the man in black armour said. 'By Styphon, it ired me to see a brave soldier used like a thievish serf!'

'His Sanctity wasn't reverently treated, nor His Holiness Vyblos. It shocked me to hear such words to the consecrated of Styphon,' he replied. 'What good can come to a realm whose Prince so insults the anointed of the god?'

'Ah!' The captain smiled. 'It's a pleasure, in such a court, to hear such piety. Now, Count Netzigon, if you could have a few words with His Sanctity — this evening, say, at the temple. Come after dark, cloaked and in commoner's dress.'

FOURTEEN

I

Kalvan's horse stumbled, jerking him awake. Behind him, fifty-odd riders clattered, many of them more or less wounded, none seriously. There had been a score on horse-litters, or barely able to cling to their mounts, but they had been left at the base hospital in Sevenhills Valley. He couldn't remember how long it had been since he had had his clothes, or even all his armour, off; except for quarter-hour pauses, now and then, he had been in the saddle since daylight, when he had recrossed the Athan with the smoke of southern Nostor behind him.

That had been as bad as Phil Sheridan in the Shenandoah, but every time some peasant's thatched blazed up, he knew it was burning another hole in Prince Gormoth's morale. He'd felt better about it, today, after following the mile-wide swath of devastation west from Marax Ford and seeing it stop, with dramatic suddenness, at Fitra.

And the story Harmakros's stragglers had told him : fifteen eight-horse wagons, four tons of fireseed, seven thousand ounces of gold – that would come to about $150,000 – two wagon-loads of armour, three hundred new calivers, six hundred pistols, and all of a Styphon's House Archpriest's personal baggage and vestments. He was sorry the Arch-priest had got away; his execution would have been an interesting feature of the victory celebration.

He had passed prisoners marching east, all mercenaries, under arms and in good spirits, at least one pike or lance in each detachment sporting a red and blue pennon. Most of them shouted, 'Down Styphon!' as he rode by. The back road from Fitra to Sevenhills Valley hadn't been so bad, but now, in what he had formerly known as Nittany Valley, traffic had become heavy again. Militia from Listra-Mouth and Vryllos, marching like regulars, which was what they were, now. Trains of carts and farm-wagons, piled with sacks and barrels or loaded with cabbages and potatoes, or with furniture that must have come from manor-houses. Droves of cattle, and droves of prisoners, not armed, not in good spirits, and under heavy guard: Nostori subjects headed for labour-camps and intensive Styphon-is-a-fake indoctrination. And guns, on four-wheel carts, that he couldn't remember from any Hostigi ordnance inventory.

Hostigo Town was in an all-time record traffic-jam. He ran into Alkides, the mercenary artillery-man, with a strip of blue cloth that seemed to have come from a bedspread and a strip of red from the bottom of a petticoat. He was magnificently drunk.

'Lord Kalvan!' he shouted. 'I saw your guns; they're wonderful! What god taught you that? Can you mount mine that way?'

'I think so. I'll have a talk with you about it tomorrow, if I'm awake then.'

Harmakros was on his horse in the middle of the square, his rapier drawn, trying to untangle the chaos of wagons and carts and riders. Kalvan shouted to him, above the din:

'What the Styphon – when did we start using three-star generals for traffic-cops?'

Military Police; organise soonest. Mercenaries, tough ones.

'Just till I get a detail here. I sent all my own crowd up with the wagons.' He started to say something else, then stopped short and asked, 'Did you hear about Rylla?'

'No, for Dralm's sake.' He went cold under his scalding armour. 'What about her?'

'Well, she was hurt – late yesterday, across the river. Her horse threw her; I only know what I got from one of Chartiphon's aides. She's at the castle.'

'Thanks; I'll see you there later.'

He swung his horse about and ploughed into the crowd, drawing his sword and yelling for way. People crowded aside, and yelled his name to others beyond. Outside town, the road was choked with troops, and with things too big and slow to get out of the way; he rode mostly in the ditch. The wagons Harmakros had captured, great canvas-covered things like Conestogas, were going up to Tarr-Hostigos. He thought he'd never get past them : there always seemed to be more ahead. Finally he got through the outer gate and galloped across the bailey.

Throwing his reins to somebody at the foot of the keep steps, he stumbled up them and through the door. From the Staff Room, he heard laughing voices, Ptosphes's among them. For an instant he was horrified, then reassured; if Ptosphes could laugh, it couldn't be too bad.

He was mobbed as soon as he entered, everybody shouting his name and thumping him on the back; he was glad for his armour. Chartiphon, Ptosphes, Xentos, Uncle Wolf, most of the General Staff crowd. And a dozen officers he had never seen before, all wearing new red and blue scarves. Ptosphes was presenting a big man with a florid face and grey hair and beard.

'Kalvan, this is General Klestreus, late of Prince Gormoth's service, now of ours.'

'And most happy at the change, Lord Kalvan,' the mercenary said. 'An honour to have been conquered by such a soldier.'

'Our honour, General. You fought most brilliantly and valiantly.' He'd fought like a damned imbecile, and got his army chopped to hamburger, but let's be polite. 'I'm sorry I hadn't time to meet you earlier, but things were a trifle pressing.' He turned to Ptosphes. 'Rylla? What happened to her?'

'Why, she broke a leg,' Ptosphes began.

That frightened him. People had died from broken legs in his own world when the medical art was at least equal to its here-and-now level. They used to amputate . . .

'She's in no danger, Kalvan,' Xentos assured him. 'None of us would be here if she were. Brother Mytron is with her. If she's awake, she'll want to see you.'

'I'll go to her at once.' He clinked goblets with the mercenary and drank. It was winter-wine, aged quite a few winters, and evidently frozen down in a very cold one. It warmed and relaxed him. 'To your good fortune in Hostigos, General. Your capture,' he lied, 'was Gormoth's heaviest loss, yesterday, and our greatest gain.' He set down the goblet, took off his helmet and helmet-coif and detached his sword from his belt, then picked up the wine again and finished it. 'If you'll excuse me, now, gentlemen. I'll see you all later.'

Rylla, whom he had expected to find gasping her last, sat propped against a pile of pillows in bed, smoking one of her silver-inlaid redstone pipes. She was wrapped in a loose gown, and her left leg, extended, was buckled into a bulky encasement of leather – no plaster casts, here-and-now. Mytron, the chubby and cherubic physician-priest, was with her, and so were several of the women who functioned as midwives, hexes, herb-boilers and general nurses. Rylla saw him first, and her face lighted like a sunrise.

'Hi, Kalvan! Are you all right? When did you get in? How was the battle?'

'Rylla, darling!' The women sprayed away from in front of him like grasshoppers. She flung her arms around his neck as he bent over her; he thought Mytron stepped in to relieve her of her pipe. 'What happened to you?'

'You stopped in the Staff Room,' she told him, between kisses. 'I smell it on you.'

'How is she, Mytron?' he asked over his shoulder.

'Oh, a beautiful fracture, Lord Kalvan!' the doctor enthused. 'One of the priests of Galzar set it; he did an excellent job . . .'

'Gave me a fine lump on the head, too,' Rylla added. 'Why, my horse fell on me. We were burning a Nostori village, and he stepped on a hot ember. He almost threw me, and then fell over something, and down we both went, the horse on top of me. I was carrying an extra pair of pistols in my boots and I fell on one of them. The horse broke a leg, too. They shot him. I guess they thought I was worth making an effort about . . . Kalvan! Never hug a girl so tight when you're wearing mail sleeves!'

'It's nothing to worry about, Lord Kalvan,' Mytron was saying. 'Not the first time for this young lady, either. She broke an ankle when she was eight, trying to climb a cliff to rob a hawk's nest, and a shoulder when she was twelve, firing a musket-charge out of a carbine.'

'And now,' Rylla was saying, 'it'll be a moon, at least, till we can have the wedding.'

'We could have it right now, sweetheart . . .'

'I will not be married in my bedroom,' she declared. 'People make jokes about girls who have to do that. And I will not limp to the temple of Dralm on crutches.'

'All right, Princess; it's your wedding.' He hoped the war

with Sask that everybody expected would be out of the way before she was able to ride again. He'd have a word with Mytron about that. 'Somebody,' he said, 'go and have a hot bath brought to my rooms, and tell me when it's ready. I must stink to the very throne of Dralm.'

'I was wondering when you were going to mention that, darling,' Rylla said.

II

He did speak to Mytron, the next day, catching him between a visit to Rylla and his work at the main army hospital in Hostigos Town. Mytron thought, at first, that he was impatient for Rylla's full recovery and the wedding.

'Oh, Lord Kalvan, quite soon. You know, of course, that broken bones take time to knit, but our Rylla is young and young bones knit fast. Inside a moon, I'd say.'

'Well, Mytron; you know we're going to have to fight Sarrask of Sask, now. When war with Sask comes, I'd be most happy if she were still in bed, with that thing on her leg. So would Prince Ptosphes.'

'Yes. Our Rylla, shall I say, is a trifle heedless of her own safety.' That was a generous five hundred per cent understatement. Mytron put on his professional portentous frown. 'You must understand, of course, that it is not good for any patient to be kept too long in bed. She should be able to get up and walk about as soon as possible. And wearing the splint is not pleasant.'

He knew that. It wasn't any light plaster cast; it was a frame of heavily padded steel splints, forged from old swordblades, buckled on with a case of saddle leather. It weighed about ten pounds, and it would be even more confining and hotter than his armour. But the next thing she broke might be her neck, or she might stop a two-ounce musket ball, and then his luck would run out along with hers. His mind shied like a frightened horse from the thought of no more happy, lovely Rylla.

'I'll do my best, Lord Kalvan, but I can't keep her in bed forever.'

War with Sask wouldn't wait that long, either. Xentos was in contact with the priests of Dralm in Sask Town; they

123

reported that the news of Fitra and Listra-Mouth had stunned Sarrask's court briefly, then thrown Sarrask into a furor of activity. More mercenaries were being hired, and some sort of negotiations, the exact nature undetermined, were going on between Sarrask and Balthar of Beshta. A Styphon Arch-priest, one Zothnes, had arrived in Sask Town, with a train of wagons as big as the one taken by Harmakros in southern Nostor.

A priest of Galzar arrived at Tarr-Hostigos from Nostor Town with an escort and a thousand ounces of gold – gold and silver seemed to be on a twenty-to-one ratio, here-and-now – to pay the ransoms of Count Pheblon and the other gentlemen taken at Tarr-Dombra. The news was that Pheblon was now Gormoth's chief-captain and was trying to reorganise what was left of the Nostori army. Gormoth would be back in the ring for another bout in the spring; that meant that Sarrask must be dealt with this fall.

He was having his own reorganisation problems. They'd taken heavier losses than he'd liked, mostly the poorly armed and partly trained militia who'd fought at Listra-Mouth. On the other hand, they'd acquired over a thousand mercenary infantry and better than two thousand cavalry. They were a headache; they'd have to be integrated into the army of Hostigos. He didn't want any mercenary troops at all. Mercenary soldiers, as individual soldiers, were as good as any; in fact, any regular army man was simply a mercenary in the service of his own country. But mercenary troops, as troops, weren't good at all. They didn't fight for the Prince who hired them; they fought for their own captains, who paid them for what the Prince had paid him. *Mercenary captains*, he could hear his history professor quoting Machiavelli, *are either very capable men or not. If they are, you cannot rely upon them, for they will always aspire to their own greatness, either by oppressing you, their master, or by oppressing others against your intentions; but if the captain is not an able man, he will generally ruin you.* Most of the captains captured in East Hostigos seemed to be quite able.

Klestreus was one exception. As a battle commander, he was an incompetent – Fitra had proven that. He wasn't a soldier at all; he was a military businessman. He could handle sales, promotion and public relations, but not management and operations. That was how he'd got elected captain-general in Nostor. But he did have a wide knowledge of political situations, knew most of the Princes of Hos-Harphax, and knew the composition and command of all the mercenary outfits in the Five Kingdoms. So Kalvan appointed him Chief of Intelligence, where he could really be of use, and wouldn't be able to lead troops in combat. He was quite honoured and flattered.

Nothing could be done about breaking up the mercenary cavalry companies, numbering over two thousand men. The mercenary infantry, however, were broken up, and put into militia companies, one mercenary to three militia-men. This almost started a mutiny, until he convinced them that they were being given posts of responsibility and the rank of private first class, with badges. The sergeants were all collected into a quickie OCS company, to emerge second lieutenants.

Alkides, the artilleryman, was made captain of Tarr-Esdreth-of-Hostigos, and sent there with his three long brass eighteens, now fitted with trunnions on welded-on iron bands and mounted on proper field-carriages. Tarr-Esdreth-of-Hostigos was a sensitive spot. The Sask-Hostigos border followed the east branch of the Juniata, the Besh, and ran through Esdreth gap. Two castles dominated the gap, one on either side; until one or the other could be taken, the gap would be closed both to Hostigos and Sask.

Ten days after Fitra and Listra-Mouth, an unattached mercenary, wearing the white and black colours of unemployment, put in an appearance at Tarr-Hostigos. There were many such; they were equivalent to the bravos of Renaissance Italy. This one produced letters of credence, which Xentos found authentic, from Prince Armanes of Nyklos. His client, he said, wanted to buy fireseed, but wished to do so secretly; he was not ready for an open break with Styphon's House. When asked if he would trade cavalry and artillery horses, the unofficial emissary instantly agreed.

Well, that was a beginning.

FIFTEEN

I

Sesklos rested his elbows on the table and palmed his smarting eyes. Around him, pens scratched on parchment and tablets clattered. He longed for the cool quiet and privacy of the Innermost Circle, but there was so much to do, and he must order the doing of all of it himself.

There were frantic letters from everywhere; the one before him was from the Archpriest of the Great Temple of Hos-Agrys. News of Gormoth's defeat was spreading rapidly, and with it rumours that Prince Ptosphes, who had defeated him, was making his own fireseed. Agents-inquisitory were reporting that the ingredients, and even the proportions, were being bandied about in taverns; it would take an army of assassins to deal with everybody who seemed to know them. Even a pestilence couldn't wipe out everybody who knew at least some of the secret. Oddly, it was even better known in far northern Zygros City than elsewhere. And they all wanted him to tell them how to check the spread of such knowledge.

Curse and blast them! Did they have to ask him about anything? Couldn't any of them think for themselves?

He opened his eyes. Why, admit it; better that than try to deny what would soon be proven everywhere. Let everyone in Styphon's House, even the lay Guardsmen, know the full secret, but for those outside, and for the few believers within, insist that special rites and prayers, known only to the yellow-robes of the Inner Circle, were essential.

But why? Soon it would be known that fireseed made by unconsecrated hands would fire just as well, and, to judge from Prince Ptosphes's sample, with more force and less fouling.

Well, there were devils, malignant spirits of the nether-world; everybody knew that. He smiled, imagining them thronging about — scrawny bodies, bat-wings, bristling beards, clawed and fanged. In fireseed, there were many — they made it explode — and only the prayers of anointed priests of Styphon could slay them. If fireseed were made without the aid of Styphon, the devils would be set free as soon as the fireseed burned, to work manifold evils and frights in the world of men. And, of course, the curse of Styphon was upon any who presumed profanely to make fireseed.

But Ptosphes had made fireseed, and he had pillaged a temple-farm, and put consecrated priests cruelly to death, and then he had defeated the army of Gormoth, which had marched under Styphon's blessing. How about that?

But wait! Gormoth himself was no better than Ptosphes. He too had made fireseed — both Krastokles and Vyblos were positive of that. And Gormoth had blasphemed Styphon and despitefully used a holy Archpriest, and forced a hundred thousand ounces of silver out of the Nostor temple, at as close to pistol-point as made no difference. To be sure, most of that had happened after the day of battle, but outside Nostor who knew that? Gormoth, he decided, had suffered defeat for his sins.

He was smiling happily now, wondering why he hadn't thought of that before. And what was known in Nostor would matter little more than what was known in Hostigos before long. Both would have to be destroyed utterly.

He wondered how many more Princedoms he would have to doom to fire and sword. Not too many — a few sharp examples at the start ought to be enough. Maybe just Hostigos and Nostor, and Sarrask of Sask and Balthar of Beshta could attend to both. An idea began to seep in his mind, and he smiled.

Balthar's brother, Balthames, wanted to be a Prince, himself; it would take only a poisoned cup or a hired dagger to make him Prince of Beshta, and Balthar knew it. He should have had Balthames killed long ago. Well, suppose Sarrask gave up a little corner of Sask, and Balthar gave up a similar piece of Beshta, adjoining and both bordering on western Hostigos, to form a new Princedom; call it Sashta. Then, to that could be added all western Hostigos south of the mountains; why, that would be a nice little Princedom for any young couple. He smiled benevolently. And the father of the bride and the brother of the groom could compensate themselves for their generosity, respectively, with the Listra Valley, rich in iron, and East Hostigos, manured with the blood of Gormoth's mercenaries.

This must be done immediately, before winter put an end to campaigning. Then, in the spring, Sarrask, Balthar and Balthames could hurl their combined strength against Nostor.

And something would have to be done about fireseed making in the meantime. The revelation about the devils would have to be made public everywhere. And call a Great Council of Archpriests, here at Balph – no, at Harphax City; let Great King Kaiphranos bear the costs – to consider how they might best meet the threat of profane fireseed making, and to plan for the future. It could be, he thought hopefully, that Styphon's House might yet survive.

II

Verkan Vall watched Dalla pack tobacco into a little cane-stemmed pipe. Dalla preferred cigarettes, but on Aryan-Transpacific they didn't exist. No paper; it was a wonder Kalvan wasn't trying to do something about that. Behind them, something thumped heavily; voices echoed in the barnlike prefab shed. Everything here was temporary – until a conveyer-head could be established at Hostigos Town, nobody knew where anything should go at Fifth Level Hostigos Equivalent.

Talgan Dreth, sitting on the edge of a packing case with a clipboard on his knee, looked up, then saw what Dalla was doing and watched as she got out her tinderbox, struck sparks, blew the tinder aflame, lit a pine splinter, and was puffing smoke, all in fifteen seconds.

'Been doing that all your life,' he grinned.

'Why, of course,' Dalla deadpanned. 'Only savages have to rub sticks together, and only sorcerers can make fire without flint and steel.'

'You checked the pack-loads, Vall?' he asked.

'Yes. Everything perfectly in order, all Kalvan time-line

stuff. I liked that touch of the deer and bear skins. We'd have to shoot for the pot, on the way south, and no trader would throw away saleable skins.'

Talgan Dreth almost managed not to show how pleased he was. No matter how many outtime operations he'd run, a back-pat from the Paratime Police still felt good.

'Well, then we make the drop tonight,' he said. 'I had a reconnaissance-crew checking it on some adjoining time-lines, and we gave it a looking over on the target time-line last night. You'll go in about fifteen miles east of the Hostigos-Nyklos road.'

'That's all right. They're hauling powder to Nyklos and bringing back horses. That road's being patrolled by Harmakros's cavalry. We make camp fifteen miles off the road and start around sunrise tomorrow; we ought to run into a Hostigi patrol before noon.'

'Well, you're not going to get into any more battles, are you?' Dalla asked.

'There won't be any more battles,' Talgan Dreth told her. 'Kalvan won the war while Vall was away.'

'He won *a* war. How long it'll stay won I don't know, and neither does he. But *the* war won't be over till he's destroyed Styphon's House. That is going to take a little doing.'

'He's destroyed it already,' Talgan Dreth said. 'He destroyed it by proving that anybody can make fireseed. Why, it was doomed from the start. It was founded on a secret, and no secret can be kept forever.'

'Not even the Paratime Secret?' Dalla asked innocently.

'Oh, Dalla!' the University man cried. 'You know that's different. You can't compare that with a trick like mixing saltpetre and charcoal and sulphur.'

III

The late morning sun baked the open horsemarket; heat and dust and dazzle, and flies at which the horses switched constantly. It was hot for so late in the year; as nearly as Kalvan could estimate it from the way the leaves were colouring, it would be mid-October. They had two calendars here-and-now – lunar, for daily reckoning, and solar to keep

9

track of the seasons – and they never matched. *Calendar reform; do something about.* He seemed to recall having made that mental memo before.

And he was sweat-sticky under his armour, forty pounds of it – quilted arming-doublet with mail sleeves and skirt, quilted helmet-coif with mail throat-guard, plate cuirass, plate tassets down his thighs into his jackboots, high combed helmet, rapier and poignard. It wasn't the weight – he'd carried more, and less well distributed, as a combat infantryman in Korea – but he questioned if anyone ever became inured to the heat and lack of body ventilation. *Like a rich armour worn in heat of day, That scalds with safety* – if Shakespeare had never worn it himself except on the stage, he'd known plenty of men who had, like that little Welsh pepperpot Williams, who was the original of Fluellen.

'Not a bad one in the lot!' Harmakros, riding beside him, was enthusing. 'And a dozen big ones that'll do for gun-horses.'

And fifty-odd cavalry horses; that meant, at second or third hand, that many more infantrymen who could get into line when and where needed, in heavier armour. And another lot coming in tonight; he wondered where Prince Armanes was getting all the horses he was trading for boot-leg fireseed. He turned in his saddle to say something about it to Harmakros.

As he did, something hit him a clanging blow on the breastplate, knocking him almost breathless and nearly unhorsing him. He thought he heard the shot; he did hear the second, while he was clinging to his seat and clawing a pistol from his saddlebow. Across the alley, he could see two puffs of smoke drifting from back upstairs windows of one of a row of lodginghouse-wineshop-brothels. Harmakros was yelling; so was everybody else. There was a kicking, neighing confusion among the horses. His chest aching, he lifted the pistol and fired into one of the windows. Harmakros was firing, too, and behind him an arquebus roared. Hoping he didn't have another broken rib, he holstered the pistol and drew its mate.

'Come on!' he yelled. 'And Dralm-dammit, take them alive! We want them for questioning.'

Torture. He hated that, had hated even the relatively mild third-degree methods of his own world, but when you need the truth about something, you get it, no matter how. Men were throwing poles out of the corral gate; he sailed past them, put his horse over the fence across the alley, and landed in the littered back yard beyond. Harmakros took the fence behind him, with a Mobile Force arquebusier and a couple of horse-wranglers with clubs following on foot.

He decided to stay in the saddle; till he saw how much damage the bullet had done, he wasn't sure how much good he'd be on foot. Harmakros flung himself from his horse, shoved a half-clad slattern out of the way, drew his sword, and went through the back door into the house, the others behind him. Men were yelling, women screaming; there was commotion everywhere except behind the two windows from which the shots had come. A girl was bleating that Lord Kalvan had been murdered. Looking right at him, too.

He squeezed his horse between houses to the street, where a mob was forming. Most of them were pushing through the front door and into the house; from within came yells, screams, and sounds of breakage. Hostigos Town would be the better for one dive less if they kept at that.

Up the street, another mob was coagulating; he heard savage shouts of 'Kill! Kill!' Cursing, he holstered the pistol and drew his rapier, knocking a man down as he spurred forward, shouting his own name and demanding way. The horse was brave and willing, but untrained for riot work; he wished he had a State Police horse under him, and a yard of locust riot-stick instead of this sword. Then the combination provost-marshal and police chief of Hostigos Town arrived, with a dozen of his men laying about them with arquebus-butts. Together they rescued two men, bloodied, half-conscious and almost ripped naked. The mob fell back, still yelling for blood.

He had time, now, to check on himself. There was a glancing dent on the right side of his breastplate, and a lead-splash, but the plate was unbroken. *That scalds with safety* — Shakespeare could say that again. Good thing it hadn't been one of those great armour-smashing brutes of eight-bore muskets. He drew the empty pistol and started to reload it, and then he saw Harmakros approaching on foot, his rapier drawn and accompanied by a couple of soldiers, herding a pot-bellied, stubble-chinned man in a dirty shirt, a blowsy woman with 'madam' stamped all over her, and two girls in sleazy finery.

'That's them! That's them!' the man began, as they came up, and the woman was saying, 'Dralm smite me dead, I don't know nothing about it!'

'Take these two to Tarr-Hostigos,' Kalvan directed the provost-marshal. 'They are to be questioned rigorously.' Euphemistic police-ese; another universal constant. 'This lot, too. Get their statements, but don't harm them unless you catch them trying to lie to you.'

'You'd better go to Tarr-Hostigos, yourself, and let Mytron look at that,' Harmakros told him.

'I think it's only a bruise; plate isn't broken. If it's another broken rib, my back-and-breast'll hold it for a while. First we go to the temple of Dralm and give thanks for my escape. Temple of Galzar, too.' He'd been building a reputation for piety since the night of his appearance, when he'd bowed down to those three graven images in the peasant's cottage; not doing that would be out of character, now. 'And we go slowly, and roundabout. Let as many people see me as possible. We don't want it all over Hostigos that I've been killed.'

SIXTEEN

I

As a child, he had heard his righteous Ulster Scots father speak scornfully of smoke-filled-room politics and boudoir diplomacy. The Rev. Alexander Morrison should have seen this – it was both, and for good measure, two real idolatrous heathen priests were sitting in on it. They were in Rylla's bedroom because it was easier for the rest of Prince Ptosphes's Privy Council to gather there than to carry her elsewhere, they were all smoking, and because the October nights were as chilly as the days were hot, the windows were all closed.

Rylla's usually laughing eyes were clouded with anxiety. 'They could have killed you, Kalvan.' She'd said that before. She was quite right, too. He shrugged.

'A splash on my breastplate, and a big black-and-blue place on me. The other shot killed a horse; I'm really provoked about that.'

'Well, what's being done with them?' she demanded.

'They were questioned,' her father said distastefully. He didn't like using torture, either. 'They confessed. Guardsmen of the Temple – that's to say, kept cutthroats of Styphon's House – sent from Sask Town by Archpriest Zothnes, with Prince Sarrask's knowledge. They told us there's a price of five hundred ounces gold on Kalvan's head, and as much on mine. Tomorrow,' he added, 'they will be beheaded in the town square.'

'Then it's war with Sask.' She looked down at the saddler's masterpiece on her leg. 'I hope I'm out of this before it starts.'

Not between him and Mytron she wouldn't; Kalvan set his mind at rest on that.

'War with Sask means war with Beshta,' Chartiphon said sourly. 'And together they outnumber us five to two.'

'Then don't fight them together,' Harmakros said. 'We can smash either of them alone. Let's do that, Sask first.'

'Must we always fight?' Xentos deplored. 'Can we never have peace?'

Xentos was a priest of Dralm, and Dralm was a god of peace, and in his secular capacity as Chancellor Xentos regarded war as an evidence of bad statesmanship. Maybe so, but statesmanship was operating on credit, and sooner or later your credit ran out and you had to pay off in hard money or get sold out.

Ptosphes saw it that way, too. 'Not with neighbours like Sarrask of Sask and Balthar of Beshta we can't,' he told Xentos. 'And we'll have Gormoth of Nostor to fight again in the Spring, you know that. If we haven't knocked Sask and Beshta out by then, it'll be the end of us.'

The other heathen priest, alias Uncle Wolf, concurred. As usual, he had put his wolfskin vestments aside; and as usual, he was nursing a goblet, and playing with one of the kittens who made Rylla's room their headquarters.

'You have three enemies,' he said. *You*, not *we*; priests of Galzar advised, but they never took sides. 'Alone, you can destroy each of them; together, they will destroy you.'

And after they had beaten all three, what then? Hostigos was too small to stand alone. Hostigos, dominating Sask and Beshta, with Nostor beaten and Nyklos allied, could, but then there would be Great King Kaiphranos, and back of him, back of everything, Styphon's House.

So it would have to be an empire. He'd reached that conclusion long ago.

Klestreus cleared his throat. 'If we fight Balthar first, Sarrask of Sask will hold to his alliance and deem it an attack on him,' he pronounced. 'He wants war with Hostigos anyhow. But if we attack Sask, Balthar will vacillate, and take counsel of his doubts and fears, and consult his soothsayers, whom we are bribing, and do nothing until it is too late. I know them both.' He drained his goblet, refilled it, and continued:

'Balthar of Beshta is the most cowardly, and the most miserly, and the most suspicious, and the most treacherous Prince in the world. I served him, once, and Galzar keep me from another like service. He goes about in an old black gown that wouldn't make a good dustclout, all hung over with wizards' amulets. His palace looks like a pawnshop, and you can't go three lance-lengths anywhere in it without having to shove some impudent charlatan of a soothsayer out of your way. He sees murderers in every shadow, and a plot against him whenever three gentlemen stop to give each other good day.'

He drank some more, as though to wash the taste out of his mouth.

'And Sarrask of Sask's a vanity-swollen fool who thinks with his fists and his belly. By Galzar, I've known Great Kings who hadn't half his arrogance. He's in debt to Styphon's House beyond belief, and the money all gone for pageants and feasts and silvered armour for his guards and jewels for his light-o'-loves, and the only way he can get quittance is by conquering Hostigos for them.'

'And his daughter's marrying Balthar's brother,' Rylla added. 'They're both getting what they deserve. The Princess Amnita likes cavalry troopers, and Duke Balthames likes boys.'

And he, and all of them, knew what was back of that marriage – this new Princedom of Sashta that there was talk of, to be the springboard for conquest and partition of Hostigos, and when that was out of the way, a concerted attack on Nostor. Since Gormoth had started making his own fireseed, Styphon's House wanted him destroyed, too.

It all came back to Styphon's House.

'If we smash Sask now, and take over some of these mercenaries Sarrask's been hiring on Styphon's expense-account, we might frighten Balthar into good behaviour without having to fight him.' He didn't really believe that, but Xentos brightened a little.

Ptosphes puffed thoughtfully at his pipe. 'If we could get our hands on young Balthames,' he said, 'we could depose Balthar and put Balthames on the throne. I think we could control him.'

Xentos was delighted. He realised that they'd have to fight Sask, but this looked like a bloodless – well, almost – way of conquering Beshta.

'Balthames would be willing,' he said eagerly. 'We could make a secret compact with him, and loan him, say, two thousand mercenaries, and all the Beshtan army and all the better nobles would join him.'

'No, Xentos. We do not want to help Balthames take his brother's throne.' Kalvan said. 'We want to depose Balthar ourselves, and then make Balthames do homage to Ptosphes for it. And if we beat Sarrask badly enough, we might depose him and make him do homage for Sask.'

That was something Xentos seemed not to have thought of. Before he could speak, Ptosphes was saying, decisively:

'Whatever we do, we fight Sarrask now; beat him before that old throttlepurse of a Balthar can send him aid.'

Ptosphes, too, wanted war now, before Rylla could mount a horse again. Kalvan wondered how many decisions of state, back through the history he had studied, had been made for reasons like that.

'I'll make sure of that,' Chartiphon promised. 'He won't send any troops up the Besh.'

That was why Hostigos now had two armies: the Army of the Listra, which would make the main attack on Sask, and the Army of the Besh, commanded by Chartiphon in person, to drive through southern Sask and hold the Beshtan border.

'How about Tarr-Esdreth?' Harmakros asked.

'You mean Tarr-Esdreth-of-Sask? Alkides can probably shoot rings around anybody they have there. Chartiphon can send a small force to hold the lower end of the gap, and you can do the same from the Listra side.'

'Well, how soon can we get started?' Chartiphon wanted to know. 'How much sending back and forth will there have to be, first?'

Uncle Wolf put down his goblet, and then lifted the kitten from his lap and set her on the floor. She mewed softly, looked around, and then ran over to the bed and jumped up with her mother and brothers and sisters who were keeping Rylla company.

'Well, strictly speaking,' he said, 'you're at peace with Prince Sarrask, now. You can't attack him until you've sent him letters of defiance, setting forth your causes of enmity.'

Galzar didn't approve of undeclared wars, it seemed. Harmakros laughed.

'Now, what would they be, I wonder?' he asked. 'Send them Kalvan's breastplate.'

'That's a just reason,' Uncle Wolf nodded. 'You have

many others. I will carry the letter myself.' Among other things, priests of Galzar acted as heralds. 'Put it in the form of a set of demands, to be met on pain of instant war – that would be the quickest way.'

'Insulting demands,' Klestreus specified.

'Well, give me a slate and a soapstone, somebody,' Rylla said. 'Let's see how we're going to insult him.'

'A letter to Balthar, too,' Xentos said thoughtfully. 'Not of defiance, but of friendly warning against the plots and treacheries of Sarrask and Balthames. They're scheming to involve him in war with Hostigos, let him bear the brunt of it, and then fall on him and divide his Princedom between them. He'll believe that – it's what he'd do in their place.'

'Your job, Klestreus,' Kalvan said. A diplomatic assignment would be just right for him, and would keep him from combat command without hurting his feelings. 'Leave with it for Beshta Town tomorrow. You know what Balthar will believe and what he won't; use your own judgement.'

'We'll get the letters written tonight,' Ptosphes said. 'In the morning, we'll hold a meeting of the Full Council of Hostigos. The nobles and people should have a voice in the decision for war.'

As though the decision hadn't been made already, here in Princess Rylla's smoke-filled boudoir. Real democracy, this was. Just like Pennsylvania.

II

The Full Council of Hostigos met in a long room, with tapestries on one wall and the windows opening on to the inner citadel garden on the other. The speaker for the peasants, a work-gnarled greybeard named Phosg, sat at the foot of the table, flanked by the speaker for the shepherds and herdsmen on one side, and for the woodcutters and charcoal burners on the other. They graded up from there, through the artisans, the master-craftsmen, the merchants, the yeoman farmers, the professions, the priests, the land-holding gentry and nobility, to Prince Ptosphes, at the head of the table, in a magnificent fur robe, with a heavy gold chain on his shoulders. He was flanked, on the left, by the Lord Kalvan, in a no less magnificent robe and an only slightly

137

less impressive gold chain. The place on his right was vacant, and everybody was looking at it.

It had been talked about – Kalvan and Xentos and Chartiphon and Harmakros had seen to that – that the Princess Rylla would, because of her injury, be unable to attend. So, when the double doors were swung open at the last moment and six soldiers entered carrying Rylla propped up on a couch, there were exclamations of happiness and a general ovation. Rylla was really loved in Hostigos.

She waved her hand in greeting and replied to them, and the couch was set down at Ptosphes's right. Ptosphes waited until the clamour had subsided, then drew his poignard and rapped on the table with the pommel.

'You all know why we're here,' he began without preamble. 'The last time we met, it was to decide whether to have our throats cut like sheep or die fighting like men. Well, we didn't have to do either. Now, the question is, shall we fight Sarrask of Sask now, at our advantage, or wait and fight Sarrask and Balthar together at theirs? Let me hear what is in your minds about it.'

It was like a council of war; junior rank first. Phosg was low man on the totem-pole. He got to his feet.

'Well, Lord Prince, it's like I said last time. If we have to fight, let's fight.'

'Different pack of wolves, that's all,' the shepherds' and herdsmen's speaker added. 'We'll have another wolf-hunt like Fitra and Listra-Mouth.'

It went up the table like that. The speaker for the lawyers, naturally, wanted to know if they were really sure Prince Sarrask was going to attack. Somebody asked him why not wait and have his throat cut, his house burned and his daughters raped, so that he could really be sure. The priestess of Yirtta abstained; a servant of the Allmother could not vote for the shedding of the blood of mothers' sons. Uncle Wolf just laughed. Then it got up among the nobility.

'Well, who wants this war with Sask?' One of them demanded. 'That is, besides this outlander who has grown so great in so short a time among us, this Lord Kalvan.'

He leaned right a little to look. Yes, Sthentros. He was some kind of an in-law of Ptosphes . . . had a barony over about where Boalsburg ought to be. He'd made trouble when the fireseed mills were being started – refused to let his

138

peasants be put to work collecting saltpetre. Kalvan had threatened to have his head off, and Sthrentros had run spluttering to Ptosphes. The interview had been private, nobody knew exactly what Ptosphes had told him, but he had emerged from it visibly shaken. The peasants had gone to work collecting saltpetre.

'Just who is this Kalvan?' Sthentros persisted. 'Why, until five moons ago, nobody in Hostigos had even heard of him!'

A couple of other nobles, including one who had just sworn to wade to his boottops in Saski blood, muttered agreement. Another, who had fought at Fitra, said:

'Well, nobody'd ever heard of *you* in Hostigos, either, till your uncle's wife's sister married our Prince.'

Uncle Wolf laughed again. 'They've heard of Kalvan since, and in Nostor, too, by the Wargod's Mace!'

'Yes,' another noble said, 'I grant that. But you'll have to grant that the man's an outlander, and it's a fine thing indeed to see him rise so swiftly over the heads of nobles of old Hostigi family. Why, when he came among us, he couldn't speak a word that anybody could understand.'

'By Dralm, we understand him well enough now!' That was another newcomer to the Full Council – the speaker for the fireseed makers. There were murmurs of agreement; quite a few got the point.

Sthentros refused to be silenced. 'How do we know that he isn't some runaway priest of Styphon himself?'

Mytron, present as speaker for the physicians, surgeons and apothecaries, rose.

'When Kalvan came among us, I tended his wounds. He is not circumcised, as all priests of Styphon are.'

Then he sat down. That knocked that on the head. It was a good thing the Rev. Morrison had refused to let the doctor load the bill with what he'd considered non-essentials, when his son had been born. He'd never say another word against Scotch-Irish frugality. Sthentros, however, was staying with it.

'Well, maybe that's worse,' he argued. 'It's flatly against nature for anything to act like fireseed. I think there are devils in it, that make it explode, and maybe the priests of Styphon do something to keep the devils from getting out when it explodes . . . something that we don't know anything about.'

The speaker for the fireseed makers was on his feet.

'I make the stuff; I know what goes in it. Saltpetre and sulphur and charcoal, and there aren't any devils in any of them.' He didn't know anything about oxidisation, but he knew that the saltpetre made the rest of it burn fast. 'Next thing, he'll be telling us there are devils in wine, or in dough to make the bread rise, or in . . .'

'Has anybody heard of any devils around Fitra?' somebody else asked. 'We burned plenty of fireseed there.'

'What in Galzar's name does Sthentros know about Fitra? – he wasn't there!'

'I'm going to have a little talk with that fellow, after this is over,' Ptosphes said quietly to Kalvan. 'All he is in Hostigos, he is by my favour, and my favour to him is getting frayed now.'

'Well, devils or not, the question is Lord Kalvan's place among us,' the noble who had sided with Sthentros said. 'He is no Hostigi – what right has he to sit at the Council table?'

'Fitra!' somebody cried, from a place or two above Sthentros; 'Tarr-Dombra!' added another voice, from across the table.

'He sits here,' Rylla said icily, 'as my betrothed husband, by my choice. Do you question that, Euklestes?'

'He sits here as heir-matrimonial to the throne of Hostigos, and as my son-adoptive,' Ptosphes added. 'I hope none of you presume to question that.'

'He sits here as commander of our army,' Chartiphon roared, 'and as a soldier I am proud to obey. If you want to question that, do it with your sword against mine!'

'He sits here as one sent by Dralm. Do you question the Great God?' Xentos asked.

Euklestes gave Sthentros a look-what-you-got-me-into look.

'Great Dralm, no!'

'Well, then. We still have the question of war with Sask to be voted,' Ptosphes said. 'How vote you, Lord Sthentros?'

'Oh, war, of course; I'm as loyal a Hostigi as any here.'

There was no more argument. The vote was unanimous. As soon as Ptosphes had thanked them, Harmakros was on his feet.

'Then, to show that we are all in loyal support of our Prince, let us all vote that whatever decision he may make in the matter of our dealings with Sask, with Beshta, or with Nostor, either in making war or in making peace afterwards, shall stand approved in advance by the Full Council of Hostigos.'

'*What?*' Ptosphes asked in a whisper. 'Is this some idea of your, Kalvan?'

'Yes. We don't know what we're going to have to do, but whatever it is, we may have to do it in a hurry and afterwards we won't want anybody like Sthentros or Euklestes whining that they weren't consulted.'

'That's probably wise. We'd do it anyhow, but this way there'll be no argument.'

Harmakros's motion was also carried unanimously. The organisation steamroller ran up the table without a bump.

III

Verkan, the free-trader from Grefftscharr, waited till the others – Prince Ptosphes, old Xentos, and the man of whom he must never under any circumstances think as Calvin Morrison – were seated, and then dropped into a chair at the table in Ptosphes's study.

'Have a good trip?' Lord Kalvan was asking him.

He nodded, and ran quickly over the fictitious details of the journey to Zygros City, his stay there, and his return to Hostigos, checking them with the actual facts. Then he visualised the panel, and his hand reaching out and pressing the black button. Other Paratimers used different imagery, but the result was the same. The pseudo-memories fed to him under hypnosis took over, the real memories of visits on this time-line to Zygros City were suppressed, and a complete blockage imposed on anything he knew about Fourth Level Europo-American, Hispano-Columbian Subsector.

'Not bad,' he said. 'I had a little trouble at Glarth Town, in Hos-Agrys. I'd sold those two kegs of Tarr-Dombra fireseed to a merchant, and right away they were after me, the Prince of Glarth's soldiers and Styphon's House agents. It seems Styphon's House had put out a story about one of their wagon-trains being robbed by bandits, and everybody's on the look out for unaccountable fireseed. They'd arrested and tortured the merchant; he put them on to me. I killed one and wounded another, and got away.'

'When was that?' Xentos asked sharply.

'Three days after I left here.'

'Eight days after we took Tarr-Dombra and sent that letter to Sesklos,' Ptosphes said. 'That story'll be all over the Five Kingdoms by now.'

'Oh, they've dropped that. They have a new story, now. They admit that some Prince in Hos-Harphax is making his own fireseed, but it isn't good fireseed.'

Kalvan laughed. 'It only shoots half again as hard as theirs, with half as much fouling.'

'Ah, but there are devils in your fireseed. Of course, there are devils in all fireseed – that's what makes it explode – but the priests of Styphon have secret rites that cause the devils to die as soon as they've done their work. When yours explodes, the devils escape alive. I'll bet East Hostigos is full of devils, now.'

He laughed, then stopped when he saw that none of the others were. Kalvan cursed; Ptosphes mentioned a name.

'That story has appeared here,' Xentos said. 'I hope none of our people believe it. It comes from Sask Town.'

'This Sthentros, a kinsman by marriage of mine,' Ptosphes said. 'He's jealous of Kalvan's greatness among us. I spoke to him, gave him a good fright. He claimed he thought of it himself, but I know he's lying. Somebody from Sask's been at him. Trouble is, if we tortured him, all the other nobles would be around my ears like a swarm of hornets. We're having him watched.'

'They move swiftly,' Xentos said, 'and they act as one. Their temples are everywhere, and each temple has its post station, with relays of fast horses. Styphon's Voice can speak today at Balph, in Hos-Ktemnos, and in a moon-quarter his words are heard in every temple in the Five Kingdoms. Their lies can travel so fast and far that the truth can never overtake them.'

'Yes, and see what'll happen,' Kalvan said. 'From now on, everything – plague, famine, drought, floods, hailstorms, forest-fires, hurricanes – will be the work of devils out of our fireseed. Well, you got out of Glarth; what then?'

'After that, I thought it better to travel by night. It took me eight days to reach Zygros City. My wife, Dalla, met me there, as we'd arranged when I started south from Ulthor.

In Zygros City, we recruited five brass-founders – two are cannon-founders, one's a bell-founder, one's an image-maker and knows the wax-runoff method, and one's a general foundry foreman. And three girls, woodcarvers and patternmakers, and two mercenary sergeants I hired as guards.

'I gave the fireseed secret to the gunmakers' guild in Zygros City, in exchange for making up twelve long rifled fowling-pieces and rifling some pistols. They'll ship you rifled caliver barrels at the cost of smoothbore barrels. They'd heard the devil story; none of them believe it. And I gave the secret to merchants from my own country; they will spread it there.'

'And by this time next year, Grefftscharr fireseed will be traded down the Great River to Xiphlon,' Kalvan said. 'Good. Now, how soon can this gang of yours start pouring cannon?'

'Two moons; a special miracle for each day less.'

He started to explain about the furnaces, and moulding sand; Kalvan understood.

'Then we'll have to fight this war with what we have. We'll be fighting in a moon-quarter, I think. We sent our Uncle Wolf off to Sask Town today with demands on Prince Sarrask. As soon as he hears them, they'll have to chain Sarrask up to keep him from biting people.'

'Among other things, we're demanding that Archpriest Zothnes and the Sask Town highpriest be sent here in chains, to be tried for plotting Kalvan's death and mine,' Ptosphes said. 'If Zothnes has the influence over Sarrask I think he has, that alone will do it.'

'You'll command the Mounted Rifles again, won't you?' Kalvan asked. 'It's carried on the Army List as a regiment, so you'll be a colonel. We have a hundred and twenty rifles, now.'

Dalla wouldn't approve. Well, that was too bad, but people who didn't help their friends fight weren't well thought of around here. Dalla would just have to adjust to it, the way she had to his beard.

Ptosphes finished his wine. 'Shall we go up to Rylla's room?' he asked. 'I'm glad you brought your wife with you, Verkan. Charming girl, and Rylla likes her. They made friends at once. She'll be company for Rylla while we're away.'

'Rylla's sore at us,' Kalvan said. 'She thinks we're keeping that bundle of splints on her leg to keep her from going to war with us.' He grinned. 'She's right; we are. Maybe Dalla'll help keep her amused.'

Vall didn't doubt that. Rylla and Dalla would get along together, all right; what he was worried about was what they'd get *into* together. Those two girls were just two cute little sticks of the same brand of dynamite; what one wouldn't think of, the other would.

SEVENTEEN

I

The common-room of the village inn was hot and stuffy in spite of the open door; it smelled of woollens drying, of oil and sheep-tallow smeared on armour against the rain, of wood smoke and tobacco and wine, unwashed humanity and ancient cooking-odours. The village outside was jammed with the Army of the Listra; the inn with officers, steaming and stinking and smoking, drinking mugs of mulled wine or strong sassafras tea, crowding around the fire at the long table where the map was unrolled, spooning stew from bowls or gnawing meat impaled on dagger-points. Harmakros was saying, again and again, 'Dralm damn you, hold that dagger back; don't drip grease on this!' And the priest of Galzar, who had carried the ultimatum to Sask Town and got this far on his return, and who had lately been out among the troops, sat in his shirt with his back to the fire, his wolfskin hood and cape spread to dry and a couple of village children wiping and oiling his mail. He had a mug in one hand, and with the other stroked the head of a dog that squatted beside him. He was laughing jovially.

'So I read them your demands, and you should have heard them! When I came to the part about dismissing the newly hired mercenaries, the captain-general of free companies bawled like a branded calf. I took it on myself to tell him you'd hire all of them with no loss of pay. Did I do right, Prince?'

'You did just right, Uncle Wolf,' Ptosphes told him. 'When we come to battle, along with "Down Styphon", we'll shout, "Quarter for mercenaries". How about the demands touching on Styphon's House?'

'Ha! The Archpriest Zothnes was there, sitting next to

Sarrask, with the Chancellor of Sask shoved down one place to make room for him, which shows you who rules in Sask now. He didn't bawl like a calf; he screamed like a panther. Wanted Sarrask to have me seized and my head off right in the throne-room. Sarrask told him his own soldiers would shoot him dead on the throne if he ordered it, which they would have. The mercenary captain-general wanted Zothnes's head off, and half drew his sword for it. There's one with small stomach to fight for Styphon's House. And this Zothnes was screaming that there was no god at all but Styphon; now what do you think of that?'

Gasps of horror, and exclamations of shocked piety. One officer was charitable enough to say that the fellow must be mad.

'No. He's just a – ' A monotheist, Kalvan wanted to say, but there was no word in the language for it. 'One who respects no gods but his own. We had that in my own country.' He caught himself just before saying, 'in my own time'; of those present, only Ptosphes was security-cleared for that version of his story. 'They are people who believe in only one god, and then they believe that the god they worship is the only true one, and all others are false, and finally they believe that the only true god must be worshipped in only one way, and that those who worship otherwise are vile monsters who should be killed.' The Inquisition: the wicked and bloody Albigensian Crusade; Saint Bartholomew's; Haarlem; Magdeburg. 'We want none of that here.'

'Lord Prince,' the priest of Galzar said, 'you know how we who serve the Wargod stand. The Wargod is the Judge of Princes, his courtroom the battlefield. We take no sides. We minister to the wounded without looking at their colours; our temples are havens for the war-maimed. We preach only Galzar's Way: be brave, be loyal, be comradely; obey your officers; respect yourselves and your weapons and all other good soldiers; be true to your company and to him who pays you.

'But Lord Prince, this is no common war, of Hostigos against Sask and Ptosphes against Sarrask. This is a war for all the true gods against false Styphon and Styphon's foul brood. Maybe there is some devil called Styphon, I don't know, but if there is, may the true gods trample him under their holy feet as we must those who serve him.'

A shout of 'Down Styphon!' rose. So this was what he had said they must have none of, and an old man in a dirty shirt, a mug of wine in his hand and a black and brown mongrel thumping his tail on the floor beside him, had spelled it out. A religious war, the vilest form an essentially vile business can take. Priests of Dralm and Galzar preaching fire and sword against Styphon's House. Priests of Styphon rousing mobs against the infidel devil-makers. *Styphon wills it!* Atrocities. Massacres. *Holy Dralm and no quarter!*

And that was what he'd brought to here-and-now. Well, maybe for the best; give Styphon's House another century or so in power and there'd be no gods, here-and-now, but Styphon.

'And then?'

'Well, Sarrask was in a fine rage, of course. By Styphon, he'd meet Prince Ptosphes's demands where they should be met, on the battlefield, and the war'd start as soon as I took my back out of sight across the border. That was just before noon. I almost killed a horse, and myself, getting here. I haven't done much hard riding, lately,' he parenthesised. 'As soon as I got here, Harmakros sent riders out.'

They'd reached Tarr-Hostigos at cocktail time, another alien rite introduced by Lord Kalvan, and found him and Ptosphes and Xentos and Rylla and Dalla in Rylla's room. Hasty arming and saddling, hastier good-byes, and then a hard mud-splashing ride up Listra Valley, reaching this village after dark. The war had already started; from Esdreth Gap they could hear the distant dull thump of cannon.

Outside, the Army of the Listra was still moving forward; an infantry company marched past with a song:

Roll another barrel out, the party's just begun.
We beat Prince Gormoth's soldiers; you oughta seen them run!
And then we crossed the Athan, and didn't we have fun,
While we were marching through Nostor!

Galloping hoofs; cries of 'Way! Way! Courier!' The song ended in shouted imprecations from mud-splashed infantrymen. The galloping horse stopped outside. The march, and the song, was resumed:

Hurrah! Hurrah! We burned the bastards out!
Hurrah! Hurrah! We put them all to rout!
We stole their pigs and cattle and we dumped their
sauerkraut,
While we were marching through Nostor!

A muddy cavalryman stumbled through the door, looked around blinking, and then made for the long table, saluting as he came.

'From Colonel Verkan, Mounted Rifles. He and his men have Fyk; they beat off a counter-attack, and now the whole Saski army's coming at him. I found some Mobiles and a four-pounder on the way back; they've gone to help him.'

'By Dralm, the whole Army of the Listra's going to help him. Where is this Fyk place?'

Harmakros pointed on the map – beyond Esdreth Gap, on the main road to Sask Town. There was a larger town, Gour, a little beyond. Kalvan pulled on his quilted coif and fastened the throat-guard; while he was settling his helmet on his head, somebody had gone to the door and was bawling into the dripping night for horses.

II

The rain had stopped, an hour later, when they reached Fyk. It was a small place, full of soldiers and lighted by bon-fires. The civil population had completely vanished; all fled when the shooting had started. A four-pounder pointed up the road to the south, with the dim shape of an improvised barricade stretching away in the darkness on either side. Off ahead, an occasional shot banged, and he could distinguish the sharper reports of Hostigos-made powder from the slower-burning stuff put out by Styphon's House. Maybe Uncle Wolf was right that this was a war between the true gods and false Styphon; it was also a war between two makes of gunpowder.

He found Verkan and a Mobile Force major in one of the village cottages; Verkan wore a hooded smock of brown canvas, and a short chopping-sword on his belt and a powder-horn and a bullet-pouch slung from his shoulder. The major's cavalry armour was browned and smeared with

148

tallow. They had one of the pyrographed deerskin field-maps spread on the table in front of them. *Paper, invention of;* he'd made that mental memo a thousand times already.

'There were about fifty cavalry here when we arrived,' Verkan was saying. 'We killed them or ran them out. In half an hour there were a couple of hundred back. We beat them off, and that was when I sent the riders back. Then Major Leukestros came up with his men and a gun, just in time to help beat off another attack. We have some cavalry and mounted arquebusiers out in front and on the flanks; that's the shooting you're hearing. There are some thousand cavalry at Gour, and probably all Sarrask's army following.'

'I'm afraid we're going to have to make a wet night of it,' Kalvan said. 'We'll have to get our battle-line formed now; we can't take chances on what they may do.'

He shoved the map aside and began scribbling and diagraming an order of battle on the white-scrubbed table top. Guns to the rear, in column along a side road north of the village, four-pounders in front; horses to be unhitched, but fed and rested in harness, ready to move out at once. Infantry in a line to both sides of the road a thousand yards ahead of the village, Mobile Force infantry in the middle. Cavalry on the flank; mounted infantry horses to the rear. A battle-order that could be converted instantly into a march-order if they had to move on in the morning.

The army came stumbling in for the next hour or so, in bits and scraps, got themselves sorted out, and took their positions astride of the road on the slope south of the village. The air had grown noticeably warmer. He didn't like that; it presaged fog, and he wanted good visibility for the battle tomorrow. Cavalry skirmishers began drifting back, reporting pressure of large enemy forces in front.

An hour after he had his line formed, the men lying in the wet grass on blankets or whatever bedding they could snatch from the village, the Saski began coming up. There was a brief explosion of smallarms fire as they ran into his skirmishers, then they pulled back and began forming their own battle-line.

Hell of a situation, he thought disgustedly, lying on a corn-shuck tick he and Ptosphes and Harmakros had stolen from some peasant's abandoned bed. Two blind armies, not a

thousand yards apart, waiting for daylight, and when daylight came . . .

A cannon went off in front and on his left, with a loud,
dull *whump*! A couple of heartbeats later, something
whacked behind the line. He rose on his hands and knees,
counting seconds as he peered into the darkness. Two
minutes later, he glimpsed an orange glow on his left, and
two seconds after that heard the report. Call it eight hundred
yards, give or take a hundred. He hissed to a quartet of
officers on a blanket next to him.

'They're overshooting us a little. Pass the word along the
line, both ways, to move forward three hundred paces. And
not a sound; dagger anybody who speaks above a whisper.
Harmakros, get the cavalry and the mounted infantry horses
back on the other side of the village. Make a lot of noise
about five hundred yards behind us.'

The officers moved off, two to a side. He and Ptosphes
picked up the mattress and carried it forward, counting
three hundred paces before dropping it. Men were moving
up on both sides, with a gratifying minimum of noise.

The Saski guns kept on firing. At first there were yells of
simulated fright; Harmakros and his crowd. Finally, a gun
fired almost in front of him; the cannonball passed overhead
and landed behind with a swish and whack like a headsman's
sword coming down. The next shot was far on his left.
Eight guns, at two minute intervals – call it fifteen minutes
to load. That wasn't bad, in the dark and with what the
Saski had. He relaxed, lying prone with his chin rested on
his elbows. After a while Harmakros returned and joined
him and Ptosphes on the shuck tick. The cannonade went on
in slow procession from left to right and left to right again.
Once there was a bright flash instead of a dim glow, and a
much sharper crack. Fine! One of their guns had burst!
After that, there were only seven rounds to the salvo. Once
there was a rending crash behind, as though a roundshot
had hit a tree. Every shot was a safe over.

Finally, the firing stopped. The distant intermittent duel-
ling between the two Castles Esdreth had ceased, too. He let
go of wakefulness and dropped into sleep.

Ptosphes, stirring beside him, wakened him. His body ached
and his mouth tasted foul, as every body and mouth on both

battle-lines must. It was still dark, but the sky above was something less than black, and he made out his companions as dim shapes. Fog.

By Dralm, that was all they needed! Fog, and the whole Saski army not five hundred yards away, and all their advantages of mobility and artillery superiority lost. Nowhere to move, no room to manoeuvre, visibility down to less than pistol-shot, even the advantage of their hundred-odd rifled calivers nullified.

This looked like the start of a bad day for Hostigos.

They munched the hard bread and cold pork and cheese they had brought with them and drank some surprisingly good wine from a canteen and talked in whispers, other officers creeping in until a dozen and a half were huddled around the headquarters mattress.

'Couldn't we draw back a little?' That was Mnestros, the mercenary 'captain' – approximately major-general – in command of the militia. 'This is a horrible position. We're half-way down their throats.'

'They'd hear us,' Ptosphes said, 'and start with their guns again, and this time they'd know where to shoot.'

'Bring up our own guns and start shooting first,' somebody suggested.

'Same objection; they'd hear us and open fire before we could. And for Dralm's sake keep your voices down,' Kalvan snapped. 'No, Mnestros said it. We're half-way down their throats. Let's jump the rest of the way and kick their guts out from the inside.'

The mercenary was a book-soldier. He was briefly dubious then admitted:

'We are in line to attack, and we know where they are and they don't know where we are. They must think we're back at the village, from the way they were firing last night. Cavalry on the flanks?' He deprecated that. According to the here-and-now book, cavalry should be posted all along the line, between blocks of infantry.

'Yes, half the mercenaries on each end, and a solid line of infantry, two ranks of pikes, and arquebuses and calivers to fire over the pikemen's shoulders,' Kalvan said. 'Verkan, have your men pass the word along the line. Everybody stay put and keep quiet till we can all go forward together. I want every pan reprimed and every flint tight; we'll all move off together, and no shouting till the enemy sees us. I'll take the extreme right. Prince Ptosphes, you'd better take centre; Mnestros, command the left. Harmakros, you take the regular and Mobile Force cavalry and five hundred Mobile Force infantry, and move back about five hundred yards. If they flank us or break through, attend to it.'

By now, the men around him were individually recognisable, but everything beyond twenty yards was fog-swallowed. Their saddle-horses were brought up. He re-primed the pistols in the holsters, got a second pair from a saddlebag, renewed the priming, and slipped one down the top of each jackboot. The line was stirring with a noise that stood his hair on end under his helmet-coif, until he realised that the Saski were making too much noise to hear it. He slipped back the cuff under his mail sleeve and looked at his watch. Five forty-five; sunrise in half an hour. They all shook hands with one another, and he started right along the line.

Soldiers were rising, rolling and slinging cloaks and blankets. There were quilts and ticks and things from the village lying on the ground; mustn't be a piece of bedding left in Fyk. A few were praying, to Dralm or Galzar. Most of them seemed to take the attitude that the gods would do what they wanted to without impertinent human suggestions.

He stopped at the extreme end of the line, on the right of five hundred regular infantry, like all the rest lined four deep, two ranks of pikes and two of calivers. Behind and on the right, the mercenary cavalry were coming up in a block of twenty ranks, fifty to the rank. The first few ranks were heavy-armed, plate rerebraces and vambraces on their arms instead of mail sleeves, heavy pauldrons protecting their shoulders, visored helmets, mounted on huge chargers, real old style brewery-wagon horses. They came to a halt just behind him. He passed the word of readiness left, then sat stroking his horse's neck and talking softly to him.

After a while the word came back with a moving stir along the line through the fog. He lifted a long pistol from his right-hand holster, readied it to fire, and shook his reins. The line slid forward beside him, front rank pikes waist high, second rank pike-points a yard behind and breast high, calivers behind at high port. The cavalry followed him with a slow fluviatile *clop-clatter-clop*. Things emerged from the fog in front – seedling pines, clumps of tall weeds, a rotting cart-wheel, a whitened cow's skull – but the grey nothingness marched just twenty yards in front.

This, he recalled, was how Gustavus Adolphus had got killed, riding forward into a fog like this at Lützen.

An arquebus banged on his left; that was a charge of Styphon's Best. Half a dozen shots rattled in reply, most of them Kalvan's Unconsecrated, and he heard yells of 'Down Styphon!' and 'Sarrask of Sask!' The pikemen stiffened; some of them lost step and had to hop to make it up. They all seemed to crouch over their weapons, and the caliver muzzles poked forward. By this time, the firing was like a slate roof endlessly sliding off a house, and then, much farther to the left, there was a sudden ringing crash like sheet-steel falling into a scrap-car.

The Fyk corpse-factory was in full production.

But in front, there was only silence and the slowly receding curtain of fog, and pine-dotted pastureland broken by small gullies in which last night's rainwater ran yellowly. Ran straight ahead of them – that wasn't right. The Saski position was up a slope from where they had lain under the midrange trajectory of the guns, and now the noise of battle was not only to the left but behind them. He flung up the hand holding the gold-mounted pistol.

'Halt!' he called out. 'Pass the word left to stand fast!'

He knew what had happened. Both battle-lines, formed in the dark, had overlapped the other's left. So he had flanked them, and Mnestros, on the Hostigi left, was also flanked.

'You two,' he told a pair of cavalry lieutenants. 'Ride left till you come to the fighting. Find a good pivot-point, and one of you stay with it. The other will come back along the line, passing the word to swing left. We'll start swinging from this end. And find somebody to tell Harmakros what's happened, if he doesn't know it already. He probably does. No orders; just use his own judgement.'

Everybody would have to use his own judgement, from here out. He wondered what was happening to Mnestros. He hadn't the liveliest confidence in Mnestros's judgement when he ran into something the book didn't cover. Then he sat, waiting for centuries, until one of the lieutenants came thudding back behind the infantry line, and he gave the order to start the leftward swing.

The level pikes and slanting calivers kept line on his left; the cavalry clop-clattered behind him. The downward slope swung in front of them, until they were going steeply uphill, and then the ground was level under their feet, and he could feel a freshening breeze on his cheek.

He was shouting a warning when the fog tore apart for a hundred yards in front and two or three on either side, and out of it came a mob of infantry, badged with Sarrask's green and gold. He pulled his horse back, fired his pistol into them, holstered it, and drew the other from his left holster. The major commanding the regular infantry blew his whistle and screamed above the din:

'Action front! Fire by ranks, odd numbers only!'

The front rank pikemen squatted as though simultaneously stricken with diarrhoea. The second rank dropped to one knee, their pikes advanced. Over their shoulders, half the third rank blasted with calivers, then dodged for the fourth rank to fire over them. As soon as the second volley crashed, the pikemen were on their feet and running at the disintegrating front of the Saski infantry, all shouting, *Down Styphon!*

He saw that much, then raked his horse with his spurs and drove him forward, shouting, *'Charge!'* The heavily-armed mercenaries thundered after him, swinging long swords, firing pistols almost as big as small carbines, smashing into the Saski infantry from the flank before they could form a new front. He pistolled a pikeman who was thrusting at his horse, then drew his sword.

Then the fog closed down again, and dim shapes were dodging among the horses. A Saski cavalryman bulked in front of him, firing almost in his face. The bullet missed him, but hot grains of powder stung his cheek. Get a coal-miner's tattoo out of that, he thought, and then his wrist hurt as he drove the point into the fellow's throat-guard, spreading the links. *Plate gorgets; issue to mounted troops as soon as can be produced.* He wrenched the point free, and the Saski slid gently out of his saddle.

'Keep moving!' he screamed at the cavalry with him. 'Don't let them slow you down!'

In a mess like this, stalled cavalry were all but helpless. Their best weapon was the momentum of a galloping horse, and once lost, that took at least thirty yards to regain.

Cavalry horses ought to be crossed with jackrabbits; but that was something he couldn't do anything about at all. One mass of cavalry, the lancers and musketoon-men who had ridden behind the heavily-armed men, had got hopelessly jammed in front of a bristle of pikes. He backed his horse quickly out of that, then found himself at the end of a line of Mobile Force infantry, with short arquebuses and cavalry lances for pikes. He directed them to the aid of the stalled cavalry, and then realised that he was riding across the road at right angles. That meant that he – and the whole battle, since all the noise was either to his right or left along the road – was now facing east instead of south. Of the heavily-armed mercenary cavalry who had been with him at the beginning he could see nothing.

A horseman came crashing at him out of the fog, shouting 'Down Styphon!' and thrusting at him with a sword. He had barely time to beat it aside with his own and cry, 'Ptosphes!' and a moment later:

'Ptosphes, by Dralm! How did you get here?'

'Kalvan! I'm glad you parried that one. Where are we?'

He told the Prince, briefly. 'The whole Dralm-damned battle's turned at right angles; you know that?'

'Well, no wonder. Our whole left wing's gone. Mnestros is dead – I heard that from an officer who saw his body. The regular infantry on our extreme left are all but wiped out; what few are left, and what's left of the militia next to them, re-formed on Harmakros, in what used to be our rear. That's our left wing, now.'

'Well, their left wing's in no better shape; I swung in on that and smashed it up. What's happened to the cavalry we had on the left?'

'Dralm knows; I don't. Took to their heels out of this, I suppose.' Ptosphes drew one of his pistols and took a powder-flask from his belt. 'Watch over my shoulder, will you, Kalvan.'

He drew one of his own holster-pair and poured a charge into it. The battle seemed to have moved out of their immediate vicinity, though off in the fog in both directions there was a bedlam of shooting, yelling and steel-clashing. Then suddenly a cannon, the first of the morning, went off in what Kalvan took to be the direction of the village. An eight-pounder, he thought, and certainly loaded with Made-in-Hostigos. On its heels came another, and another.

'That,' Ptosphes said, 'will be Harmakros.'

'I hope he knows what he's shooting at.' He primed the pistol, holstered it, and started on its mate. 'Where do you think we could do the most good?'

Ptosphes had his saddle pair loaded, and was starting on one from a boot-top.

'Let's see if we can find some of our own cavalry, and go looking for Sarrask,' he said. 'I'd like to kill or capture him, myself. If I did, it might give me some kind of a claim on the throne of Sask. If this cursed fog would only clear.'

From off to the right, south up the road, came noises like a boiler-shop starting up. There wasn't much shooting – everybody's gun was empty and no one had time to reload – just steel, and an indistinguishable *waw-waw-waw*-ing of voices. The fog was blowing in wet rags, now, but as fast as it blew away, more closed down. There was a limit to that, though; overhead the sky was showing a faint sunlit yellow.

'Come on, Lytris, come on!' he invoked the Weather Goddess. 'Get this stuff out of here! Whose side are you fighting on, anyhow?'

Ptosphes finished the second of his spare pair; he had the last one of his own four to prime. Ptosphes said, 'Watch behind you!' and he almost spilled the priming, then closed the pan and readied the pistol to fire. It was some twenty of the heavy-armed cavalry who had gone in with him. Their sergeant wanted to know where they were.

He hadn't any better idea than they had. Shoving the flint away from the striker, he pushed the pistol into his boot and drew his sword; they all started off towards the noise of fighting. He thought he was still going east until he saw that he was riding, at right angles, on to a line of mud-trampled quilts and bedspreads and mattresses, the things that had been appropriated in the village the night before. He glanced left and right. Ptosphes knew what they were, too, and swore.

Now the battle had made a full 180-degree turn. Both armies were facing in the direction from whence they had come; the route of either would be in the direction of the enemy's country.

Galzar, he thought irreverently, must have overslept this morning.

But at least the fog was definitely clearing, gilded above by sunlight, and the grey tatters around them were fewer and more threadbare, visibility now better than a hundred yards. They found a line of battle extending, apparently, due east of Fyk, and came up behind a hodgepodge of militia, regulars and Mobiles, any semblance of unit organisation completely lost. Mobile Force cavalry were trotting back and forth behind them, looking for soft spots where breakthroughs, in either direction, might happen. He yelled to a Mobile Force captain who was fighting on foot:

'Who's in front of you?'

'How should I know? Same mess of odds-and-sods we are. This Dralm-damned battle . . .'

Officially, he supposed, it would be the Battle of Fyk, but nobody who'd been in it would ever call it anything but the Dralm-damned Battle.

Before he could say anything, there was a crash on his left like all the boiler-shops in creation together. He and Ptosphes looked at one another.

'Something new has been added,' he commented. 'Well, let's go see.'

They started to the left with their picked up heavy cavalry, not too rapidly, and with pistols drawn. There was a lot of shouting – 'Down Styphon!' of course, and 'Ptosphes!' and 'Sarrask of Sask!' There were also shouts of 'Balthames!' That would be the retinue Balthar's brother, the prospective Prince of Sashta, had brought to Sask Town – some two hundred and fifty, he'd heard. Then, there were cries of 'Treason! Treason!'

Now there was a hell of a thing to yell on any battlefield, let alone in a fog. He was wondering who was supposed to be betraying whom when he found the way blocked by the backs of Hostigi infantry at right angles to the battle-line; not retreating, just being pushed out of the way by something. Beyond them, through the thinning fog, he could see a rush of cavalry, some wearing black and pale yellow surcoats over their armour. They'd be Balthames's Beshtans; they were firing and chopping indiscriminately at anything in front of them, and, mixed with them, were green-and-gold Saski, fighting with them and the Hostigi both. All he and

Ptosphes and the mercenary men-at-arms could do was sit their horses and fire pistols at them over the heads of their own infantry.

Finally, the breakthrough, if that was what it had been, was over. The Hostigi infantry closed in behind them, piking and shooting, and there were cries of 'Comrade, we yield!' and 'Oath to Galzar!' and 'Comrade, spare mercenaries!'

'Should we give them a chase?' Ptosphes asked, looking after the Saski-Beshtan whatever-it-had-been.

'I shouldn't think so. They're charging in the right direction. What the Styphon do you think happened?'

Ptosphes laughed. 'How should I know? I wonder if it really was treason.'

'Well, let's get through here.' He raised his voice. 'Come on – forward! Somebody's punched a hole for us; let's get through it!'

Suddenly, the fog was gone. The sun shone from a cloudless sky; the mountainside, nearer than he thought, was gaudy with Autumn colours; all the drifting puffs and hanging bands of white on the ground were powdersmoke. The village of Fyk, on his left, was ringed with army wagons like a Boer laager, guns pointing out between them. That was the strongpoint on which Harmakros had rallied the wreckage of the left wing.

In front of him, the Hostigi were moving forward, infantry running beside the cavalry, and in front of them the Saski line was ravelling away, men singly and in little groups and by whole companies turning and taking to their heels, trying to join two or three thousand of their comrades who had made a porcupine. He knew it from other-when history as a Swiss hedgehog: a hollow circle bristling pikes in all directions. Hostigi cavalry were already riding around it, firing into it, and Verkan's riflemen were sniping at it. There seemed to be no Saski cavalry whatever; they must all have joined the rush to the south at the time of the breakthrough.

Then three four-pounders came out from the village at a gallop, unlimbered at three hundred yards, and began firing case-shot. When two eight-pounders followed more sedately, helmets began going up on pike-points and caliver muzzles.

Behind him, the fighting had ceased entirely. Hostigi

soldiers had scattered through the brush and trampled corn-
stalks, tending to their wounded, securing prisoners, robbing
corpses, collecting weapons, all the routine after-battle
chores, and the battle wasn't over yet. He was worrying
about where all the Saski cavalry had got to, and the possibility that they might rally and counterattack, when he saw
a large mounted column approaching from the south. This
is it, he thought, and we're all scattered to Styphon's House
and gone — He was shouting at the men nearest him to drop
what they were doing and start earning their pay when he
saw blue and red colours on lances, saddle-pads, scarves. He
trotted forward to meet them.

Some were mercenaries, some were Hostigi regulars; with
them were a number of green-and-gold prisoners, their
helmets hung on saddlebows. A captain in front shouted a
greeting as he came up.

'Well, thank Galzar you're still alive, Lord Kalvan!
Where's the Prince?'

'Back at the village, trying to get things sorted out. How
far did you go?'

'Almost to Gour. Better than a thousand of them got away;
they won't stop short of Sask Town. The ones we have are
the ones with the slow horses. Sarrask may have got away;
we know Balthames did.'

'Dralm and Galzar and all the true gods curse that
Beshtan bastard!' one of the prisoners cried. 'Devils eat his
soul forever! The Dralm-damned lackwit cost us the battle,
and only Galzar's counted how many dead and maimed.'

'What happened? I heard cries of treason.'

'Yes, that dumped the whole bagful of devils on us,' the
Saski said. 'You want to know what happened? Well, in
the darkness we formed with our right wing far beyond
your left; yours beyond ours, I suppose, from the looks of
things. On our right, we carried all before us, drove your
cavalry from the field and smashed your infantry. Then
this boy-lover from Beshta — we can fight our enemies, but
Galzar guard us from our allies — took his own men and near
a thousand of our mercenary horse off on a rabbit-hunt after
your fleeing cavalry, almost to Esdreth.

'Well, you know what happened in the meantime. Our
right drove in your left, and yours ours, and the whole
battle turned like a wheel, and we were all facing in the

way we'd come, and then back comes this Balthames of
Beshta, smashing into our rear, thinking that he was saving
the day.

'And to make it worse, the silly fool doesn't shout "*Sarrask
of Sask,*" as he should have; no, he shouts "*Balthames!*" – he
and all his, and the mercenaries with him took it up to curry
favour with him. Well, great Dralm, you know how much
anybody can trust anybody from Beshta; we thought the
bugger'd turned his coat, and somebody cried treason. I'll
not deny crying it myself, after I was near spitted on a
Beshtan lance, and me crying "*Sarrask!*" at the top of my
lungs. So we were carried away in the rout, and I fell in
with mercenaries from Hos-Ktemnos. We got almost to Gour
and tried to make a stand, and were ridden over and taken.'

'Did Sarrask get away? Galzar knows I want to spill his
blood badly enough, but I want to do it honestly.'

The Saski didn't know; none of Sarrask's silver-armoured
personal guard had been near him in the fighting.

'Well, don't blame Duke Balthames too much.' Looking
around, he saw over a score of Saski and mercenary prisoners
within hearing. If we're going to have a religious war, let's
start it now. 'It was,' he declared, 'the work of the true
gods! Who do you think raised the fog, but Lytris the
Weather Goddess? Who confounded your captains in array-
ing your line, and caused your gunners to overshoot,
harming not one of us, but Galzar Wolfhead, the Judge of
Princes? And who but Great Dralm himself addled poor
Balthames's wits, leading him on a fool's chase and bringing
him back to strike you from behind? At long last,' he cried,
'the true gods have raised their mighty hands against false
Styphon and the blasphemers of Styphon's House!'

There were muttered amens, some from the Saski
prisoners. Styphon's stock had dropped quite a few points.
He decided to let it go at that, and put them in with the
other prisoners and let them talk.

EIGHTEEN

Ptosphes was shocked by the casualties. Well, they *were* rather shocking —only forty-two hundred effectives left out of fifty-eight hundred infantry, and eighteen hundred of a trifle over three thousand cavalry. The body-count didn't meet the latter figure, however, and he remembered what the Saski officer had said about Balthames's chase almost to Esdreth Gap. Most of the mercenaries on the left wing had simply bugged out; by now, they'd be fleeing into Listra Valley, spreading tales of a crushing Hostigi defeat. He cursed; there wasn't anything else he could do about it.

Some cavalry arrived from Esdreth Gap: Chartiphon's Army of the Besh men. During the night, they reported, infantry from both the army of the Besh and the Army of the Listra had got on to the mountain back of Tarr-Esdreth-of-Sask, and taken it by storm just before daylight. Alkides had moved his three treasured brass eighteen-pounders and some lighter pieces down into the gap, and was holding it at both ends with a mixed force. As the fog had started to blow away, a large body of Saski cavalry had tried to force a way through; they had been driven off by gunfire. Perturbed by the presence of enemy troops so far north, he had sent to find out what was going on. Riders were sent to reassure him, and order him to come up in person and bring his eighteens with him.

There was no telling what they might have to break into before the day was over, the long eighteen-pounders were excellent burglar-tools.

Harmakros got off at ten, with the Mobile Force and all the four-pounders, up the main road for Sask Town. All the captured mercenaries agreed to take Prince Ptosphes's colours and were released under oath and under arms. The Saski subjects were disarmed and put to work digging trenches for mass graves and collecting salvageable equipment. Mytron and his staff preempted the better cottages and several of the larger and more sanitary barns for hospitals. Taking five hundred of the remaining cavalry, Kalvan started out a little before noon, leaving Ptosphes to await the arrival of Alkides and the eighteen-pounders.

Gour was a market town of some five thousand. He found bodies, already stripped of armour, in the square, and a mob of townsfolk and disarmed Saski prisoners working to put out several fires, guarded by some lightly wounded mounted arquebusiers. He dropped two squads to help them and rode on.

He thought he knew this section; he'd been stationed in Blair County five otherwhen years ago. He hadn't realised how much the Pennsylvania Railroad Company had altered the face of Logan Valley. At about what ought to be Allegheny Furnace, he was stopped by a picket-post of Mobile Force cavalry and warned to swing right and come in on Sask Town from behind. Tarr-Sask was being held, either by or for Prince Sarrask, and was cannonading the town. While he talked with them, he could hear the occasional distant boom of a heavy bombard.

Tarr-Sask stood on the south bend of Brush Mountain, Sarrask's golden-rayed sun on green flying from the watch-tower. The arrival of his cavalry at the other side of the town must have been observed; four bombards let go with strain-everything charges of Styphon's Best, hurling hundred and fifty pound stone cannonballs among the houses. This, he thought, wouldn't do much to improve relations between Sarrask and his subjects. Harmakros, who had nothing but four-pounders, which was to say nothing, was not replying. Wait, he thought, till Alkides gets here.

Battering-pieces, thirty-two-pounders, about six; get cast as soon as Verkan's gang gets a foundry going. And cast shells; do something about.

There had been no fighting inside the town; Harmakros's blitzkrieg had hit it too fast, before resistance could be organised. There had been some looting – that was to be expected – but no fires. Arson for arson's sake, without a valid strategic reason as in Nostor, was discountenanced in the Hostigos army. Most of the civil population had either refugeed out or were down in the cellar.

The temple of Styphon had been taken first of all. It stood on almost the exact site of the Hollidaysburg courthouse, a circular building under a golden dome, with rectangular wings on either side. If, as he suspected, that dome was really gold, it might go a long way towards paying the cost of the war. A Mobile Force infantryman was up a ladder with a tarpot and a brush, painting DOWN STYPHON over the door. Entering, the first thing he saw was a twenty-foot image, its face newly spalled and pitted and lead-splashed. The Puritans had been addicted to that sort of smallarms practice, he recalled, and so had the Huguenots. There was a lot of gold ornamentation around; guards had been posted.

He found Harmakros in the Innermost Circle, his spurred heels resting on the highpriest's desk He sprang to his feet.

'Kalvan! Did you bring any guns?'

'No, only cavalry. Ptosphes is bringing Alkides's three eighteens. He'll be here in about three hours. What happened here?'

'Well, as you see, Balthames got here a little ahead of us and shut himself up in Tarr-Sask. We sent the local Uncle Wolf up to parley with him. He says he's holding the castle in Sarrask's name, and won't surrender without Sarrask's orders as long as he has fireseed.'

'Then he doesn't know where Sarrask is, either.'

Sarrask could be dead and his body stripped on the field by common soldiers – it'd be worth stripping – and tumbled anonymously into one of those mass graves. If so, they might never be sure, and then, every year for the next thirty years, some fake Sarrask would be turning up somewhere in the Five Kingdoms, conning suckers into financing a war to recover his throne. That had happened occasionally in otherwhen history.

'Did you get the priests along with this temple?'

'Oh, yes, Zothnes and all. They were packing to leave when we got here, and argued about what to take along. We have them in chains in the town jail, now. Do you want to see them?'

'Not particularly. We'll have their heads off tomorrow or the next day, when we find time for it. How about the fireseed mill?'

Harmakros laughed. 'Verkan's surrounding it with his riflemen. As soon as we get a dozen or so men dressed in priestly robes, about a hundred more will chase them in, with a lot of yelling and shooting. If that gets the gate open, we may be able to take the place before some fanatic blows it up. You know, some of these underpriests and novices really believe in Styphon.'

'Well, what did you get here?'

Harmakros waved a hand about him. 'All this gold and fancywork. Then there's gold and silver, specie and bullion, in the vaults, to about fifty thousand gold ounces, I'd say.'

That was a lot of money. Around a million U.S dollars. He could believe it, though; besides making fireseed, Styphon's House was in the loan-shark business, at something like ten per cent per lunar month, compound interest. *Anti-usury laws; do something about.* Except for a few small-time pawnbrokers, they were the only money-lenders in Sask.

'Then,' Harmakros continued, 'there's a magazine and armoury. We haven't taken inventory yet, but I'd say ten tons of fireseed, three or four hundred stand of arquebuses and calivers, and a lot of armour. And one wing's packed full of general merchandise, probably taken in as offerings. We haven't even looked at that, yet; just put it under guard. A lot of barrels that could be wine; we don't want the troops getting at that yet.'

The guns of Tarr-Sask kept on firing slowly, smashing a house now and then. None of the roundshot came near the temple; Balthames was evidently still in awe of Styphon's House. The main army arrived about 1630; Alkides got his brass eighteen-pounders and three twelves in position and began shooting back. They didn't throw the huge granite globes Balthames's bombards did, but they fired every five minutes instead of every half hour, and with something approaching accuracy. A little later, Verkan rode in to report the fireseed mill taken intact. He didn't think much of the equipment – the mills were all slave-powered – but there had been twenty tons of finished fireseed, and over a hundred of sulphur and saltpetre. He had had some trouble preventing a massacre of the priests when the slaves had been unshackled.

At 1815, in the gathering dusk, riders came in from

Esdreth, reporting that Sarrask had been captured, in Listra Valley, while trying to reach the Nostori border to place himself under the questionable protection of Prince Gormoth.

'He was captured,' the sergeant in command finished, 'by the Princess Rylla and Colonel Verkan's wife Dalla.'

He and Ptosphes and Harmakros and Verkan all shouted at once. A moment later, the roar of one of Alkides's eighteens was almost an anticlimax. Verkan was saying, '*That's* the girl who wanted *me* to stay out of battles!'

'But Rylla can't get out of bed,' Ptosphes argued.

'I wouldn't know about that, Prince,' the sergeant said. 'Maybe the Princess calls a saddle a bed, because that's what she was in when I saw her.'

'Well, did she have that cast – that leather thing – on her leg?' Kalvan asked.

'No, sir – just regular riding boots, with pistols in them.'

He and Ptosphes cursed antiphonally. Well, at least they'd kept her out of that blindfold slaughterhouse at Fyk.

'Sound Cease Fire, and then Parley,' he ordered. 'Send Uncle Wolf up the hill again; tell Balthames we have his pa-in-law.'

They got a truce arranged; Balthames sent out a group of neutrals, merchants and envoys from other princedoms, to observe and report. Bonfires were lit along the road up to the castle. It was full dark when Rylla and Dalla arrived, with a mixed company of mounted Tarr-Hostigos garrison troops, fugitive mercenaries rallied along the road south, and overage peasants on overage horses. With them were nearly a hundred of Sarrask's elite guard, in silvered harness that looked more like table-service than armour, and Sarrask himself in gilded armour.

'Where's that lying quack of a Mytron?' Rylla demanded, as soon as she was within hearing. 'I'll doctor him when I catch him – a double orchidectomy! You know what? Yes, of course you do; you put him up to it! Well, Dalla had a look at my leg this morning, she's forgotten more about doctoring than Mytron ever learned, and she said that thing ought to have been off half a moon ago.'

'Well, what's the story?' Kalvan asked. 'How did you pick all this up?' He indicated Sarrask, glowering at them

165

from his saddle, with his silver-plated guardsmen behind him.

'Oh, this band of heroes you took to a battle you tried to keep me out of,' Rylla said bitterly. 'About noon, they came clattering in to Tarr-Hostigos — that's the ones with the fastest horses and the sharpest spurs — screaming that all was lost, the army destroyed, you killed, father killed, Harmakros killed, Verkan killed, Mnestros killed; why, they even had Chartiphon, down on the Beshtan border, killed!'

'Well, I'm sorry to say that Mnestros *was* killed,' her father told her.

'Well, I didn't believe a tenth of it, but even at that something bad could have happened, so I gathered up what men I could mount at the castle, appointed Dalla my lieutenant — she was the best man around — and we started south, gathering up what we could along the way. Just this side of Darax, we ran into this crowd. We thought they were the cavalry screen for a Saski invasion, and we gave them an argument. That was when Dalla captured Prince Sarrask.'

'I did not,' Verkan's wife denied. 'I just shot his horse. Some farmers captured him, and you owe them a lot of money, or somebody does. We rode into this gang on the road, and there was a lot of shooting, and this big man in gilded armour came at me swinging a sword as long as I am. I fired at him, and as I did his horse reared and caught it in the chest and fell over backwards, and while he was trying to get clear some peasants with knives and hatchets and things jumped on him, and he began screaming, "I am Prince Sarrask of Sask; my ransom is a hundred thousand ounces of silver!" Well, right away, they lost interest in killing him.'

'Who are they, do you know?' Ptosphes asked. 'I'll have to make that good to them.'

'Styphon will pay,' Kalvan said.

'Styphon ought to; he got Sarrask into this mess in the first place,' Ptosphes commented. He turned back to Rylla. 'What then?'

'Well, when Sarrask surrendered, the rest of them began pulling off helmets and holding swords up by the blades and crying, "Oath to Galzar!" They all admitted they'd taken an awful beating at Fyk, and were trying to get into Nostor. Now wouldn't that have been nice?'

'Our gold-plated friend here didn't want to come along

with us,' Dalla said. 'Rylla told him he didn't need to; we could take his head along easier than all of him. You know, Prince, your daughter doesn't fool. At least, Sarrask didn't think so.'

She hadn't been fooling, and Sarrask had known it.

'So,' Rylla picked it up, 'we put him on a horse one of his guards didn't need any more, and brought him along. We thought you might find a use for him. We stopped at Esdreth Gap – I saw our flag on the Sask castle; that looked pretty, but Sarrask didn't think so . . .'

'Prince Ptosphes!' Sarrask burst out. 'I am a Prince, as you are. You have no right to let these – these girls – make sport of me!'

'They're as good soldiers as you are,' Ptosphes snapped. 'They captured you, didn't they?'

'It was the true gods who made sport of you, Prince Sarrask!' Kalvan went into the same harangue he had given the captured officers at Fyk, in his late father's best denunciatory pulpit style. 'I pray all the true gods,' he finished, 'that now that they have humbled you, they will forgive you.'

Sarrask was no longer defiant; he was a badly scared Prince, as badly scared as any sinner at whom the Rev. Alexander Morrison had thundered hellfire and damnation. Now and then he looked uneasily upward, as though wondering what the gods were going to hit him with next.

It was almost midnight before Kalvan and Ptosphes could sit down privately in a small room behind Sarrask's gaudy presence chamber. There had been the takeover of Tarr-Sask, and the quartering of troops, and the surrendered mercenaries to swear into Ptosphes's service, and the Saski troops to disarm and confine to barracks. Riders had been coming and going with messages. Chartiphon, on the Beshtan border, was patching up a field truce with Balthar's officers on the spot, and had sent cavalry to seize the lead mines in Sinking Valley. As soon as things stabilised, he was turning the Army of the Besh over to his second in command and coming to Sask Town.

Ptosphes had let his pipe go out. Biting back a yawn, he leaned forward to relight it from a candle.

'We have a panther by the tail here, Kalvan; you know that?' he asked. 'What are we going to do now?'

'Well, we clean Styphon's House out of Sask, first of all. We'll have the heads off all those priests, from Zothnes down.' Counting the lot that had been brought in from the different temple-farms, that would be about fifty. They'd have to gather up some headsmen. 'That will have to be policy, from now on. We don't leave any of that gang alive.'

'Oh, of course,' Ptosphes agreed. ' "To be dealt with as wolves are." But how about Sarrask and Balthames? If we behead them, the other Princes would criticise us.'

'No, we want both of them alive, as your vassals. Balthames is going to marry that wench of Sarrask's if I have to stand behind him with a shotgun, and then we'll make him Prince of Sashta, and occupy all that territory Balthar agreed to cede him. In return, he'll guarantee us the entire output of those lead mines. Lead, I'm afraid, is going to be our chief foreign-exchange monetary metal for a long time to come.

'To make it a little tighter,' he continued, 'we'll add a little of Hostigos, east of the mountains, say to the edge of the Barrens –'

'Are you crazy, Kalvan? Give up Hostigi land? Not as long as I'm Prince of Hostigos!'

'Oh, I'm sorry. I must have forgotten to tell you. You're not Prince of Hostigos any more. I am.' Ptosphes's face went blank, for an instant, with shocked incredulity. Then he was on his feet with an oath, his poignard half drawn. 'No,' Kalvan continued, before his father-in-law-to-be could say anything else. 'You are now His Majesty, Ptosphes the First, Great King of Hos-Hostigos. As Prince by betrothal of your Majesty's domain of Old Hostigos, let me be the first to do homage to your Majesty.'

Ptosphes resumed his chair, solely by force of gravity. He stared for a moment, then picked up his goblet and drained it.

This was a Hos-of another colour.

'If the people in that section don't want to live under the rule of Balthames, for which I shouldn't blame them, we'll buy them out and settle them elsewhere. We'll fill that country with mercenaries we've had to take over and don't want to carry on the payroll. The officers can be barons, and the privates will all get forty acres and a mule, and we'll make sure they all have something to shoot with. That'll keep them out of worse mischief, and keep Prince Balthemes's hands full. If we need them, we can always call them up again. Styphon, as usual, will pay.

'I don't know how long it'll take us to get Beshta – a moon or so. We'll let Balthar find out how much gold and silver we're getting out of this temple here. Balthar is fond of money. Then, after he's broken with Styphon's House, he'll find that he'll have to join us.'

'Armanes, too,' Ptosphes considered, toying with his golden chain. 'He owes Styphon's House a lot of money. What do you think Kaiphranos will do about this?'

'Well, he won't be happy about it, but who cares? He only has some five thousand troops of his own; if he wants to fight us, he'll either have to raise a mercenary army – and there's a limit to how many mercenaries anybody, even financed by Styphon's House, can hire – or he'll have to levy on his subject Princes. Half of them won't send troops to help coerce a fellow Prince – it might be their turn next – and the rest will all be too jealous of their own dignities to take orders from him. And in any case, he won't move till spring.'

Ptosphes had started to lift the chain from around his neck. He replaced it.

'No, Kalvan,' he said firmly. 'I will remain Prince of Old Hostigos. You must be Great King.'

'Now, look here Ptosphes; Dralm-dammit, you *have* to be Great King!' For a moment, he was ten years old again, arguing who'd be cops and who'd be robbers. 'You have some standing; you're a Prince. Nobody in Hos-Harphax knows me from a hole in the ground.'

Ptosphes slapped the table till the goblets jiggled.

'That's just it, Kalvan! They know me all too well. I'm just a Prince, no better than they are; every one of these other Princes would say he had as much right to be Great King as I do. But they don't know who you are; all they know is what you've done. That and the story we told at the beginning, that you come from far across the Western Ocean, around the Cold Lands. Why, that's the Home of the Gods! We can't claim that you're a god, yourself; the real gods wouldn't like that. But anybody can plainly see that you've been taught by the gods, and sent by them. It would be nothing but plain blasphemy to deny it!'

Ptosphes was right; none of these haughty Princes would kneel to one of their own ilk. But Kalvan, Galzar-taught and Dralm-sent; that was a Hos- of another colour, too. Rylla's father had risen to kneel to him.

'Oh, sit down; sit down! Save that nonsense for Sarrask and Balthames to do. We'll have to talk to some of our people tonight; best do that in the presence chamber.'

Harmakros was still up and more or less awake. He took the announcement quite calmly; by this time he was beyond surprise at anything. They had to waken Rylla; she'd had a little too much, for her first day up. She merely nodded drowsily. Then her eyes widened. 'Hey, doesn't this make me Great Queen, or something?' Then she went back to sleep.

Chartiphon, arriving from the Beshtan border, was informed. He asked, 'Why not Ptosphes?' then nodded agreement when the reasons were explained. About the necessity for establishing a Great Kingdom he had no doubt. 'What else are we, now? We'll have Beshta next.'

A score of others, Hostigi nobles and top army brass, were gathered in the presence chamber. Among them was Sthentros; maybe he hadn't been at Fitra, but nobody could say he hadn't been at Fyk. He might have envied Lord Kalvan, but Great King Kalvan was completely beyond envy. They were all half out on their feet – they'd only marched all day yesterday, tried to sleep in a wet cow-pasture with cannon firing over them, fought a 'great murthering battle' in the morning, marched fifteen more miles, and taken Sask Town and Tarr-Sask – but they wanted to throw a party to celebrate. They were persuaded to have one drink to their new sovereign and then go to bed.

The rank-and-file weren't in any better shape; half a den of Cub Scouts could have taken Tarr-Sask and run the lot of them out.

NINETEEN

I

The next morning Kalvan's orderly, who didn't seem to have got much sleep, wakened him at nine-thirty. Should have done it earlier, but he'd probably just got awake himself. He bathed, put on clothes he'd never seen before – *have things brought from Tarr-Hostigos, soonest* – and breakfasted with Ptosphes, who had also been outfitted from some Saski nobleman's wardrobe. There were more messages: from Klestreus, in Beshta Town, who had bullied Balthar into agreeing to a truce and pulling his troops back to the line agreed in the treaty with Sarrask; and from Xentos, at Tarr-Hostigos. Xentos was disturbed about reports of troop mobilisation in Nostor; Gormoth, he knew, had recently hired five hundred mercenary cavalry. Immediately, Ptosphes became equally disturbed. He wanted to march at once down the Listra Valley.

'No, for Dralm's sake!' Kalvan protested. 'We have a panther by the tail, here. In a day or so, when we're in control, we can march a lot of these new mercenaries to Listra-Mouth, but right now we mustn't let anybody know we're frightened or they'll all jump us.'

'But if Gormoth's invading Hostigos –'

'I don't think he is. Just to make sure, we'll send Phrames off with half the Mobile Force and four four-pounders; they can hold anything Gormoth's moving against us for a few days.'

He gave the necessary orders, saw to it that the troops left Sask Town quietly, and tried to ignore the subject. He was glad, though, that Rylla had got out of her splints and come to Sask Town; she might be safer here.

So they had Sarrask and Balthames brought in.

Both seemed to be expecting to be handed over to the headsman, and were trying to be nonchalant about it. Ptosphes informed them abruptly that they were now subjects of the Great King of Hos-Hostigos.

'Who's he?' Sarrask demanded, with a truculence the circumstances didn't quite justify. 'You?'

'Oh, no. I am Prince of Old Hostigos. His Majesty, Kalvan the First, is Great King.'

They were both relieved. Ptosphes had been right; the sovereignty of the mysterious and possibly supernatural Kalvan would be acceptable; that of a self-elevated equal would not. When the conditions under which they would reign as Princes, respectively, of Sashta and Sask were explained, Balthames was delighted. He'd come out of this as well as though Sask had won the war. Sarrask was somewhat less so, until informed that he was now free of all his debts to Styphon's House and would share in the loot of the temple and be given the fireseed mill.

'Well, Dralm save your Majesty!' he cried, and then loosed a torrent of invective against Styphon's House and all in it. 'You'll let me put these thieving priests to death, won't you, your Majesty?'

'They are offenders against the Great King; his justice will deal with them,' Ptosphes informed him.

Then they had in the foreign envoys, representatives of Prince Kestophes of Ulthor, on Lake Erie, and Armanes of Nyklos, and Tythanes of Kyblos, and Balthar of Beshta, and other neighbouring Princes. There had been no such diplomatic corps at Tarr-Hostigos, because of the ban of Styphon's House. The Ulthori minister immediately wanted to know what the new Great Kingdom included.

'Well, at the moment, the Princedom of Old Hostigos, the Princedom of Sask, and the new Princedom of Sashta. Any other Princes who may elect to join us will be made welcome under our rule and protection; those which do not will be respected in their sovereignty as long as they respect us in ours. Or what they may conceive to be their sovereignty as subjects of this Great King of Hos-Harphax, Kaiphranos.'

He shrugged Kaiphranos off as too trivial for consideration. Several of them laughed. The Beshtan minister began to bristle:

'This Princedom of Sashta, now; does that include territory ruled by my master, Prince Balthar of Beshta?'

'It includes territory your master ceded to our subject, Prince Balthames, in a treaty with our subject Prince Sarrask, which we recognised and confirm, and which we are prepared to enforce. As to how we are prepared to enforce it, I trust I don't have to remind you of what happened at Fyk yesterday morning.'

He turned to the others. 'Now, if your respective Princes don't wish to acknowledge our sovereignty, we hope they will accept our friendship and extend their own,' he said. 'We also hope that mutually satisfactory arrangements for trade can be made. For example, before long we expect to be producing fireseed in sufficient quantities for export, of better quality and at lower prices than Styphon's House.'

'We know that,' the Nyklosi envoy said. 'I can't, of course, commit my Prince to accepting the sovereignty of Hos-Hostigos, though I will strongly advise it. We've been paying tribute to King Kaiphranos and getting absolutely nothing in return for it. But in any case, we'll be glad to get all the fireseed you can send us.'

'Well, look here,' the Beshtan began. 'What's all this about devils? The priests of Styphon make the devils in fireseed die when it burns, and yours lets them loose.'

The Ulthori nodded. 'We've heard about that, too,' he said. 'We have no use for King Kaiphranos; for all he does, we might as well not have a Great King. But we don't want Ulthor being filled with evil spirits.'

'We've been using Hostigos fireseed in Nyklos, and we haven't had any trouble with devils,' the Nyklosi said.

'There are no devils in fireseed,' Kalvan declared. 'It's nothing but saltpetre and charcoal and sulphur, mixed without any prayers or rites or magic whatever. You know how much of it we burned at Fitra and Listra-Mouth. Nobody's seen any devils there, since.'

'Well, but you can't see the devils,' the envoy from Kyblos said. 'They fill the air, and make bad weather, and make the seed rot in the ground. You wait till Spring, and see what kind of crops you have around Fitra. And around Fyk.'

The Beshtan was frankly hostile, the Ulthori unconvinced. That devil story was going to have to be answered, and how could you prove the nonexistence of something, especially an invisible something, that didn't exist? That was why he was an agnostic instead of an atheist.

They got rid of the diplomatic corps, and had in the priests and priestesses of all the regular, non-Styphon, pantheon. The one good thing about monotheism, he thought, was that it reduced the priesthood problem. Hadn't the Romans handled that through a government-appointed pontifex maximus? *Think over, seriously*. The good thing about polytheism was that the gods operated in non-competitive fields, and their priests had a common basis of belief, and mutual respect for each other's deities. The highpriest of Dralm seemed to be the acknowledged dean of the sacred college. Assisted by all his colleagues, he would make the invocation and proclaim Kalvan Great King in the name of all the gods. Then they had in a lot of Sarrask's court functionaries, who bickered endlessly about protocol and precedence. And they made sure that each of the mercenary captains swore a new oath of service to the Great King.

After noon-meal, they assembled everybody in Prince Sarrask's throne-room.

In Korea, another sergeant in Calvin Morrison's company had seen the throne room of Napoleon at Fontainebleau.

'You know,' his comrade had said, 'I never really understood Napoleon till I saw that place. If Al Capone had ever seen it, he'd have gone straight back to Chicago and ordered one for himself, twice as big, because he couldn't possibly have got one twice as flashy or in twice as bad taste.'

That described Sarrask's throne room exactly.

The highpriest of Dralm proclaimed him Great King, chosen by all the true gods; the other priests and priestesses ratified that on behalf of their deities. Divine right of kings was another innovation, here-and-now. He then seated Rylla on the throne beside him, and then invested her father with the throne of Old Hostigos, emphasising that he was First Prince of the Great Kingdom. Then he accepted the homage of Sarrask and Balthames, and invested them with their Princedoms. The rest of the afternoon was consumed in oaths of fealty from the more prominent nobles.

When he left the throne, he was handed messages from Klestreus, in Beshta Town, and Xentos. Klestreus reported that Prince Balthar had surrounded the temple of Styphon with troops, to protect it from mobs incited by priests of

Dralm and Galzar. Xentos reported confused stories of internal fighting in Nostor, and no incidents on the border, where Phrames was on watch.

That evening, they had a feast.

The next morning, after assembling the court, the priests and priestesses of all the regular deities, and all the merchants, itinerant traders and other travellers in Sask Town, the priests of Styphon, from Zothnes down, were hustled in. They were a sorry-looking lot, dungeon-soiled, captivity-scuffed, and loaded with chains. Prodded with pike-butts, they were formed into a line facing the throne, and booed enthusiastically by all.

'Look at them!' Balthames jeered. 'See how Styphon cares for his priests!'

'Throw their heads in Styphon's face!' Sarrask shouted.

Other suggestions were forthcoming, most of which would have horrified the Mau-Mau. A few, black-robe priests and white-robe priestesses, were defiant. He remembered what Harmakros had said about some on the lower echelons really believing in Styphon. Most of them didn't, and were in no mood for martyrdom. Zothnes, who should have been setting an example, was in a pitiable funk.

Finally, he commanded silence. 'These people,' he said, 'are criminals against all men and against all the true gods. They must be put to death in a special manner, reserved for them and those like them. Let them be blown from the muzzles of cannon!'

Well, the British had done that during the Sepoy Mutiny, in the reign of her enlightened Majesty, Victoria, and could you get any more respectable than that? He was making a bad pun about cannon-ised martyrs. There was a general shout of approval – original, effective, uncomplicated, and highly appropriate. A yellow-robe upperpriest fainted.

Kalvan addressed his mercenary Chief of Artillery: 'Alkides, say we use the three eighteens and three twelves; how long would it take your men to finish off this lot?'

'Six at a time.' Alkides looked the job-lot over. 'Why, if we started right after noon-meal, we could be through in time for dinner.' He thought for a moment. 'Look, Lord Kal – Pardon, your Majesty. Suppose we use the big bombards, here. We could load the skinny ones all the way in, and the fat ones up to the hips.' He pointed at Zothnes. 'I think that one would go all the way in a fifty-pounder, almost.'

Kalvan frowned. 'But I'd wanted to do it in the town square. The people ought to watch it.'

'But it would make an awful mess in the square,' Rylla objected.

'The people could come out from town to watch,' Sarrask suggested helpfully. 'More than could see it in the square. And vendors could come out and sell honey-cakes and meat-pies.'

Another priest fainted. Kalvan didn't want too many of them doing that, and nodded unobtrusively to Ptosphes.

'Your Majesty,' the First Prince of the Great Kingdom said, 'I understand this is a fate reserved only for the priests of the false god Styphon. Now, suppose, before they can be executed, some of these criminals abjure their false god, recant their errors, and profess faith in the true gods. What then?'

'Oh, in that case we'd have no right to put them to death at all. If they make public abjuration of Styphon, renounce their priesthood, profess faith in Dralm and Galzar and Yirtta Allmother and the other true gods, and recant all their false teachings, we would have to set them free. To those willing to enter our service, honourable employment, appropriate to their condition, would be given. If Zothnes, say, were to do so, I'd think something around five hundred ounces of gold a year – '

A white-robe underpriest shouted that he would never deny his god. A yellow-robe upperpriest said, 'Shut your fool's mouth!' and hit him across the face with the slack of his fetter-chain. Zothnes was giggling in half-hysterical relief.

'Dralm bless your Majesty; of course we will, all of us!' he babbled. 'Why, I spit in the face of Styphon! You think any true god would suffer his priests to be treated as we've been?'

Xentos reached Sask Town that evening. The news from Nostor was a little more definite: according to his sources there, Gormoth had started mobilising for a blitz attack on Hostigos on hearing the first, false, news of a Hostigi disaster at Fyk. As soon as he had learned better, he had used his troops to seize the Nostor Town temple of Styphon and the temple-farm up Lycoming Creek. Now there was savage fighting all over Nostor, between Gormoth's new mercenaries and supporters of Styphon's House, and the Nostori regular army was split by mutiny and counter-mutiny. There had been an unsuccessful attack on Tarr-Nostor. Gormoth still seemed to be in control.

The Sask Town priestcraft all deferred to Xentos; it was evident that he was Primate of the Great Kingdom, Archbishop of Canterbury or something of the sort. *Established Church of Hos-Hostigos; think over carefully.* He immediately called an ecclesiastical council and began working out a programme for the auto-da-fé.

Held the next day, it was a great success. Procession of the penitents from Tarr-Sask to the Sask Town temple of Dralm, in sackcloth and ashes, guarded by enough pikemen to keep the mob from pelting them with anything more lethal than rotten cabbage and dead cats. Token flagellation. Recantation of all heresies, special emphasis on fireseed, supernatural nature and devil content of. He was pleased to observe the reactions of the diplomatic corps to this. Sermon of the Faith, preached by the Hostigos Uncle Wolf; as a professional performance, at least, the Rev. Alexander Morrison would have approved. And, finally, after profession of faith in the true gods and absolution, a triumphant march through the streets, the new converts robed in white and crowned with garlands. And free wine for everybody. This was even more fun than shooting them out of cannons would have been. The public was delighted.

They had another feast that evening.

The next day, Klestreus reported that Balthar had seized the temple of Styphon and massacred the priests; the mob was parading their heads on pike-points. He refused, however, to renounce his sovereignty and accept the rule of Great King Kalvan. Evidently he never considered his vassalage to Great King Kaiphranos, which wasn't surprising. Late in the afternoon, a troop of cavalry from Nyklos Town arrived, escorting one of Prince Armanes's chief nobles with a petition that Nyklos be annexed to the Great Kingdom of Hos-Hostigos, and also a packhorse loaded with severed heads. Prince Armanes was more interested in liquidating his debts by liquidating the creditors than he was in winning converts for the true gods. Prince Kestophes of Ulthor blew

12 177

his priests of Styphon off the guns of his lakeside fort; along with his allegiance he gave Hos-Hostigos a port on the Great Lakes. By that time the demolition of the Sask Town temple of Styphon had begun, starting with the gold dome. It was real gold, twelve thousand ounces, of which Sarrask, after his ransom was paid, received three thousand.

When he returned to Tarr-Hostigos, Klestreus was there, seeking instructions. Prince Balthar was now ready to accept the sovereignty of King Kalvan. It seemed that, after seizing the temple, massacring the priests, and incurring the ban of Styphon's House, he discovered that there was no fireseed mill at all in Beshta; all the fireseed the priests had furnished him had been made in Sask. He was, in spite of the Sask Town auto-da-fé, still worried about the possible devil content of Kalvan's Unconsecrated. The ex-Archpriest Zothnes, now with the Ministry of State at six thousand ounces, gold, a year, was sent to reassure him.

It took more reassurance to induce him to come to Tarr-Hostigos to do homage; outside Tarr-Beshta, Balthar was violently agoraphobiac. He came, however, in a mail-curtained wagon, guarded by two hundred of Harmakros's cavalry.

The news from Nostor was still confused. A civil war was raging, that was definite, but exactly who against whom was less clear. It sounded a little like France at the time of the War of the Three Henries. Netzigon, the former chief-captain, and Krastokles, who had escaped the massacre when Gormoth had taken the temple, were in open revolt, though relations between them were said to be strained. Fighting continued in the streets of Nostor Town after the abortive attack on the castle. Count Pheblon, Gormoth's cousin and Netzigon's successor, commanded about half the army; the other half adhered to their former commander. The nobles, each with a formidable following, were split about evenly. Then there were minor factions: anti-Gormoth-and-anti-Styphon, pro-Styphon-and-pro-Gormoth, anti-Gormoth-and-pro-Pheblon. In addition, several large mercenary companies had invaded Nostor on their own and were pillaging indiscriminately, committing all the usual atrocities, while trying to auction their services.

Not liking all this anarchy next door, Kalvan wanted to intervene. Chartiphon and Harmakros were in favour of that; so was Armanes of Nyklos, who hoped to pick up a few bits of real estate on his southeast border. Xentos, of course, wanted to wait and see, and, rather surprisingly, he was supported by Ptosphes, Sarrask and Klestreus. Klestreus probaly knew more about the situation in Nostor than any of them. That persuaded Kalvan to wait and see.

Tythanes of Kyblos arrived to do homage, attended by a large retinue, and bringing with him twenty-odd priests of Styphon, yoked neck-and-neck like a Guinea Coast slave-kaffle. Baron Zothnes talked to them; there was an auto-da-fé and public recantation. Some went to work in the fireseed mill and some became novices in the temple of Dralm, all under close surveillance. Kestophes of Ulthor came in a few days later. Balthar of Beshta was still at Tarr-Hostigos, which, by then, was crowded like a convention hotel. *Royal palace; get built.* Something that could accommodate a mob of subject Princes and their attendants, but not one of these castles. Castles, once he began making cast iron round-shot and hollow explosive shells and heavy brass guns, would become scenic features, just as these big hooped iron bombards would become war-memorials, Something simple and homelike, he thought. On the order of Versailles.

When the Princes were all at Tarr-Hostigos, he and Rylla were married, and there was a two-day feast, with an extra day for hangovers. He'd never been married before. He liked it. It couldn't possibly have happened with anybody nicer than Rylla.

Some time during the festivities, Prince Balthames and Sarrask's daughter Amnita were married. There was also a minor and carefully hushed scandal about Balthames and a page boy.

Then they had the Coronation. Xentos, who was shaping up nicely as a prelate-statesman of the Richelieu type, crowned him and Rylla. Then he crowned Ptosphes as First Prince of the Great Kingdom, and the other Princes in order of their submission. Then the Proclamation of the Great Kingdom was read. Quite a few hands, lifting goblets between phrases, had laboured on that. His own contributions had been cribbed from Declaration of Independence and, touching Styphon's House, from Martin Luther. Everybody cheered it enthusiastically.

Some of the Princes were less enthusiastic about the Great

Charter. It wasn't anything like the one that Tammany Hall in chain mail had extorted from King John at Runnymede; Louis XIV would have liked it much better. For one thing, none of them liked having to renounce their right, fully enjoyed under Great King Kaiphranos, of making war on one another, though they did like the tightening of control over their subject lords and barons, most of whom were an unruly and troublesome lot. The latter didn't like the abolition of serfdom and, in Beshta and Kyblos, outright slavery. But it gave everybody security without having to hire expensive mercenaries or call out peasant levies when they were most needed in the fields. The regular army of the Great Kingdom would take care of that.

And everybody could see what was happening in Nostor at the moment. He understood, now, why Xentos had opposed intervention; Nostor was too good a horrible example to sacrifice.

So they all signed and sealed it. *Secret police, to make sure they live up to it; think of somebody for chief.*

Then they feasted for a couple more days, and there were tournaments and hunts. There was also a minor scandal, carefully hushed, about Princess Amnita and one of Tythanes's cavalry officers. Finally they all began taking their leave and drifting back to their own Princedoms, each carrying the flag of the Great Kingdom, dark green with a red keystone on it.

Darken the green a little more and make the scarlet a dull maroon and they'd be good combat uniform colours.

II

The weather stayed fine until what he estimated to be the first week in November – *calendar reform; get on to this now* – and then turned cold, with squalls of rain which finally turned to snow. Outside, it was blowing against the window panes – *clear glass; why can't we do something about this?* – and candles had been lighted, but he was still at work. Petitions, to be granted or denied. Reports. Verkan's Zygrosi were going faster than anybody had expected with the brass foundry; they'd be pouring the first heat in ten or so days, and he'd have to go and watch that. The rifle shop was up to fifteen finished barrels a day, which was a real miracle. Fireseed production up, too, sufficient for military and civilian hunting demands in all the Princedoms of the Great Kingdom, and soon they would be exporting in quantity. Verkan and his wife were gone, now, returning to Grefftscharr to organise lake trade with Ulthor; he and Rylla both missed them.

And King Kaiphranos was trying to raise an army for the reconquest of his lost Princedoms, and getting a very poor response from the Princes still subject to him. There'd be trouble with him in the spring, but not before. And Sesklos, Styphon's Voice, had summoned all his Archpriests to meet in Harphax city. Council of Trent, Kalvan thought, nodding; now the Counter Reformation would be getting into high gear.

And rioting in Kyblos; the emancipated slaves were beginning to see what Samuel Johnson had meant when he defined freedom as the choice of working or starving.

And the Prince of Phaxos wanted to join the Great Kingdom, but he was making a lot of conditions he'd have to be talked out of.

And pardons, and death-warrants. He'd have to be careful not to sign too many of the former and too few of the latter; that was how a lot of kings lost their thrones.

A servant announced a rider from Vryllos Gap, who, ushered in, informed him that a party from Nostor had just crossed the Athan. A priest of Dralm, a priest of Galzar, twenty mercenary cavalry, and Duke Skranga, the First Noble of Nostor.

He received Duke Skranga in his private chamber, and remembered how he had told the Agrysi horse-trader that Dralm, or somebody, would reward him. Dralm, or somebody, with substantial help from Skranga, evidently had. He was richly clad, his robe lined with mink-fur, a gold chain about his neck and a gold-hilted poignard on a gold link belt. His beard was neatly trimmed.

'Well, you've come up in the world,' he commented.

'So, if your Majesty will pardon me, has your Majesty.' Then he produced a signet-ring – the one given as pledge token by Count Pheblon when captured and released at Tarr-Dombra, and returned to him when his ransom had been delivered. 'So has the owner of this. He is now Prince Pheblon of Nostor, and he sends me to declare for him his desire to submit himself and his realm to your Majesty's sovereignty and place himself, and it, under your Majesty's protection.'

'Well, your Grace, I'm most delighted. But what, if it's a fair question, has become of Prince Gormoth?'

The ennobled horse-trader's face was touched with a look of deepest sorrow.

'Prince Gormoth, Dralm receive his soul, is no longer with us, your Majesty. He was most foully murdered.'

'Ah. And who appears to have murdered him, if that's a fair question too?'

Skranga shrugged. 'The then Count Pheblon, and the Nostor priest of Dralm, and the Nostor Uncle Wolf were with me in my private apartments at Tarr-Nostor when suddenly we heard a volley of shots from the direction of Prince Gormoth's apartments. Snatching weapons, we rushed thither, to find the Princely rooms crowded with guardsmen who had entered just ahead of us, and, in his bedchamber, our beloved Prince lay weltering in his gore, bleeding from a dozen wounds. He was quite dead,' Skranga said sadly. 'Uncle Wolf and the highpriest of Dralm, whom your Majesty knows, will both testify that we were all together in my rooms when the shots were fired, and that Prince Gormoth was dead when we entered. Surely your Majesty will not doubt the word of such holy men.'

'Surely not. And then?'

'Well, by right of nearest kinship, Count Pheblon at once declared himself Prince of Nostor. We tortured a couple of servants lightly – we don't do so much of that in Nostor, since our beloved and gentle Prince . . . Well, your Majesty, they all agreed that a band of men in black cloaks and masks had suddenly forced their way into Prince Gormoth's chambers, shot him dead, and then fled. In spite of the most diligent search, no trace of them could be found.'

'Most mysterious. Fanatical worshippers of false Styphon, without doubt. Now, you say that Prince Pheblon, whom we recognise as the rightful Prince of Nostor, will do homage to us?'

'On certain conditions, of course, the most important of which your Majesty has already met. Then, he wishes to be confirmed in his possession of the temple of Styphon in

Nostor Town, and the fireseed mills, nitriaries and sulphur springs which his predecessor confiscated from Styphon's House.'

'Well, that's granted. And also the act of his late Highness, Prince Gormoth, in elevating you to the title of Duke and First Noble of Nostor.'

'Your Majesty is most gracious!'

'Your Grace has earned it. Now, about these mercenary companies in Nostor?'

'Pure brigands, your Majesty! His highness begs your Majesty to send troops to deal with them.'

'That'll be done; I'll send Duke Chartiphon, our Grand Constable, to attend to that. What's happened to Krastokles, by the way?'

'Oh, we have him, and Netzigon too, in the dungeons at Tarr-Nostor. They were both captured a moon-quarter ago. If your Majesty wishes, we'll bring both of them to Tarr-Hostigos.'

'Well, don't bother about Netzigon; take his head off yourselves, if you think he needs it. But we want that Archpriest. I hope that our faithful Baron Zothnes can spare us the mess of blowing him off a cannon by talking some sense into him.'

'I'm sure he can, your Majesty.'

He wondered just who had arranged the killing of Gormoth, Skranga or Pheblon, or both together. He didn't care; Nostor hadn't been his jurisdiction then. It was now, though, and if either of that pair had ideas about having the other killed, he'd do something about it in a hurry. Court intrigues, he supposed, were something he'd have with him always, but no murders, not inside the Great Kingdom.

After he showed Skranga out, he returned to his desk, opened a box, and got out a cigar – a stogie, rather, and a very crudely made stogie at that. It was a beginning, however. He bit the end and lit it at one of the candles, and picked up another report, a wax-covered wooden tablet. He still hadn't got anything done on paper-making. Maybe he'd better not invent paper; if he did, some Dralm-damned bureaucrat would invent paper-work, and then he'd have to spend all his time endlessly reading and annotating reports.

He was happy about Nostor, of course; that meant they wouldn't have a little war to fight next door in the spring, when King Kaiphranos would begin being a problem. And it was nice Pheblon had Krastokles and would turn him over. Two Archpriests, about equivalent to cardinals, defecting from Styphon's House was a serious blow. It weakened their religious hold on the Great Kings and their Princes, which was the only hold they had left now that they had lost the fireseed monopoly. Priests, and especially the top level of the hierarchy, were supposed to believe in their gods.

Xentos believed in Dralm, for instance. Maybe he'd have trouble with the old man, some day, if Xentos found his duty to Dralm conflicting with his duty to the Great Kingdom. But he hoped that would never happen.

He'd have to find out more about what was going on in the other Great Kingdoms. Spies – there was a job for Duke Skranga, one that would keep him out of mischief in Nostori local politics. Chief of Secret Service. Skranga was crooked enough to be good at that. And somebody to watch Skranga, of course. That could be one of Klestreus's jobs.

And find out just what the situation was in Nostor. Go there himself; Machiavelli always recommended that for securing a new domain. Make the Nostori his friends – that wouldn't be hard, after they'd lived under the tyranny of Gormoth. And . . .

General Order, to all Troops: Effective immediately, it shall be a court-martial offence for any member of the Armed Forces of the Great Kingdom of Hos-Hostigos publicly to sing, recite, play, whistle, hum, or otherwise utter the words and/or music of the song known as Marching Through Nostor.

TWENTY

Verkan Vall looked at his watch and wished Dalla would hurry, but Dalla was making herself beautiful for the party. A waste of time, he thought; Dalla had been born beautiful. But try to tell any woman that. Across the low table, Tortha Karf also looked at his watch, and smiled happily. He'd been doing that all through dinner and ever since, and each time had been broader and happier as more minutes till midnight leaked away.

He hoped Dalla's preparations would still permit them to reach Paratime Police Headquarters with an hour to spare before midnight. There'd be a big crowd in the assembly room – everybody who was anybody on the Paracops and the Paratime Commission, politicians, society people, and, by special invitation, the Kalvan Project crowd from the University. He'd have to shake hands with most of them, and have drinks with as many as possible, and then, just before midnight, they'd all crowd into the Chief's office, and Tortha Karf would sit down at his desk, and, precisely at 2400, rise and they'd shake hands, and Tortha Karf would step aside and he'd sit down, and everybody would start that Fourth Level barbarian chant they used on such occasions.

And from then on, he'd be stuck there – Dralm-dammit!

He must have said that aloud. The soon-to-retire Chief grinned unsympathetically.

'Still swearing in Aryan-Transpacific Zarthani. When do you expect to get back there?'

'Dralm knows, and he doesn't operate on Home Time Line. I'm going to have a lot to do here. One, I'm going to start a flap, and keep it flapping, about this pickup business.

Ten new cases in the last eight days. And don't tell me what you told Zarvan Tharg when he was retiring, or what Zarvan Tharg told Hishan Galth when *he* was retiring. I'm going to do something about this, by Dralm I am!'

'Well, fortunately for the working cops, we're a longevous race. It's a long time between new Chiefs.'

'Well, we know what causes it. We'll have to work on eliminating the cause. I'm a hundred and four; I can look forward to another two centuries in that chair of yours. If we don't have enough men, and enough robots, and enough computers to eliminate some of these interpenetrations, we might as well throw it in and quit.'

'It'll cost like crazy.'

'Look, I don't make a practice of preaching moral ethics, you know that. I just want you to think, for a moment, of the morality of snatching people out of the only world they know and dumping them into an entirely different world, just enough like their own . . .'

'I've thought about it, now and then,' Tortha Karf said, in mild understatement. 'This fellow Morrison, Lord Kalvan, Great King Kalvan, is one in a million. That was the best thing that could possibly have happened to him, and he'd be the first to say so, if he dared talk about it. But for the rest, the ones the conveyer operators ray down with their needlers are the lucky ones.

'But what are we going to do, Vall? We have a population of ten billion, on a planet that was completely exhausted twelve thousand years ago. I don't think more than a billion and a half are on Home Time Line at any one time; the rest are scattered all over Fifth Level, and out at conveyer-heads all over the Fourth, Third and Second. We can't cut them loose; there's a slight moral issue involved there, too. And we can't haul them all in to starve after we stop paratiming. That little Aryan-Transpacific expression you picked up fits. We have a panther by the tail.'

'Well, we can do all we can. I saw to it that they did it on the University Kalvan Operation. We checked all the conveyer-heads equivalent with Hostigos Town on every Paratime penetrated time-line, and ours doesn't coincide with any of them.'

'I'll bet you had a time.' Tortha Karf sipped some more of the after-dinner coffee they were dragging out, and lit another cigarette. 'I'll bet they love you in Conveyer Registration Office, too. How many were there?'

'A shade over three thousand, inside four square miles. I don't know what they'll do about the conveyer-head for Agrys City, when they go to put one in there. There's a city on that river-mouth island on every time line that builds cities, and tribal villages on most of the rest.'

'Then they aren't just establishing a conveyer-head at Hostigos Town?'

'Oh, no; they're making a real operation out of it. We have five police posts, here and there, including one at Greffa, the capital of Grefftscharr, where Dalla and I are supposed to come from. The University will have study teams, or at least observers, in the capital cities of all the Five Great Kingdoms. Six Kingdoms, now, with Hos-Hostigos. They'll have to be careful; by spring, there'll be a war that'll make the Conquest of Sask look like a schoolyard brawl.'

They were both silent for a while. Tortha Karf, smiling contentedly, was thinking of his farm on Fifth Level Sicily; he'd be there this time tomorrow, with nothing to worry about but what the rabbits were doing to his truck-gardens. Verkan Vall was thinking about his friend, the Great King Kalvan, and everything Kalvan had to worry about. Now *there* was a man who had a panther by the tail.

Then something else occurred to him; a disquieting thought that had nagged him ever since a remark Dalla had made, the morning before they'd made the drop as Verkan and his party.

'Chief,' he said, and remembered that in a couple of hours people would be calling him that. 'This pickup problem is only one facet, and a small one, of something big and serious, and fundamental. We're supposed to protect the Paratime Secret. Just how good a secret is it?'

Tortha Karf looked up sharply, his cup half-way to his lips.

'What's wrong with the Paratime Secret, Vall?'

'How did we come to discover Paratime transportation?'

Tortha Karf had to pause briefly. He had learned that long ago, and there was a considerable mental overlay.

'Why, Ghaldron was working to develop a spacewarp drive, to get us out to the stars, and Hesthor was working on the possibility of linear time-travel, to get back to the past, before his ancestors had worn the planet out. Things were pretty grim, on this time-line, twelve thousand years ago. And a couple of centuries before, Rhogom had worked up a theory of multi-dimensional time, to explain the phenomenon of precognition. Dalla could tell you all about that; that's her subject.

'Well, science was pretty tightly compartmented, then, but somehow Hesthor read some of Rhogom's old papers, and he'd heard about what Ghaldron was working on and got in touch with him. Between them, they discovered paratemporal transportation. Why?'

'As far as I know, nobody off Home Time Line has ever developed any sort of time-machine, linear or lateral. There are Second Level civilisations, and one on Third, that have over-light-speed drives for interstellar ships. But the idea of multidimensional time and worlds of alternate probability is all over Second and Third Levels, and you even find it on Fourth – a mystical concept on Sino-Hindic, and a science-fiction idea on Europo-American.'

'And you're thinking, suppose some Sino-Hindic mystic, or some Europo-American science-fiction writer, gets picked up and dumped on to, say, Second Level Interworld Empire?'

'That could do it. It mightn't even be needed. You know, there is no such thing as a single-shot discovery; anything that's been discovered once can be discovered again. That's why it always amuses me to see some technological warfare office classifying a law of nature as top-secret. Gunpowder was the secret of Styphon's House, and look what's happening to Styphon's House now. Of course, gunpowder is a simple little discovery; it's been made tens of thousands of times, all over Paratime. Paratemporal transposition is a big, complicated, discovery; it was made just once, twelve thousand years ago, on one time-line. But no secret can be kept forever. One of the University crowd said that, speaking of Styphon's House. He became quite indignant when Dalla mentioned the Paratime Secret in that connection.'

'I'll bet you didn't. That's a nice thought to give a retiring Chief of Paratime Police. Now I'll be having nightmares about –'

He broke off, rising to his feet with a smile. A Paratimer could always produce a smile when one was needed.

'Well, now, Dalla! That gown! And how did you achieve that hairdo?'

He rose and turned. Dalla had come out on to the terrace and was pirouetting slowly in the light from the room behind her. It hadn't been a waste of time, after all.

'But I kept you waiting ages! You're both dears, to be so patient. Do we go, now?'

'Yes, the party will have started; we'll get there just at the right time. Not too early, and not too late.'

And in two hours, Verkan Vall, Chief of Paratime Police, would begin to assume responsibility for guarding the Paratime Secret.

A panther by the tail. And he was holding it.

SPACE VIKING

H. Beam Piper
Author of *Little Fuzzy* and *Fuzzy Sapiens*

GALACTIC WARRIOR!
After the titanic war that had destroyed the galaxy's Old
Federation, every surviving world was on its own – and at the
mercy of the Space Vikings!

Lucas Trask was one of these renegades – a powerful warlord
commanding a deadly fighting force, hated and feared for his
plundering, terrorising ways. But few people realised that
behind his savage mask was a mind embittered by grief and
loss, and driven by an iron determination. Lucas Trask was a
man with an old score to settle. And he would stop at nothing
until he had achieved his goal . . .

Space Viking is an epic science fiction adventure in the rivet-
ing tradition of *Foundation* and *Starship Trooper*.

0 7221 6876 4   SCIENCE FICTION   85p

THE STAINLESS STEEL RAT

Harry Harrison

This book introduces Slippery Jim di Griz, cosmic criminal and the smoothest, sneakiest con-man in the known Universe. He can take any bank in the Galaxy, con a captain out of his ship, start a war or stop one – whichever pays the most.

So when the law finally catches up with the Stainless Steel Rat, there is only one thing to do – make him a cop. And turn him loose on a villainous lady who is building herself a battleship.

0 7221 44377   SCIENCE FICTION   75p

THE STAINLESS STEEL RAT SAVES THE WORLD

Harry Harrison

Someone was tampering with time, altering the past to eliminate the present, fading people out of existence into a timeless limbo. One of the victims was Angelina, the lovely, lethal wife of James Bolivar di Griz – better known as *The Stainless Steel Rat*. His determination to rescue his wife throws him dozens of centuries in both directions including an ancient nation called the United States of America. But then he didn't have much choice; to save Angelina he had to save the world.

0 7221 44369   SCIENCE FICTION   75p

All Sphere Books are available at your bookshop or newsagent, or can be ordered from the following address: Sphere Books, Cash Sales Department, P.O. Box 11, Falmouth, Cornwall.

Please send cheque or postal order (no currency), and allow 19p for postage and packing for the first book plus 9p per copy for each additional book ordered up to a maximum charge of 73p in U.K.

Customers in Eire and B.F.P.O. please allow 19p for postage and packing for the first book plus 9p per copy for the next 6 books, thereafter 3p per book.

Overseas customers please allow 20p for postage and packing for the first book and 10p per copy for each additional book.